IGNITE

A ROMANTIC VAMPIRE FANTASY SERIES

PARCHED
BOOK FIVE

Z.L. ARKADIE

FLAMING
HEARTS

CONTENTS

CHAPTER 1
IT'S A SHAM
CLARITY

"Clarity?" Baron calls cautiously, his voice echoing through the empty corridor.

He's alone as he steps out of Celeste's chambers and into a quiet, arched limestone hallway. Celeste, the vampiress who made bold advances toward him the last time we were here—deep in the core of Mount Olympus—is nowhere to be seen. Nor are any of the other inhabitants of this hidden world.

I swallow the lump of cold, stale air in my throat. "I'm here," I manage to croak, rushing to his side.

By habit, Baron reaches for my hand but glances at me when he comes up empty. I'm not fully present. He can see me, but I can't see myself

1

in this vast, hidden world. Part of me—my quarter-human side—remains in my room in Vermont, at the House of Benel, the estate my father Felix built for his seven daughters. My Encaser power allows me to exist in multiple places at once. As we agreed, after the ten-minute wait, I focused on every line and curve of Baron's remarkable face, using that connection to guide the supernatural part of me here.

During our mission to deliver the leaf from the Tree of Life to Jari, the ash-covered ground had split open and swallowed Baron and Vayle. Whatever they experienced beneath the surface terrified Vayle, and even shook Baron to a certain extent. He had seen vampires he'd once been close to—Garrett, Celeste, and the mysterious Gia. Gia had been reported dead by the other vampires on our first trip to the Mount Olympus coven, so when he saw Garrett and Celeste in spirit form alongside her, he feared they had all met the same fate.

"They're all gone," Baron says, his voice strained.

"Something happened here, and it wasn't good." A shiver moves up my divine and Enuian spine. The ghost of sheer violence lingers in this place.

"I fear you're right. The guards aren't posted in the forest, and Virgil didn't sound the call of entry."

I recall that sound—a loud, feral howl, so chilling it could freeze bubbling oil.

Baron stops to peer over the ledge of a short wall. Beyond it lies a vast opening, bathed in artificial sunlight. The first time I saw how centuries-old vampires could manufacture sunrays in the core of a mountain, I marveled at their brilliance. I feel the same awe this time, but now it's eerily empty—no sign of life.

We're thousands of stories high inside this immense inner mountain construct. Each landing is divided into compartments, with countless neon signs advertising bars. The colors, lights, and shapes of the marquees compete for attention, a chaotic display of vampiric indulgence. Baron once explained that a stiff drink can momentarily ease a vampire's parched throat. He and an old friend even sang a song about it.

"If I can't have blood, give me whiskey instead, then give me the barmaid, and I'll take her to bed…"

Suddenly, a thought hits me, and I nearly shout, "Garrett!"

"Garrett?" Baron asks, confused.

"I know what he looks like, which means I can go wherever he is."

As Baron studies my face, I notice how tightly he holds his shoulders. He's paler than his usual anemic self, and his brows are so drawn that his entire face looks pinched. I've seen him like this before—on that evening he came to me in the woods outside the Tudor-style house Fawn once shared with Lario Exgesis, a vampire transformed into a man, and eventually, into a strange and fearsome species of hyper-vampire.

I had just rescued Fawn from their basement, where Lario had kept her imprisoned in a cage made of silver. The silver wasn't meant to keep her in, but to keep other vampires out. They would tear down the Empire State Building if it meant drinking every last drop of her blood. If a Selell—a vampire—drinks me or any of my sisters dry, it would never thirst again. We are creatures who carry "lifeblood," blood derived from the Tree of Life itself. Lario managed to hold Fawn captive by weakening her with mirk, human blood.

I had been struggling to carry Fawn to the nearest portal, which led to Enu, when Baron showed up. It had only been a few days since I'd last seen him, but for him, a year had passed. He looked terrible—not just because I'd been gone so long that it broke his heart, but because my absence from this universe had taken a physical toll on him as well.

"Are you parched?" I ask, shocked by Baron's appearance. He shouldn't be parched—not with me here in Encaser form, and also on Earth.

He massages his throat. "Yes, but it's not my thirst. A vampire is somewhere nearby and alive."

I gasp. "And you're experiencing *its* thirst?"

He nods briskly. "And I can hear his thoughts."

I'm taken aback. Is Baron encasing? It seems like it. "Is this the first time you've been able to sense others outside of yourself?"

Baron frowns, concentrating as he tries to recall any instance where he had a similar ability. "Yes, this is the first occurrence."

The weight of his revelation washes over me, but there's no time to linger on it. Shaking myself back into focus, I ask, "Do you recognize the voice?"

He frowns harder. "I can't say that I do."

"What is he saying?"

"He's afraid that I might kill him. He's praying that I leave without finding him."

Out of frustration, I reach out to touch Baron's shoulder, but my hand passes right through him. It's not the only thing going wrong—my arms and legs are turning to jelly, but I don't think much of it. Not too long ago, we returned from an exhausting journey that involved camping in a frozen frontier, battling shadow phantoms made of ashes, and facing off against monsters patched together from human remains. I chalk my exhaustion up to that—residual fatigue. Despite my failing abilities and diminishing health, I'm not ready to give up.

"Well, I'll try Garrett now," I say, settling on the next logical step.

Baron gazes out over the vast emptiness. "It's worth a shot."

"Do you think he's dead?" I ask, sensing the unease in his tone.

He hesitates. "I can only hope not."

Led by Baron's hope, I picture Garrett standing beside him, singing. His bloodshot eyes, heavy lids, and the purple indentations beneath them paint the picture of someone cursed by being a Selell. His cheeks are hollow, but whenever Baron was near him, there was a spark of life, a brief return of vitality. That's why I remember Garrett's face so clearly. He loved who I love—not as much as I do, but close, very close.

Whether Garrett is dead or alive, I should be

able to find him. That's how my power has always worked. But this time, the more I reach beyond myself, the more a thick, vaporous red force pushes back, bearing down on me.

I recognize it instantly. "It's Lario. He's fighting me," I wheeze, gasping as I stop struggling against his overwhelming power.

"Exgesis? How?" Baron growls. Just the mention of Lario's name has made him more furious than the fact that his friends—and even some of his enemies—are missing, preyed upon by something.

"I wish I knew," I admit. "It has to be Tal, the Sham. She's gotten stronger over the years…"

We don't have time to figure out how to neutralize Tal, though I know we'll need to have that conversation soon. I can feel my strength slipping away with every second.

"At least we should try to save the last remaining vampire. Can you still hear him, feel his thirst?" I ask, trying to keep us focused.

"Yes…" Baron's eyes search every part of my face.

He's so worried about me, but I don't want him to ask me to leave until I know he's safe. I work hard to steady my breathing, to rely on the last scraps of strength I have left. But I'm fading fast, and the sooner we find this hidden vampire, the sooner I can be sure he's safe enough to let go of me.

But instead of focusing on the task at hand, Baron watches me more intensely. "What's happening to you?" he asks, his voice tight with concern.

"I'm fine. Just concentrate. Can you feel him? Can you feel his fear?" I fight the urge to gasp for air.

Baron stares at me, too consumed with worry to focus.

"Please," I beg, knowing this isn't the moment for me to give up and return to my body. He's still not safe. I lock eyes with him, trying to convey how crucial this is.

Baron hesitates, then shakes his head slightly, realizing I won't leave him yet. "All right. How do I find him?" His face is growing paler by the second, the vampire's thirst gnawing at him, just as my own weakness is taking over.

"Let his fear and thirst fill you, and then let yourself move toward it," I whisper, urging him to act before it's too late.

After a concerned moment of examining my health, Baron closes his eyes.

I can't tear my eyes away from Baron's captivating features, but I still wonder why I can't detect the other vampire's energy. Up until now, I've only been able to use inductive reasoning to understand the scope of my abilities as an Encaser and how they affect Baron, to whom I'm bonded. Could Baron's ability to sense the emotions of others, something I've always been able to do, be linked to our bond? Or is it something Lario has done to weaken my powers, allowing Baron to grow stronger where I falter? Or perhaps it's neither. We'll soon find out.

"I got him," Baron says, breaking through my thoughts. "Will you be able to follow me?" His eyes narrow, still filled with worry.

"I think so," I say, doing my best to steady my voice.

"If you can't keep up, promise me you'll leave, and get the rest you need."

The idea of leaving him doesn't sit well with me, but I force myself to say, "I promise."

He moves swiftly, and thankfully, I can easily match his pace in this form. We zip down hallways and massive staircases that connect the floors. Nothing blurs by. Shattered wine glasses and broken liquor bottles litter the empty tables and floors. The sharp stench of alcohol—the vampires' spirit-lifting juice—burns my sinuses. Whatever savage act interrupted their drinking, it's clear this coven put up a fight.

We pass through the lushest garden I've ever seen outside of Enu. Though we move quickly, I can still take in the thick green grass, the overripe pomegranate trees and grapevines, and limestone statues of naked men and women in provocative poses. Above it all is a sky of vaporous clouds and artificial sunlight. Once again, I'm struck by the brilliance of these ancient creatures—so clever, yet so damned.

We weave in and out of living spaces that lack the light and poshness of the common areas. Most of the cubicles are plain, holding one lone wooden bed not even equal in dimension to a twin-sized bed. Each bed is covered with a dusty white sheet that looks as if it hasn't been washed in centuries.

The deeper into the mountain we go, the danker and clammier it becomes. We've already traveled far, which tells me that Baron's senses are quite keen. Every now and then, he glances over and squints at me. I fear my suffering may overcome my will to appear well for him.

Finally, he stops. We're in one of those tight

rooms and facing the only piece of furniture—a very old, possibly Victorian era, green silk sofa pushed against a smooth black-and-white marble wall.

"He's here," he whispers as he reaches to caress my cheek. Once again, he falls short of touching me. "I don't like this." He reluctantly drops his hand to his side.

"Me either." I hate not feeling his hand on my face. I'd rather rely on the heat of his touch to keep me warm in the freezing-cold vampire lair, but since my abilities are all out of whack, I'm relying on a faint shield of warmth.

"You're shivering."

"I know," I mutter past my quivering lips. "It's fine."

The concern in Baron's eyes grows deeper, and then the next thing I know, he has his hands on my shoulders. He's actually touching me!

"What the hell?" he marvels.

We stare into each other's eyes. Despite the circumstances, I feel like this is a small victory, and so does he. Now that he has a hold of me, he pulls me into him. My breasts are pressed tightly against his firm chest. I'm nearly limp, and he's holding me as if he'll never let me go.

"I can't stay," I moan. "I can't hold on. Where is he?"

He holds me tighter and turns to the left. "There."

I follow his eyes to a spot on the floor. It's to the right of the front of the sofa. Before I get the chance to say that I don't see anything, a hatch in the ground blows open. I fly out of Baron's arms, and after a moment, I see that a strong energy force has pinned him to the ceiling. My eyes widen in horror, and then I feel a glint of hope. He's managed to grasp the blades he keeps attached to his ankles. But even though his arms are outstretched, he can't move them.

I fear that this is it. The end of my love, Baron Ze Feldis.

"Stop," I shout as loud as exhaustion will allow me.

Then I see a vampire spring out of the dark hole. My vision is becoming increasingly blurry, and I'm shivering from the cold because my shield of warmth has evaporated. I see that he's shooting the force that has Baron restrained out of one of his palms. He's just as tall and fair-haired as Baron. Although my sight and health are further betraying me, I can see that they look so much alike they could be brothers.

"Ze Feldis?" the strange vampire calls as he stops the force of energy.

Baron drops to the floor but lands on his feet. "Ben Artiste?"

CHAPTER 2

A FEEDING FRENZY
CLARITY

That's the last thing I see and hear before snapping back into my body, sitting on the edge of the bed in my room. I leap to my feet and rush to the toilet, falling to my knees as I regurgitate Goshem tea and berries.

The ache in my limbs, the nausea, and the overwhelming fatigue combine into the worst sensation imaginable. The weight of Baron being thousands of miles away presses on me like a two-ton boulder.

Fawn is suddenly there, lifting my hair away from my face. Slowly, my stomach begins to settle. The chills fade, and the shivers subside as she helps me to my feet.

"Clarity, what's happening to you?" she asks, worry etched in her voice.

"Lario," I hiss through gritted teeth.

Her eyes widen, rattled just by the mention of his name.

I drag myself to the sink and rinse my mouth with warm water. "I don't know how he weakened me, but I imagine Tal the Sham witch has something to do with it."

Frustration bubbles up inside me. Nothing is going as planned. Baron and I are supposed to be together, finding answers—not me, stuck here, sick to my stomach and fighting weakness.

"How is he—Lario?" Fawn whispers, her expression conflicted.

I can hardly believe her concern. After everything, she's still either unwilling or unable to admit what Lario really is.

"Fawn, he's a conniving, vindictive monster," I snap, my anger barely contained.

Fawn stays silent as I cup my hands under the faucet, letting the cool water pool before I scoop it into my mouth and splash it across my face. I glance at her, hearing her thoughts as clearly as if she'd spoken them. She's riddled with guilt, wondering if she's to blame for unleashing Lario on the world. When Lario had been her lover, she fed him the leaf from the Tree of Life, turning him human again—only for him to transform into an even more treacherous vampire the second time around. I've always found her strangely passive about her role in all of this.

I turn off the faucet, wiping the last remnants of water from my face.

Fawn gently curves an arm around my lower back. "Come on, let's get you back to bed," she says, breaking the long silence.

A few thoughts jostle in my mind. The first is Baron. I can relax slightly, knowing the Artiste vampire won't harm him—he was actually relieved to see Baron. But the second thought, more troubling, circles back to Lario and his relentless quest to transform from vampire to human, only to become something far worse.

"Fawn," I say as we settle into bed, "do you remember how Lario used to complain about being human? As if being merely flesh and blood was beneath him, a hindrance?"

She shakes her head as she sits at the foot of the bed. "No, I never noticed."

Her eyebrows knit together as she strains to recall any moment that might validate what I'm saying. But it's no surprise—during all the years she spent with him, Lario was a master at manipulating her memory.

For instance, she can't remember how they first met, and for the longest time, she believed Lario had killed Titus Rona, her guardian. But Titus showed up to join us on that harrowing journey through Nowhere and Jari, very much alive. Now that I think about it, I doubt Lario could have killed such a powerful creature—at least, not without serious help. From what I've glimpsed of Lario's life, it's always Tal who does the heavy lifting, while Lario simply gives the orders.

"Well, I'm pretty sure Lario never went searching for the leaf because he wanted to be human again," I say.

Fawn's confusion deepens.

"I think he orchestrated the meeting between me and Baron, and then between you and me. And if that's the case…" I trail off, pondering the most frightening part of it all.

"If that's the case?" Fawn presses, despite her slight agitation. She's eager to hear where my thoughts are leading.

"I think he wants all the sisters to be found. But I believe his plan went off track when I returned the scroll to Felix. He didn't expect that."

Fawn's eyes fill with unshed tears as she watches me. I reach out to sense how she's feeling, and the wave of emotion I get back makes my heart ache, a deep, tangible pain.

"Surely that monster didn't break your heart?" I blurt, surprising even myself. I've never felt this from her before—why now?

Fawn shrugs, then gently closes off her emotions, barring me from sensing more. She takes my hand. "It's not important. You're looking better, though. What did Lario do to you?"

It *is* important, though. Her love for that creature is a weakness, and I so desperately want to convince her to change her heart about him. But if it were easy to stop loving an abuser, so many people would have already done it. I know it will take time for her feelings to shift, and I'll be here for my sister as she moves from loving him to indifference.

With a sigh, I turn my focus back to Baron. "Okay, remember I told you about the vampire coven in Mount Olympus?"

"Yes," she says with a gentle nod.

I begin explaining about the souls in the darkness, deep beneath Jari's surface—the ones Baron saw—and how the empty coven confirmed their deaths. "The longer I stayed in that place, the sicker I felt."

Fawn rubs my thigh, offering comfort in her nurturing way. No wonder Lario picked her to manipulate. Out of all the sisters I've met, she's the one who would have the most mercy on him.

"I'm so sorry, Cl'auta," she whispers, looking away.

"About what? You didn't make me sick."

"I know, but…"

I place my hand over hers. "Don't beat yourself up about Lario, Falu. He took advantage of you." I stop myself from expressing the full extent of my hatred for him. Every time I think about how he exploited her kind soul, I become his self-appointed judge and executioner.

"Thank you, Cl'auta, but… I'm weak," she says, her voice soft and full of doubt.

"No way!" I nearly shout. "You are not weak."

Fawn opens her mouth to respond but hesitates, as if she wants to say something but can't find the words. I'm on the verge of encouraging her to speak when Zill suddenly shouts both our names in our heads.

Fawn and I sprint down the corridors, and I momentarily forget how worried I am about Baron. I'm still hoping he doesn't have to use those blades he loves wielding.

When we reach the bottom of the steps leading to the foyer, Zill and Derek are standing in front of the main door. I can feel the cold day beyond the border of our estate coming off their skin. While Zill looks flustered, Derek is cool and calm, as Weks generally are.

"The town is gone," Zill says, her voice thick with grief.

I catch a glimpse of the town she's talking about in her thoughts. "Moonridge?"

She nods frantically. "Yeah, there's no one there. It's completely empty, and the fog was rolling in…"

Zillael's memory conjures up several faces. She's remembering an older gentleman in a blue button-down shirt and a red bow tie. He's handing her a candy apple. His lips are stretched into the friend-liest smile as he winks at her. His name is Jake, the proprietor of the candy shop, and she's very worried about him.

Then I see a quite pretty high-school–aged girl with golden hair. She's seated behind Zill in a stan-dard American classroom. The girl kicks the back of Zill's desk chair. What's surprising to Zill is that she's worried about this particular classmate, along with a boy who eagerly shoots his arm in the air. Although he's not saying it out loud, Zill knows that his inner dialogue is, "Me, me, me!" She calls him Lintner, and this image of him reminds her that four years have passed. She hopes he blew that town years ago, is still alive, and that wherever he is now, he's no longer a "suck-up." What a strange thought.

"Were you caught in the fog?" Fawn asks.

I blink myself out of Zillael's head and back into the moment.

"No." Zill sighs in relief. "We left in a nick of time, knock on wood."

"But you said it's empty?" I ask.

"Wiped out."

"No, it's not," Derek chimes in. He sounds sure of this.

Our eyes shift to him, expecting an explanation.

"Humans are still there, but they're in distress," he confirms.

"Then we have to find them," Zill says with such fervor that she even surprises herself.

Something is definitely different about her. I narrow my eyes to study her. Before our journey to

Jari, she incessantly pined for Derek. Deeper within herself, she grieved the loss of the guardian she knew as Deanna, her mother. Now, neither of those sentiments seems to affect her. In the short time we've been standing here, she hasn't felt the loss of Derek's affection or Deanna's presence. She's absorbed by what she can do to help the people of Moonridge.

"Clarity, what about you?" Fawn says in a calmer tone. "Are you able to get a look around Moonridge?"

I recall what just happened at the Mount Olympus coven: the weakness, the sickness. I don't ever want to feel like that again.

"Cl'auta?" Fawn says to regain my attention.

"I believe so." I take a moment to assess my health. Zero nausea. No headache. Strength regained. Head steadied. I'm as good as new. "No, I know I'm fully recovered."

"Good," Fawn says as Zill asks, "You were sick?"

"I was, but now I'm not." I flash Zill a smile to put her at ease. "So let's get on with the show."

WE ALL MOVE TO OUR FAVORITE PATIO THAT ADJOINS the first-floor dining room. I give in to the urge to contact Baron. He's no longer in the mountain coven, nor is he alone. He and Artiste are moving fast down a damp, barely lit tunnel. I make myself visible to him. Upon seeing me, his eyes caress my face. I love when he looks at me like that.

He smirks. "You're better."

"I am." I smile back at him.

"Meet us at Chester's in Montauk at seven."

We squeeze hands, and I return to myself as the vampire walking beside him asks, "Who are you talking to?"

Montauk at seven. Got it.

We all sit on the black wrought-iron patio chairs placed around the wrought-iron table. The sun is directly above our heads. The sky is blue. Birds squawk and whistle from tree branches in the forests surrounding the estate. It's a perfect day, deep in summer here. Beyond the borders of the protection over the House of Benel, a bitter winter is whipping the land, especially the East Coast.

Fawn, Zill, and Derek watch me with expectant eyes. I let out a long, cleansing breath, but it doesn't empty all the anxiety I feel. Baron's words, *Montauk at seven*, play in a loop in my mind.

Instead of concentrating on the small town and the faces that I saw in Zill's memory, all I see is the image of Baron traveling with a strange vampire with whom he shares an uncanny likeness.

"Clarity, are you there yet?" Fawn asks.

I look at her. She knows I'm distracted.

"Not yet," I confess and close my eyes.

I don't have to shut my eyes to go the small town. My father, Felix, advised me to never close them while using my Encaser power. I'm sure he wants me to be able to see what's around my physical body while being outside of myself. Despite that, closing my eyes helps me take my mind off Baron and work to remember the small town of Moonridge and the guy in the blue shirt who'd handed Zill the candy apple. Jake, that's what she called him.

I'm stopped by a cloudy red energy shield. As I feared, all of the symptoms that ailed me earlier return. I feel as if a vice is squeezing my head at the temples. As I fight on and enter the red vapors that are trying to shove me out, my stomach turns queasy. I don't stop until the weight of something heavy knocks me out of my seat. Both the chair and I hit the ceramic floor.

Derek is the first to reach me. "You're being stopped again?" He helps me to my feet.

I nod stiffly as I struggle to regain my balance and my breath. My muscles feel as though they've been through ten rounds in a boxing ring with a heavyweight champion.

"I don't think I'll be able to fight through it without Baron," I say strenuously. "We need the full light."

"Where is he?" Zill stretches her neck to look around for him. She's thinking that he's usually not far from where I am.

"He's gone," I say.

I sound so sad that her face drops as she asks, "You mean gone, gone?"

"No," I assure her. "He returned to Greece. I'll tell you about it later. I'm supposed to meet with him at seven tonight Earth time."

"We don't have that much time," she cries.

I sigh with despair. "I know." I completely understand her frustration.

We stand in a circle, and our eyes jump from face to face. What's clear is that each of them considers me the ship's captain—even Derek, the Wek.

"Give me a second," I whisper while staring at

the tiny crystals embedded in the ceramic floor. The way the noon sun makes the tiny shards sparkle gives me an idea. "I should try it from the diamond case." I dart off, knowing that they'll follow me.

Once I'm inside the diamond-walled chamber, I glance at Zill, Derek, and Fawn, who stand outside it and watch me. Without closing my eyes, I recall Jake's face and go where the memory takes me.

From here, I can reach Moonridge without any pushback. The town is the way I remember it. The snow is at least knee high, and ice coats the leaves of the orchards, the woods, and the trees planted along the streets. I'm being pulled toward the image in my head. The closer I get to it, the stranger the energy feels. I sense that this life force isn't human, and I wonder if Jake has been turned into a Selell. He appeared to be such a happy guy; I can't imagine he agreed to become a vampire.

I'm moving across the landscape at a remarkable speed. There's life here, lots of it, but it's not human. The image of the man named Jake takes me toward a neighborhood. Quaint New England cottage homes, with their big windows and steeple-topped roofs, are separated by fields of trees and huge, unfenced yards. I stand in someone's backyard, along with a red doghouse, a fishing boat, and a large aluminum shed. I can hear the dog barking inside the house.

I head inside. The atmosphere is still here, and the stench of old trash and animal waste blows me away. The television on the short wooden stand is still on in the living room, but it's only airing loud static. The earsplitting sound forces me to rush over and, even in my state, try to turn it off.

It works!

Now that it's quiet, I notice how unnaturally dark the room is. The curtains are drawn, but where they don't meet, I see green wallpaper with a green velvet flower pattern attached to the window glass. Not a stitch of light from the late afternoon sun can trickle into the room. My observations reasonably lead me to conclude that Jake is definitely a vampire.

I hear a noise and turn to see an orange and white collie walking out of one of the rooms down the hallway. Its head is lowered as it slowly moves toward me, whimpering. The dog stops at my feet, still making that sound as it sniffs around my legs. It knows I'm here. I've never been this close to an animal, but I know it needs me to kneel and give it a hug. The poor thing is in emotional distress.

"Everything's going to be fine," I promise,

hoping that it's not an empty one. I see that he's wearing a collar with a tag. His name is Jerry. "Jerry, how is Jake?" I run my fingers through his coat.

The collie barks once and, understanding me perfectly, sprints toward the room he just dragged himself out of. I follow. When I enter the bedroom, I see the same wallpaper that's pasted on the windows in the living room covering the windows here.

But the sight that commands my full attention is an older couple, man and woman, lying on their backs under a thick layer of patchwork quilts. Their thin skins are as white as eggshells. Their cheeks are sunken, and the hair on top of their heads is as white as their skin. I've seen corpses before, and that's exactly what they look like, but they're not dead. I can feel their heartbeats and hear the slow movement of air pumping through their lungs.

Jerry, the dog, barks again, as if he's trying to answer the questions my expression is asking. Then it dawns on me that Jerry has memories. If I can see what a human or a vampire is thinking, then why not an animal?

"Can I touch your head?" I ask him before doing so. He understands me perfectly, especially when he sits on his hind legs and looks directly into my eyes, granting me permission.

I take one more glance at the couple on the bed before I kneel. In truth, this is insane! At least, that's what it feels like. I'm hoping a dog's memory will give me the answers I'm seeking? I pat the top of his head. Jerry and I look into each other's eyes. His mouth is open, and he's panting a little when all of a sudden, I absorb his memories.

The leaves of the apple trees that hover over the tiny red doghouse are barely starting to yellow. He's inside it, stretched across the threshold, bathing in another sundown. He seems to like this time of day. No, he more than likes it. The act of the sun descending beyond the horizon feels like a ritual to him, and the moment it disappears, he's stung by a sense of horror.

Jerry gallops from one end of the yard to the other, trampling the fallen twigs and leaves. He barks and whimpers as he senses approaching doom. When he reaches the back door, he scratches at the screen, howling. He wants Jake and Mary to run away with him. If they escape before the fog overtakes them, they can be safe. At least that's what his instincts tell him.

Jake pulls the door open. He's a ruddy-faced

man who appears to be in his early seventies. He's wearing a blue button-down shirt with a red bow tie. "Ey, Jerry, what did I tell ya about scratching the screen?" He pulls the door open wider. "Just come on inside."

But Jerry doesn't want to go inside. He wildly wags his tail as he lets out a series of strenuous barks while pacing in front of the threshold.

"Hanker down, Jerr," Jake says.

The funny thing is Jerry senses that Jake also feels the danger. Jerry doesn't stop pacing, yelping, and panting. He dashes across the threshold and rubs against his master's legs when the fog rolls across the yard. Jerry knows it's too late to run. He wants Jake to slam the door, lock it, and hide. *The danger has arrived*.

But Jake does the opposite. He steps outside and walks down the three-tiered cement block steps until he's standing on the edge of the summer-worn lawn. The stinging cold fog travels across him. Jerry can no longer see Jake, and he barks like crazy. Jerry runs outside to the stoop and then back over the threshold, working overtime to convince Jake to get back inside the house where it's *safer*.

Finally, it sinks in; Jake knows something isn't right. The icy air makes him cough as he stumbles up the steps to get back into the house. Before he can make it inside, someone—some thing—stands in the doorway, blocking the entrance. He's a tall, ominous figure.

Jerry barks and snaps at the backside of the brown-haired, slender man in a pair of dark jeans and a white short-sleeved T-shirt. He is young, and his life force fills the animal. I'm familiar with this harsh, invasive energy. It's that of a second-generation Selell.

The Selell turns his head one hundred eighty degrees to glare at Jerry. His eyes are red and angry. His skin is pasty brown, and his lips are so dry they show a thousand cracks. He's thirsty, and Jake is his cocktail. What I think will save the older man in the short run is that he won't give the vampire permission to consume him. But what occurs next happens so fast that I can't believe what I'm seeing.

The Selell's teeth are in Jake's neck. He appears to be drinking Jake's blood without consent. I can still only see his backside, but when he's done, he simply vanishes. Jerry is still barking his head off, beckoning Jake to come inside. Then another Selell rushes into the house. The animal is torn. He wants to dart off to the part of the house where Mary, Jake's wife, resides, but he also wants to ensure that his master hasn't met his demise.

Jake remains on his feet; he's like a beam planted in the ground. Then Jerry stops barking for a moment. I can barely explain the pervasive void engulfing every inch of the space surrounding them.

Jerry whimpers. The second Selell dashes past him and into the thick vapors. I'm unable to get a look at him or her. Since Jerry can't see into the backyard, neither can I.

Jake takes heavy steps into the house and closes the door. Mary walks into the living room, and they stare at each other as if something indescribable just happened to them.

"Jake... what..." Mary struggles to speak.

They notice the wounds on each other's neck. She touches hers. Jake touches his. Jerry walks between them, whimpering and rubbing their legs. Without speaking, they sit on the sofa.

Jerry shows me how they sat there for a very long time—I think for days—not speaking, eating, or even sleeping. He keeps himself pressed against his master's leg, and that's a very good thing, because I'm able to feel what's going on inside them —nothing. It's as if their spirits and souls have been drained. Jake and Mary are living through a state that's deeper than depression. It's a death without dying.

As I squat beside their bed, wondering how they got here from the sofa and who put the wallpaper on the windows, Jerry howls. Without noticing, I've wrapped my arms around him, and I'm petting his thick coat.

"Show me how they got here, Jerry," I say as I pat the bed.

Instead, he shows me how he's been searching for food ever since his owners fell into this state.

"Okay." I sigh as I stand.

The couple hasn't moved since I got here. I touch Jake's chest. Although it's subtle, my hand rides up then down with it. I touch Mary's chest. She's breathing too, in the same delicate manner. They're not dead, but the only sound in their heads is like white noise.

"What in the world…" I mutter.

Whatever happened to them is a mystery I must figure out. I follow Jerry to the kitchen. The trash cans are turned over, and one of the lower cabinets shows deep scratch marks. I'm sure Jerry, who's wagging his tail wildly, did it. He wants me to open the cabinet he scratched. So I do.

He gently jumps on me, panting and rubbing his orange coat against my legs as I take out a bag of dry dog food. The poor thing is starving. I hurry to a red plastic bowl near the door and overfill it. Someone has to come back and secure Jerry, at least until we can figure out how to restore his owners—if we can.

I rub his head as he chomps down on the crunchy bits. He's elated to be eating again. I don't know when I'll return, so I dump a pile of dog food next to the bowl and set the bag beside Jerry's feeding area. The last thing I see is Jerry lifting his head to whimper at me before I fade into myself.

I'm back in the diamond-walled room. Zillael, Fawn, and Derek rise to their feet as I hurry out and fill them in.

"You said they were consumed by Selells?" Derek asks.

I frown with my brows knitted. "Yes." I'm still trying to make sense of it all myself.

"Yet the humans are alive?"

"Yes, if you want to call it that. They're breathing, but that's it."

"And the Selells didn't die?"

I shake my head. "No."

"A Selell dies if he drinks a human's blood

without consent. That's the law," Derek says as if what I just told him can't be true.

"But Jake's not dead, right?" He's all Zillael is worried about at the moment.

"Not technically."

"Then we have to save him. We can still save him, can't we?"

At this moment, I have zero answers. This is all new to me, and I'm wondering where Lorenzo is. Isn't it his job to help provide me with answers? There's only one source I can reference at this juncture.

"Maybe the script can help us," I say with a sigh. "Because if vampires can suck the blood from humans and live, then something has definitely changed."

We all stand in silence, looking from one person to the next. The thought of vampires easily feeding on humans hangs heavy between us. For some reason, as I stand here, gravity feels stronger, the air stiffer, and the world more dangerous. It's as if everything around us has shifted, tilting toward something darker.

CHAPTER 3
FAWN'S GUY
CLARITY

T ime is ticking away, and the pressure is weighing on me as I read through the seven-thousand-year-old scroll I recovered from my paternal grandmother's grave. That reality is just as odd as my abilities to walk on air, run faster than a Ferrari, create shields by thinking them into existence, being in love with a vampire-like man who can drink blood to cure his thirst and travel through space at what appears to be the speed of light, and us both experiencing a heightened state of ecstasy when we make love. I have to convince myself this is all true before I can really focus on the page that's set on top of an onyx pillar in this diamond chamber.

I start by reading what I already know. I took

the leaf from the Tree of Life from Lario's heart and gave it to my father for safekeeping. Then one night, while I lay asleep on Baron's chest, Felix brought me to Enu where he gave me the leaf and instructed me to deliver it to the land of Jari. The leaf was planted in the soil of what I now read is the Branches of Restoration. Suddenly, I understand why the leaf that's able to keep a human alive forever was planted. Grass grew where ashes covered the land, and the charcoal sky gave way to a crisp, clear blue one. Restoration! I grin because I love how easy that was to figure out. The rest isn't so simple.

The script reads as if some of the old lines have new information. On line twenty-seven, I see the leaf and the key. Each sister, except the last hidden one, has her key. As the leaf was written on Lario's heart, the key is written on ours. I press my hand against my chest, wondering if I can feel it. I can't. I'm sure it's there though, because without ever learning the directions, I knew the way to Jari, just as I can instinctually find my way to any Enu portal on this great big earth.

Something happened when we planted the leaf in the Branches of Restoration. Once that is revealed to me, I'm able to read new text.

"Cl'auta," a familiar voice says, and a recognizable presence appears beside me.

"Felix... Dad," I mutter. I've only called him Dad a few times, on very rare occasions that I can't even recall.

Fawn and Zillael slowly stand upon seeing Felix in the chamber with me. Just like me, they want to explode with excitement.

"You've seen what Selells are able to do now, haven't you?" he asks. In the true Felix form, he gets quickly to the business at hand.

I always took his lack of salutations personally, especially when I was younger. These days, since I know how much he loves and cares for me and all of my sisters, I can ascertain that "getting on with it" is just a part of his personality. It has nothing to do with him wanting to hurry up and get away from me.

"Yes," I answer after the shock of seeing him wears off. "They were able to drink a human's blood without dying."

"Is that what you think? They drank the blood of the two humans?"

"That's what I saw," I say, as if I'm defending my answer.

"You saw them bite into Jake Grimes's jugular.

That part of a human's body doesn't only flow with blood; it also carries their life force. Now read the book." He sounds almost demanding. "See what's happening to this universe."

I can't stop staring at my father's face. He'll always be the most regal creature I've ever laid eyes on. He has a high forehead, dark skin, and beautiful, sharp features. He's the son of an ancient woman and a celestial being, and he's always been unreachable, unobtainable. I learned very early not to demand more than what he could give. My mommy issues far outweighed my daddy issues. Freda was a hellcat. It's still hard to believe that she wasn't simply a bad mother—she was a guardian. Who in his right mind thought she would be healthy for my psyche? Thank God Aries was around. I'd be a serious basket case if it weren't for her.

"Cl'auta," he says to refocus me on the matter at hand.

"Sorry," I say while blinking myself back into the moment.

He touches my shoulder and squeezes. *He touched me*. Don't cry, I warn myself. Do *not* cry.

"Read on," he urges me.

I take a deep breath and force it out to steady

myself. "'The air of humanity is stolen by the heart and leaf. The empty sees dark, and the dark is resurrected.'" I turn to Felix. *What the heck does that mean?*

Felix is already studying me, wearing a pinched expression. "When you saw the Selell sink his teeth into the human, what did you really see?"

I give it the old college try. I line up all the details. Humanity stolen. He bit into Jake's jugular but did not drink his blood.

"He drank his soul?" I gasp, utterly shocked by my conclusion.

"Yes. Do you know what this means?"

I think hard, trying to put the pieces together. "Jake and Mary are without their souls…"

"And remember what Ze Feldis's fears showed you."

"The souls of vampires?"

"If Zillael's friend, the shopkeeper, isn't dead, then his soul still belongs to him and to him only."

"We have to find it," I resolutely conclude.

On that note, he turns toward Fawn and Zillael, who hadn't stopped watching him since he appeared. He clearly has the same effect on them that he has on me. I hear him saying their names in my head.

"Felix," Fawn says as Zillael says, "Dad."

It's interesting to me how easily Zill calls him that, especially after knowing him for such a short period of time. Goodness, I envy her. He lifts a hand toward them. They do the same, and then he's gone. He's still the same old Felix, keeping it short and, these days, *sweeter*.

Once I'm out of the chamber, I explain to my sisters and Derek how the Selells didn't drink Jake and Mary's blood; they consumed their souls. A dreadful silence lingers in the air as everyone processes the bomb I just dropped.

"But we can still help them," I say to soothe everyone's fears. "I have to meet Baron. Fawn, you should come with me." I point at Zillael and Derek. "You two should go to Moonridge. I'll guide you to Jake and Mary Grimes's house."

"I already know the way," Derek says.

"Good. Brace yourself for what you'll find. Zill, I need you to contact me once you get to where they're sleeping. We're going to try something."

She bobs her head. Her expression tells me she's bothered by her thoughts.

"What?" I ask instead of extracting them myself.

"Are you sure they're not dead? I don't think I

can handle it if someone I know, or knew, ends up dead."

What bright, beautiful eyes my sister has—and so sad yet extremely curious at the moment.

"Yes." I'm happy to be able to tell her that. "They're still alive."

"Okay," she says with a sigh. She turns those glassy eyes on Derek, who lifts his mouth into a weak, lopsided smile.

This is the first time since they've come back with the report on Moonridge that I've seen them acknowledge each other in the "I think I like you a lot" way.

I turn to Fawn. "Then it's all settled."

"Ready?" she asks.

"Ready."

———

"Tapeetha," Fawn says out of the blue.

We're in the crystal tunnels, which still hold the rare scent of pure, untainted oxygen. The essence of Enu lingers in the air here too. The first time I traveled through these pathways, I could hardly believe it. Now I'm aware that the glassy walls and floors are made of diamond, which, like the chamber in the reading room, allows for the energy of Enu to be brought to Earth. Just like in Enu, if any forbidden creature enters the tunnels, they'll suffocate within seconds. It's a scary thought, but it makes this the safest leg of our journey.

"The second sister?" I ask, wondering why Fawn would blurt out her name.

"I remember something about her." She sounds amazed.

"What's that?"

"She went to war against the Shams in 1489. She would know how to fight them... but..."

"But what?"

She takes a long pause. "She can never leave Enu without heartbreak."

We arrive at the exit. It took us a little over six minutes to get here. As it is with Enu, time in the tunnel is slower than on Earth.

"Why the heartbreak?" I ask as we flow up the diamond steps.

"Because of the Wek, Ose. She fell in love with him and chose him over..." She struggles to remember a name.

None of this computes for me as we make our way through a hatch in the ground. To my chagrin, we're in dark, dense woods—always in the woods—and the snow is about ten inches deep. Once upon a time, I loved the icy layers of winter, but camping in the icy wilderness of Nowhere cured me of that. To combat the cold that neither Fawn nor I are dressed for, I cover us with a shield of warmth and invisibility. But not numbness. That shield keeps vampires from smelling us. We rarely run into them in the air, mostly on the ground or underground. For a second, I wonder why, but it's simply a passing thought.

It's time for us to walk the wind. We rise above the trees layered in white. A strong gust blows in off the ocean to the north of us, and Fawn uses her power to push it back.

Once we've made ourselves comfortable for this last and very short leg of our journey, I say what I've been mulling over. "So you're saying that Tapeetha's stuck in Enu because she's in love with a Wek?"

"Because they consummated their relationship."

"Had sex?" I exclaim, surprised.

"It's easy to fall in love with a Wek, but it is forbidden."

I think about Zillael and Derek. For sure, she loves him, and he loves her. I noticed him rejecting her sexual advances from the beginning. Could this be the reason?

"I think it is," Fawn says, answering my thoughts.

We move down a narrow street lined with tiny seaside tourist traps. I see the sign for Chester's about a quarter mile away, where the block dead-ends. Baron's energy stabs my heart in a magnificent way. He hasn't been gone for long, but to me, it feels as if he's been away for a lifetime.

"Well, we have to tell her," I say.

"No," Fawn admonishes me. "We shouldn't influence her decisions. You know that, Cl'auta."

"I don't think telling her that if she has sex with Derek, she'll be bound to Enu is influencing her decisions."

"Having sex with Derek will bind her to Enu only if she wants him to stay alive after the fact."

"She should know that!"

"She will, at the right time," Fawn says.

"I think the right time is whenever we tell her." I'm a little huffy about it, not because of Fawn but because of these insane rules that govern us. Do we all have to figure out everything on our own? "I mean, what about wise counsel?" I continue.

"Someone once said that the lack of it leads to the demise of the oblivious."

"And experience is the throne of the wise," Fawn responds without pause.

I snort. Silence falls between us as we land a few feet from Chester's unlit foyer.

There's one thing I must admit before I turn the knob in hopes of finding the door open. "I think you're right. Wise counsel is only effective if it's adhered to. And ready to be accepted."

"Don't worry, Cl'auta," Fawn says as she touches my shoulder. "Derek will not cross that line with her until our work is finished."

"Are you sure? He's really in love with her."

She nods. "Neither Weks nor we lust like humans or even Selells. Have you ever truly wanted a man before you met Ze Feldis?"

I take a moment to remember my past. During my deflowering debacle, lust didn't drive that awful experience. I've always been aware of my own lack of sexual burning. Up until those days in Cambridge when Baron and I first met, I'd been numb in that department. My startling answer to Fawn's question is, "No."

"So don't worry about Zill. Whatever she chooses will be the best for all of us if we don't change the course of her fate." She smiles at me under the ledge of the dark doorway.

I smile back. Then Fawn does the strangest thing. She wraps her arms tightly around her chest and hugs herself.

"Falu, what's wrong?"

Her eyes are closed, and she's breathing as though she's hyperventilating. "I don't know. I just feel—funny."

I allow myself to invade her. "Wow!" I thought she was in pain, but what's flooding her is the opposite of that. "What's going on with you?"

"I don't know." She can barely speak.

The emotions flooding her are so intense that I let go. I can't imagine where they're all coming from. I glance up the road and see a group of people heading our way. They're all bundled up in coats, sweater caps, and scarves.

"Well, let's hurry up and get inside." I check over my shoulder. Those people are getting closer.

Fawn sees them too and nods. The good thing is that the door is unlocked. We step into a wide, empty, unlit space. The folks that were walking toward us take turns shaking the locked doorknob. Since I'd dropped our shields, Fawn and I remain as still and quiet as possible, waiting for them to pass.

"I just saw it open and close," a woman says.

"You're seeing things again, Deb," another woman quips.

"Let's go! I'm freezing my balls," a guy complains. His voice is already fading.

Finally, Baron's nearness rings in loud and clear. I blink, and he's standing beside me with his arms wrapped tightly around me. I'm infused with his warmth.

"Clarity," he whispers as his lips press on my forehead. "You're better."

I smile at him. "I am, but Fawn isn't feeling too well." I move out of his embrace and wrap an arm around her waist.

He looks at her and then at me. "Did you tell her?"

"Did I tell her what?" I'm completely confused.

"About what we found hiding in the coven?"

I sigh. "No, I hadn't thought about it."

"Tell me what?" Fawn asks.

"There's a vampire with your powers," Baron says.

"Wait." Fawn shuts her eyes tight and holds herself again. "He's here, isn't he?"

"Yes."

"Ben Artiste," she whispers past her tight throat.

"Yes."

I experience Fawn's emotions. Her heart is pounding like a jackhammer, but it's not all elation. She's afraid and hesitant. Her desperate desire to flee from him is slowly fading away, and the longer we stand here, the more anxious she becomes.

"This way," Baron says with an outstretched hand.

Fawn takes his hand. It's strange for me to see her like this. She's always so good at keeping her composure, but as we walk her through a large, clean kitchen with industrial-sized appliances, she's unable to calm her angst. The floor is shiny and glistens under the dimmed light fixtures. Baron doesn't have to tell me he owns this place. The environment has his *je ne sais quoi* stamped on it.

"He's afraid to go above the surface," Baron explains as we enter a short hallway. An elevator stands open for us.

"I wonder why," I muse.

"Me too," Baron whispers. "I thought Artiste had died hundreds of years ago. The rumor was he became so thirsty that he drank a human without consent."

The doors to the elevator slide closed, and we're on our way downward.

"He would never do that," Fawn murmurs.

"You seem to know him well," I say, hoping she'll elaborate. I'm ultra-curious about their association. I've always wondered if Lario was truly Fawn's bond. Him being made for her had seemed like destiny's cruel joke. We're each much like our bonds, and there's not an evil, conniving, or manipulative bone in her body.

As I study Fawn through the mirror panel that's facing me, I see I'm smiling without realizing it. It occurs to me that this is one of the happiest moments in my life. She's a far better creature than I am, and she deserves all that's beautiful and agreeable in all universes. My eyes fall over my special gift's reflection. He's already staring at me with smoldering eyes.

The timing is perfect. The doors slide open. Fawn pulls away from Baron and me to rush out of the elevator. Baron stands behind me with his arms wrapped around me. He uses his super strength and speed to move us out of the elevator.

There's a full bar down here with round cocktail tables and chairs. Velvet red booths line the walls. The only person down here is sitting at the bar, staring at a glass of some concoction with a lot of alcohol in it. He's thankful it's no longer a momentary cure for his thirst. When he turns toward Fawn, he rises to his feet so fast that the glass topples over. First, he's momentarily blinded by a light of love, desire, and happiness. Then he feels confusion, lots of it.

"Falu?" he asks, calling her by her Enuian name.

Yes, they're very familiar with each other. Through both of their memories, I see them entangled in the throes of passion. Fawn remembers the taste of his kiss and is once again familiarizing herself with his face.

My first observation of Ben Artiste is confirmed. He more than resembles Baron. They have the same hair that looks windblown but simultaneously compact and neat, coupled with the same delicately chiseled jawline and slight yet heavy, extremely intense blue eyes. He's looking at her as if he's mesmerized. He makes a swift move, and in a flash, they're standing face to face.

"Where have you been all this time?" Fawn asks. She fears if she touches him, he might disappear.

He frowns. "I don't..." He speaks as if he's just remembering. "We were off the coast of Sardinia."

"La Isle Maddalena," Fawn says as the memory

comes to her. "But we were being chased, weren't we?"

Artiste frowns harder. "We were…"

He has a slight accent. I can't quite place it. I focus on Fawn's memories. She's on his back, and Artiste is carrying her across a white sand beach toward crystal-clear water where limestone cliffs rise out of the sea in the distance. The sun blossoms. The sky is blue. The air is warm and slightly humid. Smaller rocky islands are plopped down across the clear blue sea. Despite the apparent paradise, Fawn's expression is grim. Whoever is pursuing them is close. She hears him calling her name, warning them to give up because they won't get far.

I know that voice very well. I'll never forget it.

She's on the verge of remembering that person's face when Artiste's hand shoots up to cradle her cheek. He presses his lips against hers, but they don't kiss. They share a nostalgic gaze. Neither of them can truly believe this moment is happening.

As my heart swells and my eyes well up with tears, I hear in my head, *"Clarity, we're here. It's Zill."*

ZILL

I can hardly stomach the sight of Jake and his wife lying in bed. They look like an attraction in a haunted house, the one with the creepy old couple, pale as powder, rocking in chairs with a bone-thin canine stretched across the guy's feet.

"He's gotten skinny," I whisper to Derek, who's rubbing Jerry's head.

"Yeah," he whispers. "Did you contact Clarity?"

"I did."

"And…?"

"She said to give her a minute. I think she's with Ze Feldis."

"Okay." Derek takes care to keep his eyes on the dog, whose tail is flopping in every direction.

I take it Jake's pet is happy to see us. I notice how awkward talking to him has become. For the most part, since we left Moonridge earlier today, Derek has only looked at me when necessary. I want to shout, "What now, you moody Wek?" But this isn't the time or place for an argument, not while Jake and his wife are lying before us in a crazy kind of coma.

"They look dead already," I quietly say.

"If anyone can restore them, you and your

sisters can," Derek says, again without looking at me.

"You say that with such assurance." I stare at him, reading him. I want to see if he really believes what he said or if he's just attempting to make me feel better. I don't know why I doubt him. Derek's never been the type to say whatever it takes to calm my nerves.

He lifts his face and gazes right into my eyes, but he drops his face just as fast. "Look." He motions toward Jake and his wife with his chin.

The dog barks as the bodies light up.

"It's Clarity; she's doing something," Derek says.

Jake's eyes pop open, and so do his wife's. In the next second, crazy apparitions of Clarity and Baron become visible. He's standing on Mary's side of the bed with one hand on her head, and Clarity's on Jake's side with one hand on his head. Clarity and Baron are holding hands. My sister and her vampire boyfriend, who even in this form is so hot he sizzles, are covered in the light they're filling Jake and Mary with.

The dog has stopped barking and is watching the show, which, I must say, is pretty impressive. When it's over, we all stare at the catatonic couple, waiting to see what will happen next. The light is trapped inside them and hasn't yet faded in intensity.

"I think it's working." Clarity sounds optimistic.

"What's working?" I ask.

Clarity releases Baron's hand and presses one of her hands against my forehead. "I need you to do something."

I swallow hard. "Okay." I can't imagine what she needs me to do at this moment. I pray she won't attempt to take me inside Jake and his wife. I don't want to be insensitive, but I'd rather not experience whatever's happening to them.

Clarity smiles at me a little. She has that look on her face that she always gets when she knows what I'm thinking. "Everything will be fine," she promises.

I believe her. I let out the breath I've been holding. "Ready." I sigh.

After a moment, I see a male form in my head. He's far from where we are, and music is blasting in the background. The flickering red, yellow, and blue lights that movies use to depict seedy nightclubs swing through the air and strike the domed ceiling. The place is such a cliché. Naked women are swerving, gyrating, and pulling at the bars of cages that are suspended above the main floor. It's a packed house, and people are everywhere. I wonder if they're vampires. The guy she's focusing on is practically swallowing a woman as they kiss. Threads of saliva pull from their greedy lips. He's panting, all hot and bothered. It's gross.

"I'm going to guide you to them, and you're going to kill them," Clarity says to me.

"Are they vampires?"

"They are, and they've left these two soulless."

"So this light you gave them, it doesn't give them back their souls?"

"No," Clarity says. "They're slowly dying. The light staves off death until we figure out a way to get their souls back. I've stretched the same energy over this entire town. Thousands of others here are in the same shape."

"And you think killing the vampires can save Jake?"

"I do."

"Then that's what we'll do," I say, lifting my eyebrows at Derek.

He has no response, verbal or otherwise.

"Good." She sounds relieved but is still as intense as usual. "Do you see that?"

At first, my insides tickle. Whatever's happening

to me is unreal. A part of me—not my spirit or soul or anything like that; it's me—is rushing across a rocky desert terrain near pale, arid mountains. There are cacti, creosote bushes, and tumbleweeds. I used to dream about living in the desert. I've read up on Arizona, Nevada, and California. If all of this had never happened to me, then I think I'd be in a desert like this now, where it's warm and dry for the better part of the year. It's late afternoon, and even in the winter, I feel a tepid warmth flow up my nostrils.

We stop not too far from the towering hotels and casinos of the Las Vegas strip. I've seen it in pictures but never in real life. My consciousness hovers over a flat, tiny shack in the middle of the desert. It appears to be an abandoned garage.

"There's an entrance nearby," Clarity says.

She's right next to me, but I can't see her. I can't even see myself! She grunts from minor frustration. I think she's searching for that entrance.

"There!" she says.

We shoot across the desert so fast it takes a second for my head to catch up with my sister's presence.

"It's down there," she says, pointing at the ground.

I don't see anything because I'm too distracted by what just happened to me. "How are we able to do this?"

"Well, I searched inside you for your non-human parts and carried them with me. It was fast thinking. I'm glad it worked." She says this with the utmost patience.

"You've never done this before?" I'm surprised that I'm the first. It makes me feel kind of special.

"Not to this degree," she answers before changing the subject. "You're going to have to go down this well, and it will lead you where you need to go. Okay?"

I sense she's waiting for me to answer. I look down the hole. If I weren't standing this close to it, I don't think I would be able to see it. Spiny weeds and dry grass grow around the rim. It reminds me of photos I've seen of wolves' dens. The only difference is the positioning. Wolf dens are dug in shallow hills. This hole is not.

"That looks dangerous," I reply.

"For you, it isn't." She sounds encouraging.

"I know. But is the place you showed me down there?"

"Yes."

I try to tune in to whatever is below, but I get

nothing. I don't hear music or see flickering lights. I finally say, "Okay." I'm game to face the unknown once again and fight against it.

In the snap of a finger, I'm fully back in Jake's room, and so is Clarity, or as much as she can be. Baron, Derek, and even the dog are watching us. The light that Clarity and Baron put in Jake and his wife still makes them glow like a full moon.

This is all so weird. The Enuian part of me can jump out of my body as long as Clarity carries me? It's just one more thing that makes her great.

"I wish I could be with you, Zill, but this is your show, and Derek's, I presume," she says, glancing at him. "Stay safe."

"I will," I mumble.

She kisses my forehead. "Call me if you need me."

Then she and Ze Feldis are gone.

MOONRIDGE FEELS EERIE NOW. IN ALL THE YEARS I've lived here, the roads and sidewalks were always neatly plowed, no matter the season. The mayor kept little white lights strung through the trees and buildings, especially around those two ostentatious towers. I used to think it was over-the-top and corny. Now, I don't.

Derek and I stand in the freezing night, benefiting from the shield of warmth surrounding us. I glance up at the ashen sky, where thick clouds blot out any trace of moonlight. Soon, we'll see it when we ride the wind—it's always clearer above the clouds. It feels more magical up there, and safer.

"We should go up," I say to break the silence that's fallen between us again.

Derek does that one-nod thing, and I can hardly stand it.

"So are we not speaking anymore or what?"

"We're talking," he says with a tiny smile.

I must admit, I'm relieved to see him smiling. "Just strictly business, though, right?"

"Business is all we've been up to since you returned from Jari," he remarks.

I blurt a cynical snort. "We came here for a candy apple. Yeah, that sounds like business to me."

He laughs gently. But quickly, the deafening silence between us returns.

"So we're heading to Las Vegas, right?" he asks to fill the silence.

Although the moon can't be seen and most of the streetlamps, porch lights, and lighted marquees are out, his green eyes glisten as bright as a newborn baby's. I bet Derek has never had a bad thought or even said a bad word. I bet as long as he's lived on Earth, he hasn't made one enemy. Every girl who's ever looked at him, and I mean in just one look, became caught in a crush that they're still struggling to overcome.

"Yep," I finally croak, mesmerized by how he's watching me.

"You need to know how this works without Vayle," he says, ignoring my starry-eyed look.

That's different. Usually, he'd acknowledge it and respond with an appreciative smirk. But I can't harp on that. His mention of Vayle's name sparks a pinch of betrayal within me. I shouldn't have to do this without him. When this is all over and he's made himself human again, I'll find him and give him a piece of my mind.

"How does it work without Vayle?" I ask with a bite in my tone.

"I can't attack the living unless you're being threatened."

I feel my eyebrows furrow as I try to simplify what he just said. "Does that mean I'm on my own until I'm in a jam?"

He shakes his head. "No. After you hit, if they hit back, then I can fight. It's an easy enough rule."

"Well, it doesn't make sense."

"That's what I've been trying to convey to you. You and I are governed by separate laws because of what we are."

I stare into his eyes, detecting a double meaning in his words. "And if the laws are broken, then what?"

Derek steps closer to me. How can we be so different? His breath is warm and smells sweet. His chest rises and falls with each breath he takes. And when we're kissing and he's all over me, my body knows that his physique is exactly how it should be— perfect. But that's only his outside. Inside, he's smart and empathetic and kind. What law in Earth or heaven or Enu or Jari demands that we remain apart?

"I vanish." He enunciates every syllable, probably to get that through my thick head.

My heart takes a dive. "Vanish? Like disappear?"

"It's like dying, but I can't die. I simply won't exist any longer."

"Does that scare you?" I can't help but ask. It would scare me.

"No," he answers.

"Oh, good." I'm at a loss for words but not emotions. I'm feeling a lot of stuff at once, but I have no time to dawdle in this pool of weird sensations. I swallow the lump in my throat. "Well," I try to sound as unaffected as possible, "we should get going."

Then he shows me the smile I've been hoping to see. What an angel. Of course he's not like me. Only after forcing myself to realize the clear distinctions between us am I able to smile back at him.

It's clear that I'm the one leading us, so I take off to walk the wind first, and he goes up alongside me.

CHAPTER 4

OFF WITH THEIR HEADS
CLARITY

Baron strokes the top of my back with his strong, warm fingers. "You don't have to worry about her."

Although I want to fall calmly into his touch, I hate that Zill's out there without Fawn or me. My mouth turns down in an unsure smile. Nothing he can say will put me at ease. My worry won't pass until I see Zill, alive and well and in the flesh. However, I choose to focus on the matter at hand.

Baron, Fawn, Ben Artiste, and I are still alone in Baron's underground establishment. We're seated in a booth against a bare white wall. I'm beside Baron, and Fawn sits next to Artiste. Their forearms are touching on the tabletop. I remember sensing her feelings for Lario back when we were figuring out how to find the script. Back then, I thought she loved Lario, but those feelings were almost clinical compared to what she feels now.

Ben Artiste is telling us what he heard and the little he saw when the Mount Olympus coven was attacked.

"So the Selells who attacked the coven were second generation?" I ask.

"I don't understand what you mean by second generation." He dips his head toward Baron. "Were they different from Ze Feldis and me? Yes."

"That's right. You don't know about the leaf and Lario."

"Lario Exgesis?" he says with a scowl and balls his fists on top of the table.

I explain how Lario ate the leaf from the Tree of Life after putting a spell on Fawn and convincing her he really wanted to be human.

"You were lovers?" Artiste nearly growls at Fawn, frowning hard at her.

She stares at him like a deer stuck in headlights. She's dumbfounded, and she has no idea how to answer that question without feeling like she's incriminating herself.

"Technically no," I answer for her. "He doesn't play fair. She never loved him for real and would've never loved that bastard at all if he hadn't cast a spell on her."

I realize I'm leaning forward. My face is tense, and I've just stabbed the table with my index finger. All three of them watch me closely, especially Baron. I refuse to make eye contact with him while I feel this way. I simply hate Lario. I'm supposed to be an empathetic creature by nature, but I must have some malfunction because I can't seem to stop hating him.

Artiste narrows his eyes even more as he thinks. "Exgesis was the last face I saw before descending into the dark places in my mind. Ever been there?"

I see and feel what he's remembering. It's a place where he could recognize no one, not even his own reflection. He wondered why he couldn't go outside in the day, why the sun tormented him, why he was a man with no home, no love, not even a memory of being born. The sight of another creature frightened him so much that he lay low for hundreds of years, residing deeper in the vampire-inhabited depths of existence. And then there was the thirst—the throat-scorching, bitter thirst. Night in and night out, a thirst that couldn't be quenched.

He'd wanted to die, but nothing could kill him. He once jumped in front of a bus at night. It ran over him and dragged him a mile, but he emerged from the bottom of it unscathed. He tried to let the sun scorch him, but the pain of being in the sun for even a second was like being stabbed a million times at once for eternity. For the first time, I'm able to experience what that feels like through Artiste, and my entire body tightens from the pain. I wait for the memory to pass.

"You just took me there," I tell him.

Artiste frowns, perplexed.

"I'm able to feel what you feel," I explain.

His mouth falls open. He glances at Fawn and then back at me. He does this a few times. "The seven sisters? I kept remembering 'the seven sisters' and wondering what the hell that meant. I would see your face, Falu, and think, who the hell is she? It never dawned on me to… or maybe it did."

Fawn's mouth is slightly parted as she hangs on to his every word. "What? It never dawned on you to do what?"

He hesitates, but only because he feels dominated by the spell that Lario Exgesis cast upon him and Fawn. He looks away and mutters, "Find your face."

"She wouldn't have recognized you," I say.

"She's right," Fawn admits. "There's a lot I

forgot too." She turns toward me. "Remember when you saved me from Lario?"

"Your sister had to save you from Exgesis?" Artiste nearly shouts.

"Wait," Fawn says. "I remember something." She has all of our attention. "After Lario had me steal *The Bloods of Life* from the Vatican, he was ticked off because he couldn't interpret it. He went on the road for about a month to lecture as Dr. Dove, and then he came back." She looks at Baron. "That was the first time I met you. He said you were an old friend. I figured you'd known him for years."

"I had," Baron confirms.

"He said you were cerebral and empathetic and had superior instincts and insight into others. Lario pretended that we figured out together that you could be bonded to the sister with the power of the mind, and we, meaning he, needed her to interpret the writing." Fawn shakes her head in contempt. It's the first time I've seen or sensed that emotion in her. "He said finding Clarity and getting her bonded to Ze Feldis would put everything in motion to save the world from vampires and change vampires back to humans."

"Well, that's true," I say, at least giving him

credit for that. He'd just refrained from mentioning that once he'd turned into some sort of demigod, he'd fight us tooth and nail to make sure that would never happen.

"Yes, but Lario made me believe that being a vampire was the worst experience in the world and that he loved being human," Fawn says. "He was zealous about ridding the world of Selells. I would've never guessed he'd turn back into one. Never."

"Wait," I blurt as a thought hits me. "He knows who all seven bonds are. Artiste, did you associate with Lario before you met Fawn?"

"Yes."

"And Vayle. It was no accident he was chased into the same small town where Zillael lived," I say.

"Is she another sister?" Artiste asks.

"Yes, she is."

Silence falls between us. We're all deep in thought, asking ourselves different questions.

"There's Baron, Vayle, and Artiste. What about the other four?" I ask.

"Three," Fawn says.

I widen my eyes at her, signaling for her to elaborate.

"The fifth sister, Glo—her bond hasn't been found, and Tapeetha chose Ose."

"The Wek?"

"Yes."

"Leto Danto," Artiste says as if he's just recalling that name.

"The Selell who's bonded to Tapeetha," Fawn confirms.

"Do you have any idea where he may be?" I ask.

"No," Fawn answers with a hopeless sigh.

"But if you can remember him, then I can find him," I say without doubt. "However, you said three Selells. The third—is he connected to Adore?"

Fawn nods. "She refuses to come to Earth, which is why I've never met him."

"But is he on Earth?"

"Possibly. I would think so. Selells begin as humans, and humans live on Earth."

"I wonder if Lario knows who he is," I say.

We turn quiet because we're all wondering the same thing. I truly don't understand Adore. I wonder sometimes if she's living in a fantasyland. She's tried to convince me, and I know she's tried to convince Fawn too, to stay in Enu and forget about the earth. Adore won't interfere with our free will, but it's her will that we see things her way.

"Adore knows she has to leave Enu one day, right?" I ask Fawn.

Fawn shrugs. "She's made her choice."

"I guess we'll cross the Adore road when we get to it." I sigh, weary just thinking about it. "What about Leto Danto? Maybe he still has a portion of the power of matter."

"Maybe," Fawn says. "I think that if we want to fight the Shams, the power of matter is the easiest way to do it."

Suddenly, glass clinks in the kitchen. Baron and Artiste flick their faces toward the noise.

"Put your shields up, Clarity," Baron says.

I engage the shields of invisibility and numbness. A few seconds later, one, two, then five vampires flow into the room. They've already been served drinks, and a female bartender with blond dreadlocks and dark-green lipstick shoots through the room, serving more vampires as they rush in.

Suddenly, I'm out of the booth and on my feet. Baron's arms are wrapped around me as a vampire in a tailored business suit takes the seat we've just abandoned. Artiste has pulled Fawn out of her seat as well, and they're looking at another male vampire who's also in a nice suit. I'm surprised by how normal these guys look, guzzling their drinks and refilling them from the bottle of vodka on the table. They're discussing plans to build an underground tunnel, and they even mention Baron as one of the investors. They remind me that he's a businessman. It seems like an eternity has passed since we carried on with our earthly professions, and what's peculiar is that I yearn to be part of that life again—with Baron, as we are, Selell and lifeblood.

"We should go," Baron says.

The entire room has filled to capacity, and two more bartenders are tending to the patrons' needs. We decide to follow Baron's suggestion and finish figuring things out at the estate. To get there quicker, Baron carries me, and Artiste carts Fawn.

We break through the barrier stretched around the estate. Even before our feet touch the ground, I hear a gut-wrenching yell. Artiste is balled up on top of the thistly ground, using his arms to block his face from the sun. It soon dawns on him that he's not burning. Slowly, he unravels himself.

"The sun doesn't touch you here," Fawn says to him with an outstretched hand.

His eyes flick above my head to observe Baron, who stands behind me. Then Artiste takes Fawn's hand, and in a flash, he's back on his feet, studying the way his bare arms remain unscathed by the sunlight.

"Remarkable," he marvels. "I never thought I would—" He stops short of expressing his elation.

"I know." Fawn cups her other hand over the hand of his she's holding.

He withdraws his hand, and Fawn glances at me. I lift my eyebrows to indicate that I saw it.

"It's too soon," I say just to her. *"He's been through a lot of trauma."*

From the look on her face, she understands but is saddened by it nevertheless.

"How is this even possible?" Artiste asks, still marveling.

"There's a shift in the space-time continuum between Earth and the portion of this land that's on Earth," I explain for Fawn, who has opened her mouth but can't speak. She's still reacting to his sudden withdrawal.

He shuffles in a circle. His eyes are wide open as he takes in the trees and trails and how they all glisten in the daylight. "Do you hear that?"

"Birds, insects, yes," I say.

"Yes, that too, but I can also hear the sun." There's a catch in his voice.

We all watch a black-and-white polka-dot butterfly pass over our heads. Artiste flinches, taken aback, when the insect transforms into the shape of a human being.

"Cl'auta," Lorenzo says and nods at me. Then he notices Baron and Fawn and displays the same gesture toward them.

Artiste is the last one Lorenzo acknowledges, and I get to see what confusion looks like on a Wek's face. Lorenzo's eyes shift from Fawn to Artiste and then back to Fawn. He knows. I'm not able to detect his feelings about the situation except that he's aware Artiste and Fawn are bonded.

Fawn and Lorenzo have been getting close recently. He seems captivated by the adventurous side of her while Fawn was attracted to him at first sight. Like Derek, Zill's Wek, Lorenzo is pure beauty. His features are soft, but there's nothing boyish about his physique. Plus, Weks can enthrall women because they listen, encourage, and have an accepting manner. They're everything a good man is, both on the inside and outside.

If Baron were a Wek, our relationship would have never hit that valley years ago when Lario lied to him about me choosing to remain in Enu with Viesel Egos, of all people. Out of self-preservation,

Baron reacted to me because I'd hurt him, and I was capable of doing it again. A Wek would have believed in my heart, my head, and in me because there was nothing to lose. That's the allure. It would've been easier for us if these creatures were female. My sisters and I have one thing in common: We have a distant father. A Wek can be very appealing to a girl with daddy issues.

But what I want to confirm is, can Weks love? I'm on the road to believing that Derek sincerely loves Zillael. The look in Lorenzo's eyes says he's reacting to the presence of Artiste, but I can't get a read on him as far as love is concerned. Instead, I'm reading that he's very pleased with someone, and that someone is me.

"I've been watching, Cl'auta," he says, making sure he stays focused on my face. "You've discovered the soul snatchers."

"Yes. So now Selells can just assault humans whenever the urge hits?" I ask, glad that I'm finally having a conversation with someone who can shed more light on the matter.

"No," he says. "But that's not your concern. It's for humans to figure out."

I shake my head. "You mean there's still a way for people to save themselves?"

Lorenzo responds by blinking at me with a blank look on his face. It's his way of saying the subject is closed, discussion over.

All eyes are on Lorenzo. He doesn't often flutter in without a reason. He peeks at Fawn, and that's when I get suspicious. Maybe Lorenzo has no thoughts about Fawn, but Fawn does, and I see it all. Their lips are locked, tongues tasting each other. They're panting and moaning, and their hands are all over each other. They're in the garden right outside the bedroom in Fawn's area of the house. The grass beneath them is a perfect plush green, and there's a white pearl statue of a female Enuian with bushy long hair. She has no breasts, but she makes up for it with rich, seductive curves. The way the moon hits the stone makes it look almost alive. Then Fawn slips off his shirt. He slips off her shirt. From what I see, a Wek has sex like a regular person or vampire.

"Cl'auta," Fawn calls only to me.

I face her.

"Did you see that?" she asks.

I nod subtly. *"But I thought Lorenzo would vanish after, you two, you know…"*

"He's not my Wek, he's yours, so…"

I'm still a little shocked by their encounter. It

looks as though Lorenzo has been following our every word to each other. As my Wek, he has my abilities, so more than likely, he heard everything we said. Still, he has no emotional reaction.

"If you were right about killing the Selells who took the Grimes's souls, then what should your next step be, Cl'auta?" Lorenzo asks, getting on with the real reason he's here.

The funny thing is, Artiste senses that something is going on between them. With narrowed eyes, he watches Fawn, Lorenzo, and even me.

"I have to identify the thieves." I know there's more to it, but I can't get the picture of Fawn and Lorenzo doing it out of my head.

"We have to kill them all," Baron says, picking up my slack.

"Yes," I say, putting my thoughts back on track. "We have to identify and kill all the second-generation vampires."

"And how will you do that?" Lorenzo asks, seemingly nonreactive to what I learned about him. He's in schoolmarm mode, leading me to an answer that he feels I already know.

"The identifier," I reply. "The fang and the heart."

"That is not correct," Lorenzo says.

"Really? Then what is correct?" I sound irritated. I really dislike Schoolmarm Wek.

Again, he gives me the blank look. "I'll be watching," is all he says before transforming back into the black-and-white polka-dot butterfly and fluttering away. Normally, he says good-bye to the group first.

We waste no time getting inside the house. I haven't been gone long, but every time I go away, this place feels more like home. Neither Cambridge nor Manhattan ever felt like that, which makes this a novel sensation.

Baron and I go to the study to wait for Zill and work on figuring out our next step. Fawn takes Artiste to show him their living space. I wonder how they're getting along, but it's hard to concentrate on anything outside of this room when Baron paces across the marble floor. He's moving so fast his feet aren't touching the ground, and the breeze he stirs up blasts me whenever he passes me.

Watching him makes me weary. I pat the empty space beside me on the brass-colored leather sofa. "Baron, sit, please?"

He stops and turns to face me. His expression exposes the heaviness that's burdening him at the moment.

I give him a tiny smile. "You're giving it too much thought. Maybe you should just rest for a moment. You know vampires need to relax too."

He walks over at regular speed to take that seat I just offered him. He leans back, closes his eyes, and pinches the skin between his eyes as if a vampire can truly have a headache. "The sooner we're done with this, the sooner we can—"

"Spend time together, alone," I finish.

He gazes at me with those hypnotic eyes of his and lifts his mouth into the equally spellbinding smirk only he can do. "I have plans for us."

"What sort of plans?" I'm grinning like the Cheshire cat.

He makes a swift move, and I find myself sitting across his lap.

"You'll have to wait and see," he whispers before pressing his lips to mine.

My head goes floating again. I wonder if kissing him will ever stop feeling like the first time we made out on Longfellow Bridge in Cambridge.

"You should tell me now," I say, "because we might be at this world-saving stuff for a very long time." Every part of me is throbbing. As I lean against his chest, I'm reminded of how perfect his anatomy is.

"We'll find our moments, Cl'auta." His tongue and lips taste my neck.

I feel his fangs pushing against my skin. Like other parts of him, they're pulsating. He wants me. I want him, but the tragic truth is there's simply no time to make love.

"I love it when you call me that." I gnaw on his bottom lip.

"Cl'auta," he whispers. "Cl'auta, what's the power of matter?"

Although that question throws me like a curve ball gone astray, I can't tear my lips away from his. "I don't know." I literally can't form a thought right now. I'm dizzy, and the room is spinning.

"Remember, we have to remain on the offense…" He gropes my left breast.

"I remember…" I lick his fangs. I love the way the sharp end throbs against my tongue.

Baron's teeth retract, and he stops kissing me. In a microsecond, I'm off his lap and seated next to him. That magnificent light-headedness is gone. He's stiff, and his eyes are shut tightly.

"Don't ever do that again, Clarity. Please," he pleads.

I remain very still, waiting for Baron to recover.

After a handful of seconds pass, he turns his eyes toward me.

"Sorry," I say.

"Don't be. This is my curse, not yours."

"Don't say that."

Baron searches my face. For the life of me, I want to know what he's thinking. After a short while, he cracks a smile and stands.

"So," he says to put our focus back on the matter at hand, "once we learn more about the power of matter, we'll know how or if we'll need to use it."

"Right." I search over my left shoulder, wondering what's taking Fawn so long to get here.

FAWN

My feet are planted so firmly on the ground that I visualize feeling the hardwood floor right through the soles of my lambskin boots. Only on rare occasions does my skin run hot, and this is one of them. I watch Ben move around the room, picking up objects and then putting them down.

"It smells like you in here," he says and lifts a

crystal vase that holds a single blue rose. "It looks like you too." He smooths a petal between two fingers.

Was that a compliment? Should I say thank you? I don't know. And now he's standing only an inch away from me. *Am I still breathing?*

"We once loved each other, didn't we?"

"Yes," I croak. There's a lump in my throat.

"And all this time, you've been with Lario Exgesis?" The way he asks that question isn't harsh. Rather, it's something close to an affectionate confirmation.

"I think so." My heart is pounding, and I think I'm going to choke. I hope he doesn't ask me the one question I can't answer.

"Did you love him?"

Inwardly, I sigh with relief; that's not a hard question to answer. "I thought I did, but now I know I didn't."

"Do you remember what happened after La Isle Maddalena?"

I wish the vase he's clutching would fall out of his hand and break. I want the sound of the crystal shattering against the floor to disturb the painful silence. I shake my head stiffly.

"What do you remember?"

I want to say everything, but there's nothing I should share with him because, in retrospect, much of it is awful. The most dreadful part is the fact that I no longer have a Wek, his demise orchestrated like a perfect symphony by Lario. "It doesn't really matter since I was given false memories and realities."

"What were those false memories and realities?"

"Why do you need to know?" I snap.

He stares into my eyes for what seems like an eternity. I work hard to keep my knees from buckling. The heaviness of the moment weighs me down. This is worse than fighting the evil at the Tis Issat Falls and the monsters in Jari combined—almost.

He unleashes a crooked smile. "I'm happy you got the better part of the deal. I've been living like a rodent."

"I'm sorry to hear that." I drop my face. If he intended to make me feel guilty, then it worked.

"You shouldn't be," he says. "If either of us received the bitter end of the deal, I pray it was me."

I suddenly realize that he's touching me. His hand is on my lower back—a familiar spot. The heat. It's been so long since I indulged in it. So many centuries have passed, but I feel as if we stood close like this only yesterday.

"So tell me, Falu, what bedlam has fate whipped up for us these days?" He's still smiling at me.

I can't smile back. I'm a fake, a fraud, a cheater. People say that speaking the truth sets one free, but I'm afraid it may cause me to lose what I'm craving: true love—this reclaimed love that guilt keeps me from embracing.

I tear my eyes away from his face. "More Shams doing vampires' dirty work."

"And Ze Feldis is part of this?" he asks in a highly curious tone.

"You sound shocked. How do you know Baron anyway?"

"We're related, sort of. He denounces us, but it doesn't change anything."

I'm shocked. "But you're much older than Ze Feldis, by at least three hundred years."

"I met him once, at the Counsel of Eir. Both sides of the bloodlines were negotiating a truce with Ze Feldis."

"A truce with Ze Feldis?"

"He went mad and started a war with the Elos and Askins after they destroyed his family's haven." He stares into my face with a fire burning in his eyes. "I miss this," he whispers, completely changing the subject. "I remember your body. It's... extraordinary. I can't imagine another man touching it, but the Wek has. Hasn't he?"

I think I want to faint. I'm woozy with guilt. One of my worst fears has come to pass. A large part of me wants to lie. I feel his warm hands pressing against the small of my back, and I notice how close our faces are. He leans in a few inches closer, and our noses are touching. I wonder if he'll want to be this close to me if I speak the truth.

"What do you want to hear?" The strain of my thoughts is reflected in my voice. "I forgot you even existed until I saw you again."

"So you have made love to the Wek," he concludes.

I refuse to validate his conclusion. Instead, I press my lips together and let my watery eyes stare into his beautiful hazel eyes. He runs a finger over my lips to smooth the tension out of them.

"There," he whispers and gently presses his lips against mine.

My chin is shivering, and no matter how hard I try, I can't stop it. Although he's kissing them, my lips part. A deep sigh escapes me. Desire almost smothers me as, one button at a time, he works on freeing me from my white cotton blouse. Then his fingers stop. He steps back from me. His eyes are closed.

When he's gathered himself, he says, "Whatever demon the Shams put inside me made me afraid of my own shadow. I had forgotten I was a vampire. I didn't think I was human or even an animal. I thought I was a thirsty, evil demon who'd somehow escaped from the pit."

"I'm sorry," I whisper, choked up.

After a moment, he says in a more enthusiastic voice, "It's over."

"Yeah," I say, still sympathetic. "Although I don't know what's worse: believing I loved a man who caused you all of that pain or you living through the pain he caused you." Tears well up in my eyes again. I feel so helpless. "I'm so sorry." It's the least I can say.

After a rapid movement, Artiste once again stands before me. To my relief, our noses are touching.

"This is the third time you've apologized for something you did not do," he says.

"I'm sorry for the things I did do," I confess.

"I forgive you, but you couldn't have helped it, could you?"

I think hard, placing myself back into those days with Lario and then after Lario. Could I have helped it with Lorenzo? I gulp just from picturing him. If Ben hadn't showed up, then I would be in love with Lorenzo.

"No, I couldn't help it," I answer with certainty.

We stand in silence. Currents of desire flow between us like volts of electricity. It takes Clarity's voice in my head to weaken the lust consuming me.

"It's my sister," I whisper.

"What is she saying?" he whispers too.

"She wants to know when I'll join her."

"Well…" His warm lips are on mine. "Not yet."

He moves so fast that all I can see is light. I'm down to my bare skin and lying on top of the red-and-pink floral-print quilt on my bed. Artiste slows down to study my face and then my exposed body. His fangs grow, and so does that glorious part of him. Before I know it, both are inside me. I'm tripping off the highest high in my life, the most pleasurable sex ever. It was never like this with another man, only Artiste. Long forgotten noises escape me. I'm moaning and whimpering, and if I could be rational, I'd probably be embarrassed by my actions. But I'm not embarrassed; I'm in ecstasy.

Memories of my former life return to me as

well. I've always believed that I had lived in the Arctic in isolation when I ran away, alone, from the ugliest decades on Earth. Now I realize I hadn't been alone. Artiste was there with me. We had thousands, probably millions, of moments just like this. Now I know Lario *did* cast a spell on me. Everything I've done in ignorance was because of the evil that ripped my heart, my life, my love away from me.

"I love you," I sigh.

His lips press against mine. It feels like only yesterday our tongues touched like this.

"I hope so," he whispers back.

"We should go meet Clarity…"

"No." He licks that swollen vein that protrudes against the skin of my neck. "Let's get away from here. Mozambique. You liked Mozambique?"

"I did," I say. I want to run away with him. I want to get those lost years back. I want to take back all the mistakes Lario made me make. Like the one I have yet to confess to Ben…

"I don't have a Wek anymore." My eyes are shut because I don't want to see his face when I can no longer feel his lips upon my neck. "I didn't know why I was so drawn to him, but I seduced him, and he couldn't resist me," I say with shame.

"Open your eyes," Artiste tenderly demands.

I take a deep breath, let it out, and open my eyes.

Like old times, he's looking at me as if I'm all he'll ever need. "That makes revenge that much more necessary. We'll take care of that first and then Mozambique."

I don't wait for him to put his lips back on me; I put mine on his chest. He shifts his hips, and I bathe in bliss again, just like old times.

ZILL

Derek and I stand at the edge of the well. So far, twenty-seven vampires have plunged down it. They were moving so fast that the average human eye couldn't see them.

"I really love this invisibility deal," I say to Derek. "Wish I'd known Clarity back in high school. It would've made the whole hellish process much easier."

When Derek chuckles, I stop staring down the hole and glance at him. It's always strange when that happens. I wasn't attempting to be funny.

"You're not nervous, are you?" he asks.

I shake my head. "Not as long as I'm invisible. We're like ninjas. They'll never know what hit them."

"Then, after you."

I leap down the rabbit hole. I have complete control of my senses, limbs, and muscles. I'm strong and energized, as if I'm fueled by a burst of adrenaline times ten thousand. But unlike adrenaline, my energy isn't a quick fix; it's constant.

I miss Vayle. He would love this, I think—diving into the unknown, spiraling downward for what seems like forever. I'm wondering how deep we'll go when I land on my feet.

Derek and I aren't alone. We're in what looks like a gigantic metal drum, and I see thirteen vampires in here with us. What an unlucky number. Six of them are coupled, kissing greedily as if their mouths are food. I can't stop frowning because it's gross. I mean, one of the guys has his hand so far up the girl's short skirt that he just might injure her down there. Another one is clearly finger banging his chick, and no one seems appalled! Maybe they think it's hot. But no, it's definitely gross.

Then something strange happens. The kissers and gropers stop cold turkey, and they eye each other suspiciously. One sniffs, then another, and then they're all sniffing. They're searching upward and downward. One by one, they pound on the metal with balled-up fists. *Bang, bang, bang.* The force of their blows is hard, and even the floor under our feet is vibrating. Just like me, they're strong.

"Out, out, out…" they chant.

"Impatient, I think," I say to Derek.

They all turn toward me. They heard that, and deep down inside, I'm screaming, *What the hell!*

I get lucky, because the walls lift and reveal a wide-open space. There are thousands of vampires down here. Most of them are facing a stage where band members wearing only tight black leather pants and black leather hoods are playing instruments under harsh lighting. The one who is yelling into a microphone sounds as if he's being strangled. I can hardly stand the noise, yet I'm pumped. I search the faces of the vamps guzzling vodka and bourbon and other libations by the bottle, looking for the two soul-snatchers.

I turn to see if Derek's getting an eyeful of this, but hot damn, I'm alone! I panic for a second before something within my brain resets itself. I have a job to do, and fear can't keep me from completing it. A picture of Jake and Mary is stuck in my head. I'm responsible for waking them up.

This is like one of those supercharged rave parties I've heard of. They look as though they're on hardcore drugs. A lot of them are jumping, shaking their heads, wiggling their tongues, shifting their eyes, yelling and howling at the top of their lungs. It's kind of insane.

My feet don't touch the ground. As I pass the vampires, they turn in my direction and sniff like the ones who were in the container with me. One male vampire pinpoints the source of the smell and charges in my direction. He hits the shield Clarity set around me and knocks over a load of people— well, vampires—as he falls to the ground, quivering as if he's having convulsions.

What a trip.

Then things go from bad to worse. They're fighting and sinking their teeth into anyone who's close to me. Teeth end up in each other's arms, necks, faces, anywhere there's exposed skin, tasting blood before convulsing and howling in pain. Another one jumps at me, then another. Complete pandemonium has broken out. Clarity made me invisible, but they obviously sense my presence. Like hounds, they must be able to smell my blood.

I rise higher, and their heads tilt back so that they can inhale in my direction. Derek's disappeared, and the Selells can smell me. For a second, I wonder where Mr. Lux, my old geology teacher, is. He's supposed to help me in these situations. I can't take them all on, can I? But he's not here. So I force myself to remain composed and keep my head in the game.

I gaze at the ceiling. The disco lights flicker white in this area. Like angry, bloodthirsty bats swarming a fat cow, the vampires spring into the air toward me. I search across the ceiling while dodging them until… Bingo! There's the blast of red, yellow, and blue lights and the dancing girls in cages.

The couple I'm looking for is still at the table, but they're not alone. Six Selells have joined them: three males, three females, all couples. They're engaged in the normal activities—drinking and making out—but what's different is that the vampires at this table are actually talking to each other.

The male vampire Clarity showed me shoots to his feet and yells while stabbing a finger at one of the other male vampires. The one who is still sitting doesn't like being yelled at. After a moment of staring at the standing vampire, he opens his mouth to let out a gut-wrenching growl. These guys are on the verge of tearing each other's heads off. Their altercation keeps them from realizing when, on the other side of the room, the band stops playing. Their peers are still making themselves sick by sinking their teeth into each other.

When my mark growls back at his challenger, it becomes clear to me that there's no better time to strike. I have no weapons, but energy pumps through my palms and into my fingers. I once saw this old cartoon with a sailor guy who had gulped down a can of spinach and then all this energy shot to his hands and feet. That seems to be what's happening to me.

The girl has now inserted herself into the squabble. She's standing, which makes things easier for me. I soar toward them while dodging vampires. My eyes are narrowed as I zoom in on my marks. I hear the one vampire accuse the other of finishing his bottle of cognac before he could taste it. Really, their argument is that petty.

"Buy another bottle," the accuser demands.

"Go to hell," my mark roars back.

"We don't need your shit," his girlfriend hisses.

My hands become daggers as they slice through his neck and then hers. I pant as I stand over my victims. That happened so fast, the other vampires at the table are stunned. They eye each other as if asking, "Which one of you did that?"

Two by two, they dart off, and so do I. As I take off, heading in the same direction I entered, a familiar hand clamps down on my shoulder. I stop to face Derek.

"This way," he says.

"Where the hell did you go?" I yell through clenched teeth as mayhem continues around us. I don't even think I'm the cause anymore. The chaos has taken on a life of its own.

"I have limitations, Zill," he says and grabs my hand. "We have to go."

Once upon a time, I would've dug in my heels and refused to leave until he'd satisfied my curiosity, but this time, I let him lead me. It's turned feral in here. Some of the vampires are dead on the floor or tabletops. Some are splayed across chairs, blood dripping from their mouths. It is the most insane sight.

Derek and I move fast. He pulls me through a white plastic cylinder. When we get to the end of it, a blast of strong air lifts us into the night sky. We hover under the ominous clouds that are pelting the earth with rain. There's a factory below with long white spherical structures that are blowing vapory fumes into the atmosphere.

"Let's go where it's dry," I say to Derek.

We rise above the rain clouds to keep from getting wet. When all the ugly weather is beneath us, I turn toward him.

"So what are your limitations?" I bark. I'm still sort of pissed off I had to do all of that alone.

"I have to listen to my instincts when it comes to you," he says.

"And your instincts told you to bail on me?"

"Yes, they did."

I stare into his pure green eyes and realize that not one bone in my body is truly angry at Derek. He's just so perfect and pure. Although my thoughts are completely off subject, it occurs to me that he's never had to live a real life. No mother, father, sisters, or brothers. He used to go to school every day, and he seemed to love it. He was on a first-name basis with all the superiors. The teachers, the principal, nurses, the dreaded Mrs. Lowenstein, and every single student at school loved him.

Truly, a lot about Derek Firth is still a mystery to me, but to think that he was created to watch me or watch out for me or something like that is insane. It's finally sinking into my thick head. Just like me, he has a job to do, and I have to stop making it harder for him. He's already chosen to do the same for me.

"Come on," I say and rush back toward Moonridge.

He grabs my arm before I can get too far.

"What?" I ask, looking into his eyes.

"You're leaving it like that?"

"Yeah," I say.

At first, he frowns as if he's bothered, but then he seems to force himself to smile. "Then lead the way."

All I can think about is how weird our last exchange was as we head back to see if my handiwork helped Jake and Mary.

CHAPTER 5

IN SEARCH OF MATTER
CLARITY

Fifteen minutes ago, I called for Fawn, but she chose to ignore me. When I checked in on her, for a brief moment, I realized why. She'd been overtaken by her passion, which I completely understood. Two minutes later, Zill reported that she'd killed the Selells and was on her way back to Moonridge.

Baron and I decided we should meet her there, so now we're standing on Jake and Mary's porch. From somewhere deep inside the house, Jerry is yapping. I turn the doorknob. It's locked.

"Here, let me," Baron says. He turns the knob, and it opens.

"Right," I say with a smile.

"It's all in the wrist." He winks at me.

Baron takes my hand and enters first. The rush of warmth from his touch floods me. I'll never get used to how the initial jolt of our energies colliding feels. It's much more comforting than the shields I create. Once we're inside, Jerry's barking turns more intense, then he lets out a loud whimper. Someone, likely Jake, is trying to keep him quiet.

"They're hiding," Baron says.

I examine our surroundings. There's a distinct difference between being here in full form and being here as an Encaser. The television, wool sofa, and scratched-up coffee table appear more tangible. So do the shelves that hold fragile, old-fashioned trinkets. The weight of what we're doing here is heavier and the danger more immediate.

"This way," Baron says as he takes my hand.

He guides me down the hallway toward the back of the house. We follow the whimpering, moving past the room where Jake and Mary had rested. We both observe that they're no longer lying on the bed. I sigh with relief. So far so good.

Jerry is quiet, so I reach out to latch onto the living energy in the house. "They're in the basement."

"Yes, I know," he whispers back.

"They're afraid of us."

"But Jerry isn't, is he?" he asks.

How could I miss that! "Jerry!" I walk faster.

We end up in a tiny carport where there's a huge paint-stained sink. On the opposite side of that sink is a white wooden door. The entry to the basement is behind it. Baron steps over to the door and grips the knob.

"Wait," I say only to him.

Jake's breathing accelerates as he experiences an all-out panic attack. While experiencing Mary's fear, I feel her wrap her arms around her husband in an attempt to keep him calm. It's funny how love works. She's no longer afraid of what we could possibly be or what harm we could inflict upon them. At the moment, her only fear is losing Jake forever.

"Jerry," I call.

The dog barks again.

"Let Jake and Mary know we're here to help."

The couple focuses on their pet as he licks their faces and jubilantly turns in circles. I feel Jake recovering from his earlier attack, and that's a relief.

"Who are you?" Mary shouts. Her voice is still shaky.

"I'm Clarity, and I'm here with Baron. We

know what happened to your town, and we're here to help."

After a long moment, Jerry's barking becomes louder as he gets closer. I hear his feet tapping up the stairs, and now he's scratching at the door. Baron reaches out to open it, but I place my hand on top of his.

"No," I whisper, shaking my head. "They should open it. Gives them back their power."

Of course, Baron catches my drift and kisses me on the forehead.

"Geez," I hear in my head, *"do you guys ever take a break?"*

Baron and I turn to see Zill and Derek walking toward us. I can still feel the chill on their skin from walking the wind. Her cheeks are nice and rosy, and her windblown hair makes her look like a walking, talking, grinning ad for an expensive perfume. As the door to the basement opens, I let go of Baron's hand and hurry over to throw my arms around her. I hug her tight, happy to see her safe and sound.

"Is that you, Derek?" Jake asks. He stands on the threshold still wearing the baggy, apple-print pajamas.

I stifle a gasp at how deathly thin he's become, even since I last saw him.

"It's me, Jake." Derek's entire face is squeezed into a severe frown.

Mary steps up behind Jake. After seeing all of us, their fear turns into relief. Derek convinces the couple we'll be just as safe in the living room as in the basement, and we all gather there. I notice how, while sitting on the sofa, Mary can't take her hand off Jake's fragile thigh, and vice versa.

"It happened fast," Jake says. "All of it." He touches the side of his neck as he remembers that he was bitten.

The marks are faint.

"I remember the sun was burning our eyes," Mary adds.

"That's why you covered the windows?" I gently ask.

"We had to, or we'd go blind. I'm sure of it," Jake says. "That was just the start. We kept getting weaker and weaker until all we could do was crawl in bed and lay there. I thought…"

Mary squeezes his leg. "We thought we were dying."

"What about now?" Zill asks.

The couple takes a moment to assess their health.

"I'm okay. What about you, honey?" Mary asks Jake.

"I think I'm okay too, but we haven't gone out in the day yet."

"May I tell you what happened?" I ask.

Jake narrows his eyes, studying my face, then Zill's, and then mine again. It's as if he's realizing we're almost carbon copies of each other. There's a glimmer of fascination in his eyes, but instead of addressing the bizarre, he says, "If you can explain it, then by all means."

I tell them what the sort of creatures the fog dragged in and how instead of drinking their blood, they were somehow able to consume their souls.

"That's not possible," Mary insists, shaking her head.

"I'm afraid so," I say.

Over the years, I've noticed the capacity for the human brain to forget unfortunate events. It's a biological coping mechanism, and already the Grimeses are reestablishing the rules of what can and can't be real. Bloodsuckers, soul suckers, and a town that has been drained by them can never exist in the realm of truth. My heart aches for them because more than anything, I wish they could live in blissful ignorance. Heck, I wish *I* could! But unfortunately, none of us in this room can.

"You'll be able to take the coverings off your windows," I say, continuing with the business at hand. "But everyone in your town is still in the state you were in—soulless."

Jake and Mary look at each other with dread.

"Why were we saved?" Jake asks. "I'm nobody special."

"Because Zill's memories of you led me to you."

Jake glances at her again and then at Derek.

"All we wanted was a candy apple," Zill says with a shrug.

For the first time since we've arrived, Jake smiles. Zill's good at making people smile without trying.

I assure them that we're going to get everyone back to normal as soon as possible. We know that we have to kill the vampires who ravished Moonridge. I follow Jake and Mary's eyes to Zill's hands, which are covered with a black, tar-like substance. I can smell it. It's the scent of dried Selell blood. Unfortunately, I fear that before this is over, my sister's hands will be stained with a lot more of it.

When we return to the estate, Fawn and Artiste are already waiting for us in the study.

"I'm so sorry," she says as she stands to receive us.

In order to ease her guilt, I smile nonchalantly and say, "An apology isn't necessary, Fawn. But you have to fill me in when or if we get a moment." I raise my eyebrows.

While wearing a coy grin, she sweeps right past me on her way to hug Zill. "You're safe." She heaves a sigh of relief.

"Of course I am," Zill mutters, taking care not to get vampire residue on Fawn's white blouse.

I sense that she's beginning to feel a little smothered by her sisters. I see an eighteen-year-old girl when I look at her, but in truth, four Earth years have passed since her senior year of high school. Fawn and I whisked her away before she could officially graduate, but from this moment on, I will see her as an adult, equal to me in ability and duty. At least I'll try.

"Fawn," I say as she lets go of Zill, "what are the nuances of the power of matter?"

"It's simple. Tapeetha can actually move mountains. She could cut the Andes out of Venezuela and set them in Manhattan if she wanted to."

"Wow!" I turn to look at Baron, who's reacting the same way that I am.

"This means she can make thousands of vampires appear wherever we need them to be, right?" Baron asks.

"That's how she annihilated the first crop of Shams. See, before 1489, there were more Shams in the world than Selells."

"So why did she choose to go to war with them?"

"They hunted her and... and me," she says, as if surprised by that fact.

"Wait, that means you're way older than three hundred?"

"Yeah," she says and looks at Artiste. "Ben, we fought with her, didn't we?"

"Yes," he answers while scowling at the collection of Lario's books.

I can't imagine being in Fawn and Ben Artiste's shoes. To have my memories manipulated to such an extent? Centuries lost, experiences gone, growth, wisdom all wiped away and reprogrammed with whatever lies suited Lario's purpose.

"She was able to lure them into a place called the Revere Capsule," Fawn says.

"I've never heard of it," I say.

"That's because it doesn't exist. Tapeetha created it because she had to lure them to one place. Then she destroyed it with a flammable substance called sentakuloc."

"What's that?"

"It's hotter than fire. Any human being within seven hundred miles of its flames will melt to ashes, and it can destroy the earth down to the core."

"Sentakuloc," I repeat the word. "It's an Enuian substance, isn't it?"

"Yes, it is."

"How did you lure them to the Revere Capsule?"

"We created a myth," Artiste says.

"A hundred years in the making," Fawn adds. "According to the myth, it was a mysterious place where a powerful eclipse could bring Shams ultimate power on the fifth day of Nisan."

"The month of happiness," I mutter as I remember this.

"Over the years, we planted clues that would lead them to this made-up place. We left scripts in caves they frequented and sent humans to drop hints of the existence of the Revere Capsule," Fawn says. "Vampire Shams put a lot of faith in human prophets."

"You worked with humans?" Zill sounds shocked by that.

"They used to be our strongest allies against Selells and Shams since they couldn't be touched without permission."

"But Shams are Selells, right?"

"Well, yeah, but once they practice magic, their essence is transformed into something far more sinister."

"Do they still crave blood?"

Fawn can't answer that, so she looks to Ben Artiste for help.

"Yes," he says, "but they find ways to get around it."

"Oh," Zillael says.

We all take a moment to reflect on what Artiste just told us. I must admit, it's pretty interesting in a horrific way.

"Well," I say, "that's changed. It seems second-generation Selells can sink their teeth into humans whenever they feel like it. At least, they can if the human doesn't know how to stop them."

"And we don't have a hundred years to indoctrinate them and lure them to a made-up place," Baron says.

"No, we don't." My mind works overtime to put together a plan.

All eyes are on me. I know how strange I look to

others when I'm thinking like this. My eyes shift around, and my mouth twitches in all directions.

"I think we can use the power of matter to bring all the second-generation vampires to one place," I say.

"How?" Fawn croaks.

I twist my mouth in a frown. "I don't know yet, but I'll figure it out."

"Well, also, this time, we won't be able to destroy them with sentakuloc," Fawn says.

"Why not?" Zill asks.

"Because it was mined out of the Demur Mountains in Enu, and we had to use all of it. None of this plan works without Tapeetha's power anyway, and she won't leave Enu without Ose."

Fawn sounds sure of that, but I'm not sure she's right. We all would rather be languishing with our lovers, but we share a sense of duty. Tapeetha feels it too, I believe.

"I don't think that'll be a problem," I say, shaking my head. My brain maps out another solution though, just in case. "What about the Selell she's bonded to? Is he still alive?"

"Leto Danto," Artiste says.

"Leto Danto?" Baron asks. It sounds as if that name has rung a bell for him.

"Danto, yes."

Baron scoffs bitterly. "So that filthy bloodline is why I'm part of this?"

His reaction is alarming and catches everyone off guard—or at least me and my sisters. Artiste isn't surprised by Baron's outburst. Baron is still snarling, and I'm very much afraid that he's on the verge of turning his back on us. Then his eyes move from Zill's face, to Fawn's, and then to mine. For a moment, I swear he's reading their thoughts.

"I apologize," he whispers while still looking at me.

"That's okay," I barely say.

I touch his shoulder. After my hand makes contact, he draws me into him. I kiss him quickly to assure him that I'm fine. He lets me go, but he still keeps his arm curled around my waist.

I know a little about his familial issues, but only as far as him avenging an invasion on the Ze Feldis household. From what I've gathered, Artiste and Baron are related. I don't quite understand what the point of contention is for Baron.

"Just to be clear," Zill starts, "you're not going to quit on us, are you, Baron? Because that's really not like you. You always, you know, have it together."

Fawn laughs. She was thinking the exact same thing. But she doesn't stop laughing, and it becomes infectious. I can't help but join her. It's uncontrollable and so silly, and now both vampires, the Wek, and Zill are watching us, wondering if we've gone mad. Maybe we have. Maybe we have present traumatic stress syndrome.

We're so knee-deep in this hell of fighting vampires and Lario Exgesis, there's no running off on a romantic get-away with the Selell I love. I can't sit down, lounge, and think about nothing but deepening my bond with my wonderful new sisters. I want to run off to Enu and spend the rest of the day with Adore. It may take me from Earth for a year or so, but I love Baron, and since that's an unwavering fact, he can come with me! My love for him would keep him alive in my mother's universe. Speaking of my mother, I'd rather be hunting for her than figuring out a way to make thousands of soul-sucking vampires appear out of nowhere so that we can slay them.

ALTHOUGH IT'S TWO THIRTY IN THE MORNING, WE decide lack of food is the culprit for our hysterical laughter, so my sisters and I head to the patio to eat.

Baron goes to his office to check on business, and Artiste decides to explore the woods.

"Do you miss Vayle?" Fawn asks Zill as we tear into our berries and bread.

Zill takes a bite of bread and berries and shrugs.

"Ah, I see…" I say.

"What?" Zill asks with cat-like nervousness. She always worries about what information I'm retrieving from her thoughts.

"Don't panic, I didn't read your mind," I say. "I'm starting to figure you out by observing you, that's all."

"Do tell," Fawn croons playfully.

"First you," I retort.

She flips a hand nonchalantly. "Yes, the bond and I have bonded. But you know that, Cl'auta."

"What about Lorenzo?" I ask.

"You mean your Wek?" Zill asks, surprised.

"Yes, my Wek," I say.

Fawn says, "I love Ben, but I was attracted to Lorenzo. He's a Wek, after all. It's complicated."

We fall quiet for a little as we eat and think. I've experienced how that complexity feels second-hand but never directly. Fawn's feelings for Ben Artiste are real, and so are Zill's for Vayle. But I remember my initial reaction to Lorenzo. I thought he was the most gorgeous being I'd laid eyes on since Baron Ze Feldis. Not only that, he's my second brain. He's in my DNA somehow. What if we had met before I fell in love with Baron? He definitely had the chops to awaken the romantic feelings that had been dormant in me since forever.

Zill sighs and whispers, "Yeah, it *is* complicated."

"But do you know what's going to be even more complicated?" Fawn asks as she takes a sip of hot Goshem tea. "Convincing Leto Danto to help us. From what I remember, he was infuriated when Tapeetha chose Ose over him. Looking back, it does seem that her choice was sort of peculiar."

"Please elaborate," I say.

"Well, she loved Danto a lot. They were as close as you and Ze Feldis. Then all of a sudden, she started developing these feelings for Ose. At the time, I just figured the heart wants what it wants."

"So she met her bond first, not the Wek?"

"Yeah…" She narrows her eyes at me. "What are you getting at, Cl'auta?"

I explain my theory about how meeting the Wek first could interfere with the bond. "And you, Zill…"

Her eyes widen at me as if she dreads what I'm about to reveal.

"There's something strange about the order in which you met Derek and Vayle," I say.

She does that shrug of hers. "I knew Derek for a long time, but not as a Wek. I didn't really think about him much. He was cute and all... I mean, everybody liked him. But we never said anything to each other until the fog."

"That's it!" I blurt. "The fog forced him to reveal himself to you before it was time."

"Well, later we had that fight, and Vayle showed up," she adds.

I can't help but feel her heart drop when she says Vayle's name. My mind works to see how all of this connects. We're definitely weaker without our bonds, and it seems as though outside forces have worked like the dickens to destroy all of those relationships. In Fawn's situation and even mine, Lario was the culprit. Could he have orchestrated the imbalance between Zill, her bond, and her Wek as well?

"You know what I think?" I sit on the edge of my seat, so filled with angst I'm about to burst.

They watch me expectantly.

"We're not the only ones with a plan. A serious,

serious plan. I think Lario has been trying to destroy our connections with our bonds while, at the same time, orchestrating our meetings with our bonds on his timeline."

"He does know a lot about us," Fawn muses.

"I think he's behind severing Tapeetha's bond with Leto Danto, and I wonder…" I stop myself from saying the worst.

"What?" Fawn asks.

All of the energy this successful elucidation stirs up in me makes me leap to my feet. "I think I saw it in the script!"

"What?" Fawn sounds even more eager to know what I'm thinking.

"I think Leto Danto has his power and Tapeetha's too. That's what he gained when Tapeetha chose the Wek over the bond and left Earth. That's what all of our bonds will gain if we make the same choice. Finish eating. I'll be back." My heart races as I gallop off.

"Where are you going?" Fawn shouts at my backside.

"To confirm whether or not Leto Danto is the answer to our soul-snatcher problem," I yell over my shoulder, still running.

BARON RUSHES INTO THE READING ROOM. HE stands right outside the diamond chamber, watching me closely. I lift a finger at him to assure him that I see him and will fill him in as soon as I'm done.

This time as I read the script, I see that it does show how the Selells are able to steal souls from humans. There's no mention of them also being able to drink their blood, so that rule still must be valid. The script says that a multitude of leaf-marked Selells are scorched by the fire, and then I see the sun and what looks like a lunar eclipse. I'm not sure what the eclipse means, but I'm convinced that we can find the power of matter and possibly convince him to work on our behalf. He may be brokenhearted, but that's a state ignited by love. The more he hates Tapeetha, then the more he loves her, which may give us a chance to convince him to help us.

I rush from the chamber and tell Baron that I have to find Leto Danto. He refuses to let me make contact with the lost vampire alone. Without speaking a word, I hold out my hands, palms facing up. He rests his palms on top of mine.

Every moment spent with Baron Ze Feldis is a reminder that I'm a woman who is no longer an island. He rewards me for being so amenable from time to time by showing me my favorite of his expressions. He smirks, and my legs want to turn to butter. But it's time to stand firm.

So I refocus, and I take the image of Danto, another Selell who resembles Baron, from Fawn's memory. I tell myself that he's the person I want to find, and I smack into an impenetrable barrier. The impact is so hard, so real that I'm actually shaken by it.

"Did you feel that?" I ask Baron.

"Let's try again, but this time, generate more light," he suggests.

I take in a deep breath and force it out. This time, I press my hands closer to his, and he returns the favor. The light is ignited within me. I push it toward my hands and wait for it to connect with Baron. Once it's fully ablaze, I drink it up to carry it with me. Once again, we get nowhere. I squeeze my eyes shut and push harder. Still, even together, we make no headway.

"Damn!" I curse so loud I startle myself. "This is so frustrating!"

"This is not the work of Shams," Baron concludes.

"No, it's not," I strongly agree. "I think it's Danto. The only people who can block me like this are my sisters. Adore did it once when I tried to pull some answers from her. If he's taken Tapeetha's powers, then he must be making a conscious effort to use them against me, which means he knows I'm looking for him. Me, Baron." I point at myself. "He knows about *me*. You know what that means, don't you?"

Baron looks confused, and I remember that I never shared my theory with him about Lario interfering with the sisters' bonding processes. I recount my hypothesis beat by beat, starting with Fawn and Ben Artiste and ending with Zill and Vayle.

"I see," he says.

"Lario's gotten to Leto," I conclude.

"I would say so," he concurs, to my relief.

After a moment of silence, I say, "I'm going to have to go to Enu and convince Tapeetha to return to Earth. It's our only option."

I hear the growl purring deep in Baron's throat. I've gotten used to the sound over our accelerated years together. It's one of the indicators that he's reacting to something I've said or done, pleasurable or not.

"How many years will you be gone this time?" he asks with a bite.

"It should only be days. But why don't you come with me?" I ask.

He lifts his brows, presumably surprised by my offer. "Is that possible?"

"If I love you, which I do, then yes, it is."

He mulls something over. I'm wondering what that is until he says, "We can't forget about the coven."

I sigh hard and rest my forehead against his chest. Just remembering how the Mount Olympus coven was wiped out, and the fact that we don't have any real answers as to why, is already mentally exhausting.

"We just can't let Exgesis get too far ahead of us," he mutters.

I lift my face to look him in the eyes. "I know that, but... you don't want to go with me?" Goodness, I sound so dejected.

"Of course I do," he answers without hesitation. "But I think it's time you rely more on your sisters. They're quite formidable, Clarity."

I turn the corners of my mouth down. I know

that already. "I still think it would be easier to use the power of matter to put Lario face to face with Zill. She can rip his heart out and then"—I wipe my hands together—"we'll be done with him. The end—of him at least."

"That easy?" He sounds doubtful.

"Yes, that easy," I say with confidence.

"You're oversimplifying."

"I don't think so."

"You don't?"

"No, Baron Ze Feldis, I don't." I'm aware that we're engaged in a spat. However, unlike Baron, I see the power of matter as the answer to all of our problems. With it, we can find and destroy everything that has to die, which definitely includes Lario and his soul-sucking vampire imps.

"You have to remember the problems Lario caused at the coven. And," he says before I can cut him off, "as you've already concluded, Danto has chosen to stop you from reaching him. Why do you think that is? What did you already say?" His expression says he's expecting an answer.

"Because he's somehow connected to Lario," I reply hesitantly.

"Exactly. If Exgesis orchestrated our meeting and, as you said, ruined the relationships between your sisters and their vampire bonds, then think about it. He even tried to ruin what we have." He clenches his teeth as anger flashes across his face and passes. "Understand this, Clarity. Although I never trusted Exgesis, in a bizarre way, I was loyal to him. Remember when we met in Cambridge after being imprisoned by Zina and her vampire imps?" He leers at me in jest.

I smile weakly, but I'm desperate for him to finish making his point.

"I often wonder why I believed you'd be safe in Veil Green. I can't remember being able to say no to Exgesis, not once. He's always more than a step ahead."

"And he knows my abilities," I add.

"Your powers, Clarity. I have them now," he confesses. "I can see your sisters' thoughts. Hear them too."

I feel my entire face drop. "And what about emotions? Can you feel those too?"

"I can," he confirms. "And Fawn is keeping something from you. She has flashes of Exgesis. She sees him."

"Why would she keep that from me?" If I look conflicted, it's because I am. I thought she trusted me enough to tell me everything.

"She's riddled with self-doubt. She thinks Exgesis still has a hold on her, and if she stays close to you, then she'll remain free of him."

"Do you think he does? Is that why she dreams of him?"

"I don't know. It could be fear. It could be more." He cups my chin. "But she can't find out if you're babysitting her."

"I'm not babysitting her," I feebly protest. I know that's exactly what I'm doing.

"Good," he sings as if that's settled. "So while we're away, Fawn and Zillael should look for Exgesis. Just to get a line on him, just to keep things turning here on earth." He's testing me.

"Without me?" I sound doubtful, and my own tone catches me off guard. Realizing I just failed the quiz, I take a deep sigh. "All right. You're right."

He grins at me. "Good. Now, when do we leave?"

BEFORE BARON AND I TAKE OFF TO ENU, WE ALL meet in the study.

"We just wait and do nothing," Zill complains.

I glance at Baron, who's standing behind the sofa where my sisters sit, watching me. This is an interesting scene. They're seated; I'm standing, lording over them.

Without another word, I extend my hands for each of them, which they take. I pull them to their feet. Funny, we're standing eye to eye. We have virtually the same body shape and height, although Zill is slightly stronger than we are, being that her power is her strength.

"We have a common enemy. None of us should rest until we stop him." I turn to Fawn. "If you can get close to him, then you should."

Her eyes expand. "What do you mean?"

For a second, I sense that she's panicked, but then it passes. That's exactly what Baron told me. She's choosing to withhold certain things about herself from me.

"If something inside you is leading you to Lario, then you shouldn't be afraid of that." I squeeze her hand to put her at ease. "You can call anytime you need me or Zill. Listen, this isn't going to be a cake-walk. We have to remain on the offense."

She narrows her eyes at me. "Then you know about my thoughts."

"I do," I admit, leaving out the part about Baron revealing them to me.

"But what if he's trying to lure me into a trap?" She sounds so afraid.

I lift my hand that's holding Zill's hand. "Then kill him," I suggest. "And remember to stay on the offense. That's what's different this time around, Falu. You're hunting him."

On that note, Fawn and Zill stare at each other. I love seeing that determined look in their eyes. Baron winks at me. I think he's proud of me. I love that too.

CHAPTER 6

IT'S NICE
CLARITY

I t's almost sunrise, but a skeleton of last night's full moon is still lodged in the sky and tilting to the east. Birds sing on the spiny branches overhead that block the sky. Baron and I are in a part of the forest, beyond the gates of the estate, that's dense with gigantic birch trees. For the most part, we've walked at a normal pace all the way here to the Enu portal. Baron only used his intense speed to lift me over the gate. He's been quiet since we left the study. Every once in a while, he looks at me with a strained smile, but that's it. He's nervous, and his anxiety is rubbing off on me.

To the human eye, we're facing a tree trunk that's about five feet in diameter. However, I see the glow of light beyond its rigid bark. I glance at

Baron, who hasn't let go of my hand since we left the house. The pucker of skin between his eyes deepens. I'm pretty sure he sees this magnificent phenomenon too.

I squeeze his hand. "Are you sure you want to do this?" I hope he hasn't changed his mind.

There's heaviness in his hesitation. "You're Enuian, aren't you, Clarity?"

"Half," I answer, unsure where this line of questioning is going.

"You're good, pure. I'm not." He studies me with a sad intensity that my heart breaks a little.

How can such a beautiful, smart, caring, loving creature doubt his goodness? I've been linked to emotions and behaviors long enough to realize that there's nothing I can say to change his mind about himself. Only life can teach him differently.

But to convince him for the moment, I point at the entrance. "Do you see that?"

"The light, yes," he says.

"That's a start. If you couldn't enter, then you wouldn't be able to see the portal."

"Really?" He sounds surprised, and he's beaming a little.

"Really."

Without further delay, he sweeps an arm around

my waist. In an instant, we're inside the cloud of light, speeding forward, and then we're out.

At first, my eyes are open, but then I close them and tilt my face up toward the magnificent Enuian sun to bathe in its perfect—and I mean perfect—warm rays. I almost forget that I'm here in the land of bliss with the man I love. When I turn toward him, he's already watching me. That crease of skin between his eyes has softened, but there's something different about his face. There's a hint of pink in his cheeks, as if he's blushing, and his blue eyes are lighter, nearly powder blue.

"You're so beautiful."

I hear him say it without speaking. But it's more than that; I'm able to experience the emotions that formed that declaration. I'm able to feel how intimidated he is by this world with its powder-blue skies that twinkle with pink lights.

We're standing near the edge of the same grassy hill I stood on the first day I entered Enu. The same valley is beneath us. It still holds trees with yellow, red, and purple leaves. Baron is taken aback by all of this. Even the lazy streams cutting through the valley without being pushed by a larger water source enthrall him.

"So this is where you're from?" He grins at me.

"I wish," I whisper, looking across the basin.

"Are those trees down there silver?"

I look at the ones he's referring to. "Yeah, they are. Interesting, huh?"

"Very," he barely says. "You know, it smells like you here. Feels like you too."

I snort, amused by that.

"Ah, I see," he says.

I narrow my eyes at him. "You see what?"

"This place isn't complex enough for you."

Wow! He grabbed that feeling from very deep down inside me. He's good at this.

All I can say is, "We should get going."

I'm fully ready to race down the hillside. I want to get far away from the secret I've kept hidden that he just spoke out loud. Plus, a large part of me is eager to show Baron that I can keep up with him here in Enu.

But he's not budging. Instead, he's undressing me with his eyes. I become aware that I'm wearing the same slinky, navy blue dress I slipped on before Fawn and I took off to meet him and Artiste in Montauk. That was two Earth days ago. Time is an elusive entity for me these days. Baron doesn't see the dress the same way as I do. To me, it's an article of clothing I should've changed before leaving. He loves the way it slides over my frame, the way the slinky material slips over my curves. He's viewing it like it's my second skin, and to him, there's no difference between me wearing this dress and me being naked.

Dear God, I've never thought I was so desirable. He can no longer concentrate on the sparkling trees, and he's lost the desire to step through the crystal streams. He wants me out of this dress. He wants to get an eyeful of my soft, sensitive nipples and touch me in places that'll make me hot for him. This drive, this need for me is so potent that he can hardly contain himself.

"Don't worry, I'm not going to seduce you," he says with a smirk. "I want to rip your clothes off and do dirty things to you every second of every day."

I can't help but chuckle. "I want you too, but alas…"

"Lead us on, love," he says.

His calling me "love" doesn't go unnoticed.

He frowns. "Is that uncomfortable for you? My calling you 'my love'?"

I can't avoid his question. "A little," I answer honestly. I can't lie; he already knows the truth.

That pucker of skin between his eyes returns. "I

knew you were uncomfortable with it, but I didn't know why until now."

I'm thoroughly curious. Does he now have insight into me that I'm too afraid to tap into?

"Why?" I sound desperate. Even I don't understand why a nickname so sweet makes me fight the urge to cringe.

Instead of answering me, Baron uses his speed to draw me into him. Our lips connect, and our tongues relish the taste of each other. To him, my mouth tastes of sweet lime with a hint of mint. I pull in every sensation he's experiencing, and by how deep he's falling into me, I ascertain he's unable to help doing the same.

My throbbing heart, my hard nipples pressing against his chest, my warmth that's the same temperature as the Enuian sun is driving him crazy. Just the same, his solid chest and strong hands, caressing and groping me everywhere, are causing me to lose my mind!

We're a millisecond away from doing something about all of these sensations when I hear, *"Cl'auta."*

I use my Enuian super speed to roll out from under Baron, who still has a hand under my dress. I jump to my feet so fast that my stomach drops a little.

"Adore?" I say, breathing heavily.

Baron, who is now on his feet, pulls my backside into him. He's hard in all the right places.

Adore can't take her eyes off of him. Her mouth has fallen open. At first, I think she's having the normal initial reaction to the glory that is Baron Ze Feldis, but that's not it. To Adore, his looks and physique are ordinary; it's what he is that fascinates her. I think this is the first time she's ever seen a Selell in real life.

"You're the Selell, Baron of the Ze Feldis clan?" Intrigue colors her tone.

"Yes, and you are…" he says.

"Adore, the first daughter of the House of Felix Benel." Still, she can't take her eyes off him. "I think you say hello in your world?" She's being quite careful with him.

"Yes, that would be appropriate," I answer, grinning.

"Well, then." She bows her head. "Hello, Baron Ze Feldis." One of her arms flings up toward us. "May I?"

Her ebony hand moves toward Baron's face. Her fingers are long and graceful with skin so smooth they look as though they've never engaged in a hard day's work or been burnt by the sun.

She stops short of touching him to wait for his answer.

I'm in Baron's thoughts, and he's confused about whether or not he should allow her to touch him. He still wants to ravish me. At the same time, he's admiring Adore's exotic beauty, which can't be helped. And then there are his animalistic instincts. Her fingers have crossed the boundary of safety. Normally, if someone got this close to him without invitation, they'd face his daggers.

"It's okay, Baron," I say to him only.

With that, he nods stiffly at Adore. She doesn't hesitate after the permission is granted. I turn to watch her fingers press against his cheek and slide up to his forehead.

"Oh," she says, carefree as her hand drops to her side.

"So what's the verdict?" I can't help but ask.

Baron is also wondering what that was all about.

"There's not much difference," she answers. "He almost feels like us."

I nudge him with my elbow. "That's what I've been trying to get him to realize," I say jokingly.

Adore's gaze falls to Baron's hands pressing against my abdomen. "But he hasn't stopped holding you so that I can hug you. I miss you all the time, Cl'auta."

Baron, who's now just as charmed by my sister's peculiarity as I am, lets go of me. We hug, and Adore's touch fills me with warmth. I've never felt so happy—like pink balloons, birthday cake, white ponies, and laughing at something silly with Fawn kind of happy.

"You're here for Tapeetha?" she says.

I give her one last squeeze. "I am." We pull apart from each other.

"You need her on the Earth, don't you?" She sounds so sad.

"Yes."

She extends a hand toward me. "Then I'll take you to her." She glances at Baron. "Follow us, Ze Feldis."

Without further ado, we take off down the hill-side at the speed of light. Just when it looks as if we'll collide with the ground, we hit another cloud of light. The rays aren't blinding, and I turn to look behind me to make sure Baron is still with us. I can't hear his thoughts or sense his emotions at the moment. Our eyes meet as our feet hit ground. He smiles and winks to put me at ease.

We're not walking on solid material like cement

or asphalt or brick or rock, but this is a road that our feet now cross. It's made of a cloudy vapor that is sturdy yet plush. Multicolored buildings—built with a glassy element that separates the rays of the sun into red, orange, yellow, green, blue, indigo, and violet—flank us on both sides of the misty street. One is directly ahead of us too, and I think that's where we're headed.

"Does anyone live in those buildings?" I ask Adore.

"Live in them?" she asks, confused by what I mean.

"Does anyone ever enter these buildings?"

"Oh, yes, we do. We are in every place here. If we don't use it, then it shouldn't exist. Isn't it the same on Earth?" Her attention flickers between Baron and me.

Baron is still reacting to her question. He can't believe she's never been to Earth.

"No, it isn't," I answer.

Adore grunts and leaves it at that.

We get to the building and climb a set of foggy steps. I can't help but study my feet in the flat, peep-toe sandals as they hit the white, vapory blocks. We walk right through the crystal block wall that glows yellow, and we end up on a shimmery golden floor that overlooks what reminds me of a vast metropolis with hundreds of monumental bridges running across it. The bridges are not held up by posts; they are suspended in midair and run so far out into the distance, I can't see where, or if, they end.

"What is this?" I ask.

Baron stands next to me. I hold his hand and tilt my head onto his shoulder. The light of day falls over us and the millions of structures that look like roofless houses. Some are round; others are square, rectangular, or triangular. I see L-shaped, U-shaped, and V-shaped buildings. All are placed in such a way that each house appears to be an extension of the neighboring ones. They're separated by plush green grass or crystal-clear streams and watering holes, fruit trees, and beds of colorful flowers. Water gushes into deep, rounded gorges. Countless natives are having a ball riding the current down, down, all the way to the unseen bottom.

"What are they?" Baron wonders.

There are so many Enuians, and they're all different colors, like a box of jumbo-sized Crayolas.

His gaze veers to my chest. I smile because he's noticing that the Enuian women have no breasts, but I do. He's comparing me to this place in what seems like a constant quest to know more about me.

"They're Enuians," I reply.

"We must continue, or you will miss her," Adore says. She continues down the golden walkway.

Baron and I tear our eyes away from the land below to follow her under a high archway of green rock that looks like a cross between marble and sandstone. The sun filters through the solid arch, and the golden floor glimmers below our feet. The combination of both makes it appear as if tiny sparks of light are twinkling in the rock.

The farther we walk, the more I sense Tapeetha. At the same time, I feel as if I'm fighting a force that's trying to stop me, although its resistance is meager.

"Not yet," Adore warns me. "Don't reach for her yet."

"How do you know what I'm doing?" I'm deeply curious about that. Not even Fawn can tell when I'm using my ability to pull in an energy other than hers.

"I'm sensitive," she says. "I'm more sensitive to good than to bad." Her mouth turns down into a grimace.

"Is it because you've only known good?"

She stops in her tracks and pins her focus on Baron. "Yes," she says, not answering my question.

Baron's eyes widen. Apparently, he has some inner dialogue going on that she can hear. I knew it wouldn't take Baron long to figure out how to keep my ability from working on him as long as we're in Enu.

Adore looks at me. "And yes, Cl'auta. Good is all I have to know." Her eyes shift to the left as I give her permission to read my thoughts.

"Not for long, Ad'ru." Instantly, I feel how insensitive my words are, but they are necessary.

"We're here," she barely says. Her eyes are watery, and she's avoiding eye contact with both of us now. "She won't be able to resist you here."

There's another pillow of light in front of us. Adore is right. Tapeetha is coming in loud and clear, and she's dreading my arrival.

"So are you leaving us?" I ask my now-gloomy sister. The look on her face makes me cradle her cheek in my hand, and just like that, my touch brings back that wonderful sparkle in her glassy eyes and puts a smile on her lips.

"Never, Cl'auta. I'm always with you."

I ignore the fear that's gripping her. "Until next

time, Ad'ru." I kiss her other cheek and then her forehead.

I'm surprised that I'm moved to be so affectionate with her. I'm surprised that I love someone so much. Her fears worry me, and her sadness breaks my heart. She's awfully stubborn, choosing to ignore reality for the sake of indulging in good. It's safe but selfish, which contradicts what we are as creatures.

Unfortunately, I'm unable to give Adore's emotions the attention they require. I'm being flooded by Tapeetha's energy. She can't fight me now, and time is of the essence. From beyond this realm, Fawn is showing me a picture of a woman and asking me to find her. Mental multitasking is getting easier.

I grin at Baron. "Follow me, Selell." I leap toward the wide-open field of grass that lies beyond the pillow of light.

At the same time, I take Fawn to a white stone chateau on top of a mountain range surrounding the port town of Nice, France. Inside the manor, the halls are full of stark white light. I'm unable to see what surrounds us, and that worries me a bit. We stop inside a tight, windowless room. A green glow fills the room, which is strange in itself. A thin-faced woman with dark skin and tired eyes reaches out to us. She's a Selell, and Fawn knows her. She tells Fawn to come to her soon, and with a flick of her fingers, I'm fully back in myself.

I want to be worried about Fawn and Zill and demand to know who the woman is, but I force myself to stay out of it. I have to trust Falu so that she can learn to trust herself. I refocus on the task at hand, starting with the scenery—acres of green grass extending into forever. I've been to Enu enough to know that this is simply a transitional port that will lead us to Tapeetha's ideal reality, her "heaven."

"You're ten times faster here," Baron says, grinning back at me as we shoot across the picture-perfect blue sky.

"You're just now noticing that? I've been showing off ever since we got here." I grin at him.

All of a sudden, a heavy force weighs on me, threatening to slow me down. It's not Tapeetha; it's her environment. Baron feels the same strain, so he takes my hand. I'm overtaken by the force of the power flowing through him. Together, we overcome the will of Tapeetha's environment.

I'm able to see my new sister more clearly. She's a long way off, but her eyes are trained on me as

Baron and I soar over a thick rain forest. The tree-tops are so high they're close enough to tickle our soles. It looks like the real world down there. Farther in the distance, framed by gorgeous purple mountains, a herd of gazelles leaps across savanna woodlands. Elephants, zebras, antelope, and giraffes lounge at a sparkling waterhole. I notice that there are no predatory animals on the ground.

Tapeetha stands on top of one of those mountains, watching us. I see her long platinum-blond hair being stirred by a light wind. Her skin is the color of snow, and her eyes are yellow like the sun. Her mouth is pink and caught open in awe. She's standing on the highest peak, wearing a brown leather skirt that fits low on her waist and a vest made of white fur.

"Cl'auta and bond," she says. She watches Baron with narrowed, unwelcoming eyes after he and I land in front of her.

There's a lump in my throat. I did not expect such hostility from her. She wants me to go away just as much as she's determined to remain in Enu with the Wek. She doesn't soften her expression or take her eyes off of me, and I'm pretty sure she hasn't blinked.

"Then you know why I'm here?" I timidly say.

"I know why you are here." She sounds as if she's carefully speaking a language that's not her native tongue. "Tek luk," she says, more comfortably and clearly. She throws in a snarl.

I glance at Baron, who's frowning at Tapeetha. I think he understands what she just said.

"You bring the blood of Danto to torture me?" Once again, she's glaring at Baron.

Baron wants to roar at her for connecting him to Danto, but he holds his anger inside. I hear a growl rumbling deep inside his throat, though.

"It's time," I say to her. "It's time," I repeat more sternly.

She steps closer to me and gives me a warning growl. "Tek luk."

Baron releases a more menacing rumble. He really doesn't like this sister of mine, and he's making that clear to me and to her. I touch his chest to calm him down. This is an act she's putting on, I'm sure of it.

I stand my ground. "You can't stay, so no Tek luk, Pan'a'tua," I say, using her Enuian name. "You know what we have to do."

For the first time, she turns away to glare at the valley below. It's interesting that this is where Tapeetha is most comfortable. Not Manhattan or

Los Angeles. Not Rome or Paris or London. Nowhere that most would consider civilization.

"Come," she says.

Before Baron and I can consent to follow her, she takes off. We're right behind her, racing down the purple mountain until we're shooting past trees. The deeper we go, the darker it turns. Mist hovers over the muddy ground, and we weave through exotic trees I've never seen in my life. Some have trunks as thin as broomsticks, but the tops explode into wiry branches as thick as smoke-stacks. I'm amazed to see the frail trunks support their weight.

Tapeetha is walking at a normal pace now, leading us toward a hut made of mud and straw. As we get closer, a man steps out of it. His skin is a perfect shade of bronze, and his narrow eyes are as blue as the sky. I've never seen anyone who looks like him. He's a Wek, and he's simply beautiful. What's strange is he's wearing a pair of white cotton pants, and despite all the mud and dirt surrounding him, there's not one stain on those pants.

"Oh, Cl'auta," Ose says, bowing toward me. By nature, he's more hospitable than my sister.

"Oh, Ose," I return his greeting.

He glances at Baron and then at Tapeetha, who rushes to his side.

"If I go," she says, sniffing back the wetness that threatens to drip from her nose, "Ose dies. You want that for me, Cl'auta?"

Her heart is on the line, and I'm smothered by her sadness. This is the softest she's been since we arrived.

"Of course not," I whisper past my tight throat. I shake my head. "But I'm here to collect you regardless."

"How long?" she asks.

"Now."

Tapeetha and Ose face each other. They're speaking to each other without words. She's begging him to tell her what she should do. Her tears are flowing freely. Ose assures her that he cannot impose his will on her.

"Don't you love me?" she begs.

"I do," he replies. "But you were not created to love me." He holds her tightly. "We both knew this time would come. I chose this sacrifice a long time ago, Tapeetha. What do you choose?"

She drops her face to look at the grass. Her thoughts are turning. Her love for him is very strong but ineffective. It strips her of the power of matter, restricts her to Enu, and keeps her from fulfilling her destiny.

"I no longer hold the power of matter," she says to me, as if that's an excuse for her to stay.

"You will, once you return to Earth."

She glances at Baron. "What about Danto? Can't he help you?"

I let out a loud, cynical snort. She's worn my patience thin. I can't believe she's willing to put our destiny in the hands of her Selell.

"No, he can't," I bark as a flash of anger grips me. I'm fighting the urge to give her a piece of my mind while simultaneously trying to put myself in her shoes.

"Ose," she whimpers.

He touches her lips before kissing them. He glances at me and opens his mind to me so that I can be aware of the fact that he knows he and Tapeetha should have never crossed this line. If he's seeking forgiveness, then I cannot grant it. I'm not his maker. If he's seeking understanding, well, *that* I can give. So I show him my warmest smile and turn the corners of my mouth down to display a little sympathy.

The ground quakes. Baron draws me into him to keep me safe as a blast of light overcomes us.

Once it passes, Tapeetha is wearing a blousy white dress that matches Ose's white trousers. The landscape has given way to the transitional port of pure green grass under a perfectly blue, cloudless Enu sky.

We're in the transport zone.

Mission accomplished.

FAWN

TWO DAYS AGO...

"I remember this feeling," I say to Ben, who's sitting beside me on the bench in my—no, our—garden. I take his hand. "This is how I felt before Cl'auta showed up in Veil Green. Even though I have you here, again. I have Zill, but Cl'auta... I'm that character in the *Charlie Brown* cartoons. You know the one who needs the blanket to feel secure? Linus. I'm him."

Ben watches me with his brows furrowed, shaking his head. Of course he's confused. He missed the entire twentieth century!

"Are you referring to a safety blanket?" he asks.

I chuckle. I'm amazed he actually got that reference; it's generally a modern phrase. "Yes, definitely. A security blanket."

"And your sister makes you feel safe?" He looks confused by my confession.

"I think so. She's solid. She doesn't even know how together she is. Way more than any of us." I stand and pace even though I just ended a proper round of pacing not too long ago. I'm waiting to get a flash of where Lario may be. I've been trying for the last two hours, even working very hard to recall my dreams, but I have nothing concrete.

"What happened to you, Falu?" There's a hint of concern in his voice.

I stand still to study him. "That's a good question. I'm lost. I don't even recognize myself, Ben."

In a flash, he's standing in front of me, blocking my path. I couldn't continue pacing even if I wanted to.

"I used to have passion and fight," I say as if I'm some elderly person remembering how life was fifty years ago. I feel like that. Like a part of me is long gone and I'll never get it back.

"Thirteen zero nine, A.D.," he says. "That's when I first saw you. You were venturing through

Ngoyo on an expedition. You were with your father."

The experiences and words of the past return to me so quickly I can hardly keep up. "And I was with the Woyo."

"Yes." Ben grins and nods.

I imagine pictures of the past are playing through his memories as well. I giggle at the next memory. "Your people thought I had been kidnapped because of my skin color, and they tried to take me, but I—"

"Blew them back to the dark sea they sailed in upon," he says with a laugh.

"And that was the beginning of an all-out war. You were turned into a Selell by Akili two days later. Wait," I nearly shout as I grab Ben by his washed-out T-shirt.

"Wait, why?" His interest is beyond piqued.

"Akili! She's a Sham!"

"No way," Ben protests with a growl.

"You let her drink you; she's a Selell. It wasn't personal. And she used to be my guardian. She wouldn't hurt me or you."

Ben clenches his teeth, flexing his jaw. Funny, I've seen Ze Feldis display the exact same expression. Unlike my sister's lover, he's being stubborn.

I sigh hard. "Listen, if I'm going to follow my gut, then Akili is who we need." I take my hand off his chest and square my shoulders. I feel the strength that used to spark my actions. "Are you coming or not? Because Zill and I are going to find Akili." My tone is assertive, and it fills me with a power stronger than the force that I wield.

Then it happens so fast that for a moment, I think I'm being whisked away by lightning. I end up on my back on top of my perfectly made bed.

Ben is stretched on top of me. "You're back," he whispers, wearing a wicked snarl.

His teeth are flashing and fangs pulsating. The sight captivates me. Every inch of my being is on fire as my lips find their way to his. His fang punctures my lip, just a tiny prick. I taste a tiny amount of my sweet blood, then Ben tastes it too. He throws his head back to growl like a wolf at the climax of a hunt; he's on the verge of indulging in the captured.

I used to think this was lethal. Why did I think that? This isn't dangerous. Lario made me believe it was, and now I remember why. I press my cheek against the pillow and stretch my neck, exposing the major vein. The prick of Ben's teeth tickles at first, but as he feeds from me, my body feels as if it's suspended in air. I fall in love with him like it's the first time for the billionth time since that day in 1309.

I remember that there's something I have to say to keep him from draining me dry. Especially if he loses his head and forgets to withdraw his fangs from my neck.

"Stop," I moan.

His fangs withdraw from my neck, and I notice I'm naked and Ben is inside me. The sensation of his shifting hips has me practically immobilized, overwhelmed by pleasure. I've missed this. The fact that Lario and his magic could make me forget making love to Ben proves without a doubt that he's a dangerous opponent.

Ben's warm tongue circles the pink tip of my breast, making me feverish with desire. I gasp. I wholly remember my lover. He's not even close to arriving at his peak, and I won't rush him. We'll hit the road when we're done. Lario may get a few more steps ahead of us, but right now, who gives a damn? Not me.

TWO AND A HALF HOURS LATER, AFTER WALKING THE wind, Zill, Ben, and I arrive at Teterboro in New

York. It was the only airport that would give us clearance to charter a flight to Paris, France, within an hour of my call.

It's cold. Although snow isn't falling, it's thick on the ground. It seems that for the last five years, we've been stuck in this never-ending Earth winter. As we stand on the tarmac, watching the loading ramp drop, I'm itching to experience another Earth spring. I hope we won't miss the next one.

I glance at Ben, who's already staring at me. For a beat, I wonder what he's thinking. I see the pure lust in his eyes, but there's something else. For sure, he's full of me: my scent, my power, even my spirit. He drank my blood, which intensified his love for me and mine for him.

I glance at Zill. She's watching the slice of moon that's just become visible between the clouds. She hasn't said much to me since we left the house. After I told her where we were going and the reason, all she offered was a dismal, "Okay." We rushed off to my closet to change into heavier winter clothing, and even though we were pulling from my wardrobe, she was ready way before I was.

I've noticed that her tastes have changed a little. She seems to have retired the faded, paint-stained denim jumpers, like the one she wore the first day we met her. I remember Cl'auta's face when Zill walked out in the outfit. Her expression was classic. Cl'auta is a borderline fashionista, and the hilarious part is that she doesn't even notice it. But since that day, I've given Zill free access to my closet, and she's taken it.

Right now, she's wearing a pair of my black, fitted jeans, a peach V-neck sweater, and black leather boots lined with lambskin. She looks good in my clothes. I live for the days when we'll be able to wear them when we fly into De Gaulle for reasons other than finding a Sham. One day, she and I will hit French boutiques during the day and nightclubs at night. We'll shop and dance without a care in the world, and the only Selells that exist will be our bonds.

As the clouds pass back over the moon, the light disappears from her soft skin. Her gleaming eyes embrace me as she flashes me a smile. Something is definitely weighing heavily on her mind.

"Where's Derek?" I ask.

She pulls the black peacoat tighter around her torso to keep herself warm. I wish I could transfer the warmth I'm feeling from holding Ben's hand to her, but I can't.

Zill shrugs. "I don't know. *Watching*, I guess."

Well, that sounded sarcastic. I put my arm around her shoulder and draw her toward me to make her a little warmer.

"He'll show up," I tell her to comfort her. "He's doing his job."

"And what's that?" she snaps.

"Well, when you made the decision to meet Akili with me, it gave him the freedom to go collect information you might need for later."

"I still don't get it," she says.

"He's your eyes and ears, Zill. That's what a Wek does. He's a gift, not a necessity." She still looks confused, so I explain further. "Okay, let's say when we land at De Gaulle, there's a cyclone between us and our destination. You say, 'I wonder if there's a barricade preventing us from getting to point B, Derek my Wek?' Now that you've asked, he can say, 'Yes, there's a cyclone ahead of us.' That's what a Wek does—one of the things, at least."

She ponders that as the green lights that run up and down the handrails cut on. It's time for us to board, and we do. Zill chooses to sit alone in the back of the airplane, but I insist that she join us. I use the excuse of needing to give her more information about Akili before we arrive, and I promise to let her go hibernate in the back once I'm done. But the good thing is, even before the jet lifts off the ground, Ben has her laughing as she tells us about how the vampires in the underground rave smelled her blood and started biting into each other's necks, which made them sick.

"It was so gross. They were hacking all over the place, sticky, gooey blood and junk."

"But it sounds like it was easy for you to put an end to them," Ben says.

"Yeah," she says, recollecting. "Too easy."

"That's how it should be."

"Really? Shouldn't I at least have a conscience about it? Yeah, it was crazy mass confusion, and I really wanted to laugh. But it was also the saddest thing in the world."

"Do both," Ben tells her. "Feel it all with no regrets because that makes you honest."

"Yeah," she whispers and stares out into the darkness.

"Have you met your vampire?" Ben asks, in an effort to fulfill my wish to keep her talking.

"Yes," she says without looking our way.

"Is that so?" He sounds shocked.

"Yeah, but he doesn't want to be a vampire. He's a mommy's boy."

"Oh come on," I say in the "mommy's boy's"

defense. "Don't be so hard on Vayle. He's new to this."

"And now he's old to it," she says through tightly clenched teeth.

I didn't realize how angry at him she was. "If he comes back, you'll be sorry." I want to gauge how she feels about the idea of his return.

She turns to look at me. "He should've come back with us in the first place. I mean, Ze Feldis didn't sit there like a wimp and whine about his mommy and being human again." Her face is contorted, and I think she's on a roll. "I darn near begged him to stay, and all he could do was cry about how I don't love him. I mean, really? Is that what it would've taken? Me lying about loving him? I do love him, I love him a lot, but he's such a… a… I begged him to stay, and he didn't."

"Well…" I try to be delicate, knowing she won't like what I say next, even though it's the truth. "You *ordered* him to come with us and even sort of insulted him a little, but did you ask? Nope." I shake my head. "You didn't do that."

She looks out the window. She's probably remembering how she harshly asked him, "What's your problem, guy?" Then she inadvertently accused him of ditching the power of the sun to run home to his mommy, or something to that effect.

"What's done is done," she mutters.

I've been around long enough to know she's not "done" with it, not even a little.

"So what's this all about? You said you needed to tell me something before we get to Paris?" Her tone is acerbic.

I sigh, exasperated, and widen my eyes at Ben to ask him for more help with her. At times like this, I wish I possessed Cl'auta's power of the mind.

Ben leans into her. "In five seconds, your head will explode."

I can't help but burst into laughter. This moment. This is us, Ben and I. Together.

Zill snorts as she slightly smiles, rolls her eyes, and shakes her head. Of course she remains a little defiant, but even she melts under the power of Ben's natural charm.

"Okay," she says as if she's giving up, "so I'm mad at Vayle." She crosses her arms. "I mean, you guys get to be warm, but I'm cold because he's not here to hold my hand. I just…"

"You chose Derek," I remind her.

She shrugs. "Derek's not a choice." She takes a long pause. "I don't choose anyone anymore. I just want to do this, you know? With you and Clarity." She takes another pause. "I mean, I don't need a vampire."

"Not if you don't mind the cold," Ben says.

Zill rolls her eyes at him. "Where did you get this one, Fawn?"

"Ze Feldis found him in a cave." I laugh and touch Ben's chest.

He takes my hand and kisses the back of it.

"How did you get those marks on your neck?" Zill asks out of nowhere.

Ben taps one of his fangs. "From these."

"You bit her?" She sounds repulsed. "You can do that?"

"Well, yeah," I say. "For a long time, I thought we would die if a vampire drank our blood. I think Lario inserted that belief into my memories because we're both stronger after he drinks me. But you know what I think?"

"What?" Zill is on the edge of her seat.

"I think Lario wanted me to tell Clarity that if Ze Feldis drank her blood, then she would die."

"Why would he do that?" Zill asks. She realizes the answer just as fast. "Oh… to keep them as weak as possible."

"Exactly."

"I can't wait to kill this guy."

"That's the spirit!" Ben exclaims.

Then he asks the flight attendant to bring us a deck of cards, a bottle of tequila, and, of course, Goshem tea. We play blackjack, and Ben and I down a couple of glasses of tequila. Zill reminds us that she's twenty-two, so we decide to celebrate her twenty-first birthday by letting her have her first taste of the "devil's juice."

"And thousands more…" Ben sings in tribute as we lift our glasses and drink to her birthday.

"You know, Ben, you're the true king of the one-liners," Zill says before taking her first drink. She spits it out, spraying the liquid on the empty leather seat across from her. "This stuff tastes awful!" She gags and coughs at the same time.

I hand her a cup of Goshem tea. "Stick to this."

Zill gladly takes it.

As the seven and a half hours rush by, Ben and I recount the days before our memories were stolen from us. I'm happy to have Zill's full attention. She's pepped up, and whatever thoughts had brought her down earlier seem to be gone now.

"So who's this Akili?" Zill asks with her cards fanned before her face.

"She used to be my guardian,"

She drops the cards to her lap. "Like Deanna?"

"Yep."

"Hit me," she says to Ben, and he passes her a card. "Does that mean that Deanna's still alive?"

"If she isn't dead, then she's still alive. Akili is a Selell, but she wasn't one when she was my guardian." I glance at Ben. "Hit me."

He deals me a card.

"So Deanna's a regular human being? Hit me."

"Sort of. She's anatomically human, but certain gifts are given to them to protect us."

"And this Akili, she's African?"

"Hit me. She's from the Woyo nation. Don't call her African. She doesn't like that."

"Okay," Zill barely says, frowning hard. "So Deanna was real?" She sounds amazed by that. "Hit me."

I give her a tight-lipped smile and nod. "Yes. She was." I try to sound reassuring.

After a moment spent deep in thought, she snorts. "Figures."

"What do you mean?" I'm almost afraid to ask.

"She was just so high maintenance. I would hate to think that she was really something special. Although she was special to me, most of the time." Zill nods with a sentimental expression. "I still want to see her again. It's good to know that I can."

I stare at Zill, who's looking at her cards again. She's such an enigma to me.

"Hit me," I say to Ben.

"Can't," he says.

I look down at my hand and see that I have ten cards. Zill has eleven. I have five cards too many, and she has six more than necessary.

"I was wondering how long you two would keep this up," he says.

Zill slams her cards on the round table between our seats. "What can this Akili do for us?" she asks, blowing off playing cards in order to focus on more important issues.

"She's a nolotuka," I reply as I toss all ten of my cards on the table. Five pair. "By the way, I won." I wink at Ben.

"And she's not a nice little vampire either," Ben adds, winking back.

"She turned him, but—" I start to explain.

"No buts about it! She deceived me," he complains for the millionth time.

I touch Ben's knee. "He was a religious zealot. He would never have chosen to turn. Ben and his buddies came to 'civilize' the savages."

Zill blurts an amused laugh.

"What I found strange was Akili told me he was coming before he arrived. Apparently, he was two years late."

"That's frightening but true," Ben mumbles. "I bailed on three earlier missions because—"

He stops short of saying what I've waited centuries to hear. He's never told me why. I always assumed there was some sort of contention between him and his father.

"Because?" Zill presses.

He glances at me and then turns his attention on Zill. I can see the thoughts churning in his head. I'm compelled to lean toward him, curious to hear his answer.

"Because I changed my mind."

"Why did you change your mind?" Zill won't let it go. She gets like that sometimes. Like a dog with a bloody bone.

"Because I had obligations."

"What obligations?" She snaps her face toward me. "He's being evasive, Falu. Don't you think so?"

I shrug. Over the years, Ben has generally been an open book. This is the only secret he's ever kept from me, and I've let him have it.

"It's okay," I say to her and rub his leg. *"It's his secret, and I'm letting him keep it."*

She nods, agreeing to let it go. "So how did she seduce him?"

"She's a nolotuka."

"Yeah, you said that. What does that mean?"

"Have you ever heard of a Seirên?"

"Of course I have." She twists as she's suddenly struck by illumination. "Oh, I see. She made Ben think she was Falu. How does it work? Being turned into a vampire?"

"First, he gave her permission to drink him, almost to death. Then he drank her Selell blood, and she killed him before he could recover. The Selell blood overtakes the human blood instantaneously, and the transformation begins."

I had no knowledge Akili planned to turn Ben into a Selell. I'd barely known Ben at the time, and I certainly didn't love him. He was simply a pesky missionary who, like the rest of them, wondered what I, a girl with skin the color of snow and eyes like emeralds, was doing living amongst the Woyo.

We land late in the afternoon. Zill and I hit the air running, and Ben stays on the airplane waiting for nightfall. The late December cold nips at my nose and fingers. I'm tempted to contact Cl'auta and ask her to cover us with one of her warmth shields, but I'm determined to see how far we can get without her aid.

We get a little warmer once I blow the clouds away from the sun. I'm guessing meteorologists could've never predicted this. It's about sixty degrees now, and that's a more agreeable temperature. I have the ability to change the weather, but I use that ability sparingly and responsibly.

I absolutely adore Paris. If I had to choose any city to live, it would be here. I'd take one of those old little apartments lining a cobblestone street, close to the marketplaces, cafés, and clubs. I love strolling across the many bridges and along the lakes. Then there are the fountains, courtyards, and cathedrals. I remember the Revolution and Versailles under siege. The tension in the streets could've been cut with a knife. There was the Nazi occupation in the 1940s and then being hammered by the Allied forces. This lovely city has taken some major blows, and yet here it stands. It will probably remain just like this even after the end of time.

We soar over the countryside full of rolling hills, valleys of grapevines and olive groves, dirt roads, and streams that twist through the high grass that's tickled by the wind. It's all so picturesque. Some of the landscapes threaten to rival those of Enu. Although people can be ugly, much of Earth is awfully beautiful. The closer we get to the French Riviera, the less the cloud coverage demands my attention.

"So this is France?" Zill says.

"You've never been?" I asked, surprised. A daughter of the House of Benel should've visited almost every part of this earth! We have no limitations as far as that's concerned.

"Nope. Of course Deanna's been here thousands of times, but she never took me." It sounds as though she's complaining.

"You know her job was to protect you, right?"

Zill doesn't answer. She seems struck by the sight of the bulky chateaus with their high windows and rounded towers. They line the coast, once the summer homes of the elite, and for the most part, they still are. But as the years passed, many of these mansions were converted into boutique hotels. The water that ripples onto the white sand is a little foggy this time of year but still vibrant. Not even the slight chill can keep the many winter tourists from catching a tiny amount of rays from the descending sun.

We journey away from the port toward the

mountains. High up, a thick conglomeration of trees circle a single white-stone chateau with a red-brick rooftop. The sight of it makes me stop abruptly.

Zill follows in suit. "Is that where we're going?" She senses my apprehension while scanning the thick tree line.

I nod stiffly. My jaw is so tight I can't open my mouth to speak. I have no idea why, but all of a sudden, I'm nervous. We're visceral beings, and my instincts are warning me to approach with caution.

We're not alone. Cleotis Lux has joined us. Only Lux, not Titus Rona. Lux's sword isn't drawn, but his hand is in his pocket. His sudden appearance can only mean that something Zill is determined to battle is nearby.

"Mr. Lux?" Zill exclaims. She's shocked to see him.

Lux's gaze is pinned on the house. "If we enter, then our battle will be hard won."

Zill and I look at each other, determined to heed Lux's warning.

"You think this is a trap?" she asks me.

I'm too confused to respond. If danger is something one can feel, then I feel it. But I feel trust in equal parts. There's no way Akili would double-cross me. Not on purpose. But I have to admit that something has definitely gone wrong.

"To the ground," I say.

We all drop down. The soil is dry, and it crackles beneath our feet. The leaves that brush our faces lack moisture. It hasn't rained here in weeks. One of the great things about Nice is its dry weather.

Zill searches over her shoulders. "Feel that?"

"I do," I say.

"I feel like we're being watched," she whispers.

"Yes, I feel the same way," I say. "But we are on the ground, and we don't have a shield of invisibility, so…"

The wind rustles the leaves. From somewhere far away, I hear a car engine purring and some sort of generator roaring.

Zill studies the ground beneath us. "This way."

She darts into a grove of olive trees. Soon, I'm following her up a narrow trail. We move around the perimeter of the property. Cleotis Lux's sword of fire is now burning. Since we're all on our guards, I call my powers to my palms, to my fingertips. I'm ready.

Zill lifts a hand, and I stop behind her. She squats, shovels the dirt and rocks with one hand,

and then looks at me, pointing at the spot she just cleared. That's where I aim my palm. I use a quiet force by thinking of soft air. With one strong burst, I clear away the debris and reveal a hatch made of dry wood. I blow it open. She and I look inside it. If Selells are down there, we're still safe. They can't come out in the daytime even if the sun is descending. But we see nothing but an empty concrete floor.

"After me," Zill says and jumps into the hole.

I take the plunge after Cleotis Lux. The drop is only about seven feet. We face a long, narrow hallway.

"What the ..." I whisper.

"It looks like some sort of escape route," Zill answers. "Kill the first face you don't recognize because this place is infested with vampires. If you want to find your guardian, it'll be over their dead bodies."

I did not expect this. My heart is thumping like crazy. I want Ben here with us, and Cl'auta and Ze Feldis. But as I watch Zill skulk down the tight space, it occurs to me that we are enough. She's the fighter, and I have the force. We are pure power. So I let courage lead me.

The farther we move, the deeper into the earth we go. I feel as if we're walking through a casket. I stir up a wind to give us some air until we finally get to the end of the walkway. We make a sharp right only to face a wide-open, pitch-black space.

Zill turns to lift her eyebrows at Cleotis Lux, who shoots into the blackness. It happens so fast, but I see his sword whipping through the air. I hear cries, growls, and grunts. Zill stands in front of me. I see faces trying to get at us, but her hands are working, snatching and ripping and penetrating.

"Start your engines," she calls over her shoulder before leaping into the pit of vampires.

I shoot a steady wall of force in front of and behind me. I can't see Zill, but I do see Lux's sword slicing away. His swinging stops abruptly. I stifle a gasp when, out of nowhere, Zill steps in front of my shield. She's covered in the black tar that is Selell blood.

"Are you okay?" she asks, searching my face.

"I'm fine." My voice isn't shaky, and I'm already thinking of a way to make this easier. "They're all through here, aren't they?"

"Yeah." She's breathing heavily.

The fire of Lux's sword intensifies and lights the room. I can see now. Black goo and dead Selells litter the floor. Hot ashes settle in the air. The ghost of violence remains in the room. I have to walk through it, this reminder that this is all real.

"There's still sunlight out there," I say, figuring out a way to get this done with less of a body count.

"At least for a little while longer," Zillael says.

Cleotis Lux stands ready to fight. He's staring in one direction, waiting for the next group of Selells to arrive. Guardians like him are always ready to fight. I have to work fast. I step inside the room, rising off the floor to avoid trampling on Selell blood and bodies. At the ceiling, I shove my hands against it, testing its resolve.

"It's made of wood," I announce.

Zill whips around to face a half-opened door. "Get back in the hallway, Falu."

But I continue with my plan. I aim both of my palms above my head to blow the top off this place. There's an earsplitting crashing. A geyser of dirt and wood shoot up into the dusky sky. The weaker rays of the late day are still strong enough to burn the Selells who intended to make a late afternoon cocktail out of us. Just as I planned, smoking like chimneys, they retreat deeper into the tunnels.

"Glad you ignored me," Zill says as she stares at the sky.

"I think we should get out of here before nightfall. This place is infested with Lario's Selells." I squat, swipe a finger through the black sludge on the lacquered wooden floor, and sniff it.

Zill blinks as if I've lost my mind. "You know what's going on, right?"

"Yes, I do, but there's no way we can get in, recover Akili, and get out alive. In less than fifteen minutes, it's going to be night."

"We've done all right so far. Let's just finish it."

I sigh hard. She widens her eyes at me, beckoning me to get on board with her plan. I shake my head because I know she's right.

I take a gut check. "All right, let's get to the house. Fast."

Zill, Cleotis, and I power through the air, over the spiky trees, toward the chateau. Time is ticking away. We land on a veranda with stained-glass windows. I choose not to waste a second. I blow the door off its hinges and then the glass from over the patio.

Zill and Cleotis are already inside slaying our aggressors. For a second, I notice how possessed the Selells look as they strike the shield of force I've surrounded myself with. They look like young men who've lost all reason. They don't look ashen and demonic, as if the process of once being human and now being the walking, talking dead has turned them into monsters. The only difference between them and me is that they have bulging, throbbing fangs, their lips are dry, and the skin around their eyes is swollen and purple. It looks as if thousands of years have passed since they've had a decent night's sleep or a solid meal. It's the saddest thing I've ever seen, and I wish we didn't have to destroy them.

I work faster. Surely Selells are equipped with survival instincts. If they're exposed to the descending sun, then maybe they'll choose to retreat. I blow the entire front of the house to smithereens. Shards of plaster, brick, wood, and other materials shoot out around us. I stack what I can one on top of the other, but I keep moving forward.

I make an effort to stay away from the Selells. Their thirst is driving them mad. Their growling and screeching and wailing threaten to disrupt my concentration, so I zone out. Their sounds become faint background noise. I clear the silky, very French furnishings from my path. I blow the walls off the first floor but leave the beams that hold the house intact. Although the sun's rays are weaker than they were five minutes ago, they're still strong enough to gradually turn the vampires to ashes. The higher the sun is, the faster they burn.

We're fighting against time. There must be thousands of Selells here! I take the stairs and catch a glance of Zill. Her movements are just as precise as mine. She's strong, and with each swipe of her hands and kick of her legs, she's taking their heads off. Blood, body parts, and ashes hit my shield, and the stomach-souring scent of rot invades my senses. I blow away all three flights of stairs, and in the attic at the very top of the house, I see the green light.

In a panic, I snatch a wall from the opposite side of the house to cordon off the area where the green light comes from. At least now I know where the zone is that I have to preserve. Fragments fall around me like snow. I'm covered in soot, but none of it breaks my concentration. I dismantle the rest of the house bit by bit while keeping that one small area intact. By the time I'm done, all of us, including the room I'm holding together, are floating above the foundation. As we set our feet back on the ground, I place the room in front of us.

"Drop the walls," Akili shouts from inside it.

I hesitate. The day is almost done. When night comes, Ben will join us, but a number of Selells have dug themselves deeper into the earth, and they're lying in wait. I have no choice but to follow Akili's instructions.

I blow out the walls and stack them on top of the others. There she is, positioned in the center of the room, surrounded by the green haze. It seems to be keeping her safe from the remaining sunlight. Nothing about her has changed over the centuries; she looks the same.

"Come, both of you," she calls to Zill and me.

"Wait," Cleotis Lux orders as he looks at the sky.

Something is happening to me. My body is so light that it's mixing with the air. My breaths are shallow. I'm…

CHAPTER 7

THE GATHERING

CLARITY

I'm holding my breath, counting down from ten. I have no doubt that what I've asked Tapeetha to do will work, but I can't help but be concerned. My sisters faced a heavy assault, and I'm kicking myself for not seeing the ambush ahead of time. I should've known the blinding light was a smokescreen. That's strike one for me for missing it. So now I'm standing on the front lawn of the Vermont estate, squeezing Baron's hand while we watch Tapeetha. Her yellow eyes turn sapphire blue, and her long hair takes on a life of its own. The strands flow toward her face as if blown by an unfelt wind.

I'm at the count of five when one by one, Fawn,

Zill, and the woman Fawn asked me to guide her to materialize before our eyes. Artiste shows up behind them. Tapeetha's managed to get all four of them home. Finally, I can breathe easily again.

Fawn and Zill twist this way and that, jarred by the change of scenery and circumstances. Upon seeing the new sister, they get an inkling of what just happened to them.

It's Ben who makes the first move. He goes to Fawn when she starts coughing. Zill coughs too.

"Are you hurt?" Ben asks while running his hands up and down Fawn's body as if he's giving her a physical examination. He embraces her then steps back to examine the grimy, oxygenated Selell blood and soot that covers her.

"I'm fine," she says while reaching out to squeeze one of Zillael's hands. "What about you?"

Zill looks as if someone has painted her with Selell blood. Her entire face is contorted in a grimace as she searches across the lawn, the massive wrought-iron gate, and the enormous cedars pressing against it. Her heart is in her throat. Something's coming, or shall I say someone.

"I'm fine," she croaks, but she's not quite sure of it.

A lot is happening right now; even I'm over-whelmed by it all. Fawn has just noticed Akili, who's hugging herself. Akili appears very vulnerable at the moment, and her eyes shift from face to face and then toward the sky. Appearing captivated, Tapeetha walks over to Zill, swipes a finger down one side of her face, and smells the substance she gathered.

"What's this creature?" she asks.

Zill is looking into Tapeetha's eyes, but she's not really seeing her.

"It's a new kind of Selell," I answer for Zill.

Tapeetha grunts. Then she becomes distracted by the sight of three individuals.

"Vayle?" Zill whispers.

He's not alone. A woman is with him, and by her long, wavy brown hair and height, she's one of our sisters. She must be Glo. And there's no doubt that the Selell strolling gracefully beside her is her bond. Like Baron, he's something to look at, even at a distance. His steps are deliberate, his chin slightly tilted. I'm drinking in his energy. He's on guard.

"Finn Elo," Baron hisses. Before I can respond, he's left my side to stand face to face with the myste-rious new vampire.

"I cannot be here," Akili mumbles in a distinct French accent.

Fawn rushes over to catch Akili before she collapses. At first, Ben is distracted by Baron and the vampire named Finn, but then he shoots over to help Fawn keep Akili on her feet.

My attention is being pulled in two directions, toward Vayle and company and toward Akili, who's gulping air and struggling to breathe.

"You, the Encaser," Akili says.

I tear my focus away from Baron and put it on her.

"I need you to take me to Catskills." She struggles to hold up her arms, which is her way of asking me to come to her. She's having trouble keeping her arms up, so I move quickly to her side. Akili presses her ice-cold hands against my head.

"You come to me in two suns; I'll have answers for you," Akili says and then gasps for air like a fish out of water. Our environment is killing her.

I bring Tapeetha's inner consciousness with me, and we ride up the snow-covered Slide Mountain in the Catskills until we penetrate the million-year-old rock. We drop into a vast open space that resembles the Mount Olympus coven.

"Bring her here," I tell Tapeetha.

I'm getting better at this. I'm able to see Akili dematerialize right before all the eyes that are watching her while I'm still in the belly of the mountain. When Tapeetha and I fully return to ourselves, she turns around in a circle, confirming our surroundings. Then she whips her face forward and pins her attention on me. She's breathing heavily, her eyes wild with exhilaration.

"Tek maka luk menta lak?" she asks.

"Yes, I was able to take you there."

For the first time, Tapeetha smiles at me. Her entire face brightens. It's a good look on her. She turns to Fawn. "Oh, Falu."

"Oh, Pan'a'tua." Fawn reaches out to take Tapeetha's hand. "I know it wasn't easy to leave Ose. Thank you for getting us out of there." She sounds gracious enough for the both of us at the moment.

I can't take my eyes off Baron and the Selell named Finn. They're still speaking, and now they're watching us observe them. After a few seconds, the three strong, virile vampires and an equally stunning daughter of the House of Benel move toward us. They're extraordinary specimens, and if anyone can carry the weight of the world on their shoulders, they can.

I look from Fawn, Tapeetha, and Zillael to the new sister, who has to be none other than Glo, the fifth sister. This is our new dawn. We are on the verge of fulfilling some kind of purpose.

I used to think our purpose was creating a path for Selells to turn back into their human selves, but so much has happened since we began our journey. Lario's a vampire again, and a more menacing one at that. Humans' souls are being stolen. Covens of first-generation Selells are being wiped out because second-generation vampires are feeding on them. Who knows what else the future has in store for us?

Soon the three new arrivals join us. Zill and Fawn decide to get cleaned up before extending a proper greeting to Glo. On her way to her rooms, Fawn walks Tapeetha to her space. I can't imagine where that will be. I haven't seen any décor that appears to suit her rugged tastes.

Baron and I stay with Glo, Finn, and Vayle. It's warm outside, and it's on the verge of evening. We move to the patio, and all of us except Finn sit around the wrought-iron table. After we sit down, another individual materializes beside Glo.

My mouth falls open. "Raz!" I'm filled with excitement and bewilderment.

"Hey, Clarity," he says in that draggy voice of his. That's about as excited as he ever sounds.

I know it's juvenile, but I leap out of my chair, run to him, and throw my arms around him. It's funny how in this moment, I'm back at Paradise Cove, watching him and Aries goof off in the foamy waves before they crash against the shore.

"What in the world are you doing here?" I exclaim.

"I'm with Glo," he replies.

"How? Why?" I still sound overexcited.

"Yeah," he says in that lazy tone of his. "I'm a Wek."

My mouth falls open in shock. But of course he's a Wek! He hasn't aged a day since I saw him last. Sure, he's quite scruffy, but like every Wek I've seen, he's quite beautiful. He's very agreeable and extremely likable. From the age of eleven to about fourteen, I had a slight crush on him. He was the model of the perfect boyfriend, one that Baron Ze Feldis has definitely lived up to.

"Unbelievable," I say and turn my excited eyes on Baron. I want to tell him all about growing up with Raz and Aries, how they created all the happy memories in my life before he came along.

But Baron still has that disturbed expression that formed when Finn showed up. Something about the vampire, who actually looks more like him than Artiste, gets his goat. I try to pull information from Finn's thoughts in order to figure out what's going on between them, but Finn's a single-minded being. He's only thinking about the new breed of vampires and the many ways he can put an end to them. I hesitate to experience the thoughts that are playing out in his memories: a small, vacant town; people in cages; a fight; another celestial guardian who wields a sword; a Selell in a tunnel who warned him to lie low because the new vampires are attacking the old ones and killing them. It's all looping in his thoughts. I even get a bird's-eye view of Glo's power, and she can do some major damage. But I also sense that Finn is growing impatient as we sit here under the sun, on our fancy furniture, in front of the spread of berries, flat bread, cream, and Goshem tea.

"You know Aries?" Glo asks me.

I can feel the slight ache in her heart the second she mentioned Aries. "Yes, years ago. She was my—"

"Nanny," Glo finishes for me.

I smile at her while nodding.

She smiles back but barely. Through a tight throat, she says, "She was my best friend. My sister before I knew I had sisters. And…" Glo looks off toward the swimming pool. She notices how grandiose it is but only briefly.

I see their last conversation in her memories. Aries does look a lot different than she did back when I knew her. She's not in over-washed, faded cutoff jean shorts and a turquoise bikini top that's an accessory to her brown skin. She's wearing a red-and-white form-fitting dress and actual high heels! She looks like a million bucks.

I also see them in Glo's living room, a space that's designed in the modern, minimalist décor. Aries tells her that she's Glo's guardian. Glo feels betrayed, but it doesn't change how much she loves Aries. We clearly have a lot to talk about, but there's a low rumbling in Finn's throat. He's hit the limit of his patience.

"Have you ever eaten any of this before?" I ask Glo, changing the subject.

She shakes her head. "No, but it looks delicious."

She's making an effort to be agreeable, which I

must admit I find very interesting. But it doesn't look delicious to her at all. Her palate is far more refined.

"I'll be back," Vayle says before hurrying away from the table. He's been distracted ever since Zill went to get cleaned up.

"Ze Feldis, I take it you've heard about the Olympus coven?" Finn asks, getting right down to business, as he's been itching to do.

"Finn, sit, please," Glo says.

He does what she says without protesting. It's what Baron would do for me. I can't keep my eyes off them. They're a beautiful pair. Her eyes are almost the color of glass, and so are his. She has very brown hair and white skin with a deep peach undertone. There's probably no one in the entire world who looks like her—or Tapeetha, or Fawn, or Zill, or Adore. Am I really that beautiful?

"I have," Baron says, but he's still quite tense.

"It's Exgesis. Are you still buddying up with him?" There's outright condemnation in Finn's tone.

"No, are you?" Baron gives it back to him.

Glo and I look at each other. She's wondering if I sense the hostility between the two of them.

"They don't like each other much, do they?" I say only to her.

She flashes me a slight smile. *"Finn doesn't like anyone. He's socially challenged."* She's clearly joking.

I chuckle but decide to end the faceoff between Baron and Finn. They look as though they're only seconds away from ripping off each other's heads. There's definitely bad blood between them.

"Well," I say to get both of their attention. They turn to face me. "The new vampires have devastated a town named Moonridge. I think I saw where you two have faced a similar problem. What was that place you were thinking about earlier, Finn?"

He's frowning so hard I think his entire face is on the verge of crumbling. "You can know what I'm thinking?"

I'm not intimidated. "I can."

"I can too," Baron adds, but he sounds as though he's dangling his abilities in·Finn's face.

This is strange...

Now Finn's thinking of something other than killing Lario and second-generation vampires. I see a memory of a woman with long, straight black hair, big brown eyes, and a very pretty face. Baron and this woman are on a bed in a cave with a single candle illuminating it. Their limbs are entangled as they engage in the wildest sex I've ever seen. I look away and shut my eyes to erase the image from my head.

When I open my eyes, Baron is glaring at Finn as if he's going to rip off Finn's head. He knows what Finn showed me. It was quite cruel, actually. If I were a different individual, then that memory could have devastated our relationship. But Baron and I have made a pact to never let those we loved in the past influence our present.

I force out a deep breath to cleanse the tiny bit of jealousy I feel. "So this is where we are…" I fill Glo and Finn in on our plan to use the power of matter to round the new vampires into one place and destroy them, like Tapeetha did in 1489.

"I remember that," Finn says.

"The only problem is," I continue, "I have to find a feature that differentiates them from your kind of vampire. That may be the impossible part of the plan." I sound as defeated as I feel.

"Like a physical feature of some kind?" Glo asks.

"Yes, inside or out."

"I might be able to help. I can see through things if I choose too."

"So can I," Finn says, giving Baron the one-up glare.

"So you can see through bodies?" I ask, deciding to keep on planning.

"If I want to." She sighs. "Like you have a key on your heart, and so do I, and the other sisters."

"The key to Jari," I say.

"We just came back from there." Glo recounts how they had to race to collect Vayle. Lario wanted him because he has the power of the sun.

"How did you figure it out?" I say, sitting on the edge of my seat.

"Before this Exgesis guy got away from Finn, he pointed at the sun. Then Raz provided a few clues."

"He was that close, and you let him get away from you?" Baron scoffs.

Finn glares at Baron.

"Thank God you were right, Glo," I say, extra loud to keep the peace.

"Are you aware that those vampires can feed on humans?" Finn asks Baron. He sounds as if he's forcing himself to be civil.

"It's not their blood they're drinking," Baron replies quite unpleasantly.

"It's their souls," I say before Finn can mirror Baron's temperament. "It's just that the initial pierce of the skin…" I pause, distracted by the marks on Glo's neck. "Did you bite her?"

"Yes, I drank her." Finn looks at Baron and then back at me.

Baron and I stare at each other, dumbfounded.

"And you're both still alive." I actually feel the muscles in my face twisting to show how perplexed I am.

Glo turns to look toward the sunroom that leads to the hallway that leads to Fawn's living quarters. "He drinks her too, Fawn's vampire."

"Artiste?" I ask, shocked by that information. I shake my head profusely. "No, she's the one who warned me against it."

Glo shrugs. "I saw the marks on her neck."

To Glo, it's no big deal. I really want to see how it's done. I want to pull the act of them engaged in biting from her thoughts, but Glo isn't thinking about it.

"But Exgesis survived her heat," Finn says as he turns to gaze at Glo. For the first time since he's arrived, he has something on his brain other than the task at hand. He's fighting the urge to touch her neck, where he last left his mark.

He stops himself from remembering the act of biting her by ripping his eyes away and putting them on Baron. He can barely look at me because seeing me reminds him of Glo. He's got it bad, and I don't blame him. She's exquisite, and she has a very agreeable energy. It's inexplicable. I mean, I like being here, sitting across the table from her, comparing what she and Finn Elo know to what Baron and I know so that we can charge forward with our plan.

"The power of fire," I whisper mostly to myself.

Finn says, "But before I could kill him, he disappeared."

Baron pounds his fist on the table with a snarl. "That's because he has Leto Danto."

The table is still vibrating from Baron's assault on it.

"The power of matter," I say, while shaking my head. "Lario's controlling Leto Danto and exploiting the power of matter."

ZILLAEL

Nothing, think of nothing, I tell myself over and over while focusing on the sound of the water spraying out of the shower head. I study the vampire blood as it washes down the drain. It turns red again when water mixes with it.

Vayle has returned. I'm kind of freaking out about that too.

Think of nothing.

His eyes. The way he kept looking at me. He has questions for me, and I wonder what they are. Am I in love with Derek? I don't know anymore. Derek has pulled so far away from me that I hardly recognize him. Do I love Vayle? I don't know, but my heart is thumping like crazy.

Every part of me remembers Vayle's hands exploring my body and the way he tastes when we kiss. But it's not only that. I want to hear him laugh again, joke with me, make a case for me ending up flipping burgers in Foreversville if I don't choose him over the Wek. It would've been nice to have him with me when I ventured through the dome of doom, the place where I had to behead the two Selells who stole Jake and Mary's souls. It would've been cool if he'd gone to Nice with us. Vayle holds the other half of the power of sun. At least he and Ben could've gone with us in the daytime. Man, I miss him. I don't want him to go away again—ever.

I hit the button that turns the water off and step out of the shower. The floor-to-ceiling mirrors surrounding the double bowl sink catch all my angles. Usually I try not to look at myself, but this time, I can't help it.

My hips are more rounded and breasts more plump. My legs are long but strong, and there are tiny cuts on my shoulders. It's the body of a woman who is feminine but strong. Personality wise, I have the strong part down, but the woman part? Let's just say I'm no Clarity. But I want Vayle to look at me the way Ze Feldis looks at her. I can see them spending forever together in pure happily-ever-after bliss. Not me and Vayle though. It's that actuality that keeps me from falling completely in love with him.

Once that's settled, the enigma of why I feel so strongly for Vayle at the moment passes, and I step over to a grandiose contraption in the corner of the bathroom. It's a body dryer! One steps into it, and the air turns on and dries one off. I only use it because I like the idea that my father, my actual father, had it built into my bathroom because he wanted to give me the finer things in life. That's what I want, a guy who simply wants to give me the best things.

When I'm dry, I feel the pressure of wanting to hurry back to the patio. I want to see him. I wonder if he's there. Hot damn, Vayle is back! I run out of what I call the dry-my-butt corner and down the short hallway to my bedroom. When I see him sitting on the bed, I gasp in shock.

"All right," Vayle sings, clearly digging the scene, "I'm just going to look at your face." But then his eyes fall downward over my body and then return to my face. "Starting now."

I grunt nonchalantly as I walk over to grab a long T-shirt out of my dresser and slip it on. "So you came back." I turn my back on him and shuffle through my closet, containing my excitement. I can't look at him right now. My strong feelings have returned, and frankly, Vayle hasn't done anything to earn them.

"I figure if I was born to do this, then I'd better."

"What made you come to that conclusion?"

I notice that I've never seen some of these clothes before. By the style of them—very skinny jeans and corduroy pants, thick, fitted sweaters, screen-print long- and short-sleeved T-shirts with words like, "Life Is What You Make It" written across the front, and three pairs of cozy, furry snow boots—I'd say Fawn had them placed in here. I smile because it's such a sisterly thing to do.

"I guess I always knew it." Vayle takes a long, thoughtful pause. "I don't like being dead, and I don't like that this happened to me. But I can't cry over spilled milk, can I?"

I turn to face him. "Well, that's one way of looking at it."

"You're being cynical, Zill."

I nod. "Sarcastic, actually. I'm being sarcastic. I mean, aren't you the college student?"

Now he snorts a chuckle. "Miss me?" He smirks at me. He's cute when he does that.

"Hell yeah," I sing, feigning enthusiasm.

"Are you being sarcastic?"

"No." I shake my head. "Cynical."

In a flash, he's off the bed and standing in front of me. "I missed you too."

All of a sudden, my breathing is all over the place. He's wearing the same sooty shirt we left him in last week. Without thinking, I take grab the hem and pull it up over his head.

"You should get cleaned up," I barely say.

Vayle smashes his lips against mine. His tongue finds mine. I feel as if my head is floating somewhere above my shoulders.

"You look good," he whispers between kisses.

His fangs are throbbing as if they have a heartbeat of their own. In a fraction of a second, I'm stretched out on my bed, and Vayle is positioned between my legs. His private parts press against me.

"What's been going on since I've been gone?" he whispers, our noses are touching.

I gulp. "Moonridge has problems."

"What kind of problems?"

"Vampires came through there and stole everyone's soul, or something like that."

"Sounds dire."

"It is," I say.

"That's all?"

"I had to kill two vampires the other day, and then a lot more not too long ago. I've been doing a lot of killing…" I don't know what I'm saying. I'm so hypnotized by his dark eyes.

"Are you still a virgin?" he whispers as his mouth consumes my lower lip.

"Of course." The impulses running through my body make me squeal. I can't believe how much I don't want to be a virgin right now. I want him to touch me all over. I want him to enter me and change my virtuous status.

He pecks my lip, which is a stark shift in his mood, and says in a jolly voice, "Good." He gets off of me and shuffles toward the bathroom. "You're right; I have to get this stuff off of me!"

"Hey!" I shout and run after him.

He whips around and presses me against the wall. "I told you, Zill. When I deflower you, you're going to want it because you love me."

He gently kisses me one more time before shuffling to the bathroom. While he's in there, I slip into a pair of black corduroy skinny pants and a long-sleeved white T-shirt with "Smiles not Frowns" written across the front of it. I slip on a pair of knee-high black sheepskin boots and look toward the bathroom. The water is still running.

I'm not sure if I should stay or go. Four days have passed since I saw him last, and it seems that's all it took to get us to this new stage in our relationship—if we can even call it a relationship. I'm not in love with him—at least, I don't want to be—but I'm so in lust of him. I want to seduce him. I want to make him change his mind about deflowering me, but I know a temptress doesn't live inside me.

I sigh as I leave and head down to the patio. Apparently, Vayle hasn't changed his mind. I can still hear the water spraying as I walk out the door.

FAWN

Ben has chosen not to leave my side as I follow Tapeetha down the long corridor. She appears to know where she's going. Her expression sours, and she turns her nose up as we pass a modern-designed space.

"Who could live here?" she criticizes in carefully crafted English.

I remember two major things about Tapeetha: she's flippant about empathizing with humans, and she hates life on earth. The only contemporary life she's had was in a villa outside of Rome in the 1500s. Leto Danto convinced her to live there with him for at least two years. She tried, but every second she spent away from the African highlands, lowlands, and rain forests depressed her. That was the main point of contention between them. Tapeetha considered Africa home.

We have that in common, she and I, because we're the earliest sisters. Africa is the homeland of our grandmother, Zillael, our last human ancestor. It's where the earliest nations resided, although Pan'a'tua rejected those cultures as well. She's always lived as though the sky is her ceiling and the oceans are her walls. Out of all us, she understands best how indestructible we truly are. She's swum black seas thousands of miles deep. Pan'a'tua will tell anyone that we aren't hindered by altitudes, the stifling cold, or fire; none of it can kill us. It'll make us uncomfortable, torture us possibly, or make us wish we were dead, but not kill us.

"Not you," I say, still grinning at my memories of her.

We walk down the staircase that's at the end of the hallway. Ben lifts his eyebrows at me. We both wonder where the steps lead, but Pan'a'tua is confident about where they're leading her.

At the bottom is a wide-open cave. The ceiling is low, and the entire cave is made of rugged black-, white-, and gray-flecked rock. The floor is covered from wall to wall with leopard fur, and a deep fire pit burns on the left side of the cave. A swing bed extends from one corner of the room to the middle of it, but what's most fascinating about the space is that it opens up to the outside. On the other side of the large opening, prairie land stretches as far as the eye can see. Tall blades of yellow grass wave in the wind under a sky that's congested with white rolling clouds. Yes, the sun is covered. The room is cool but still comfortable, maybe sixty-five degrees.

What really catches my eye is the lake. A lazy

geyser shoots up from the middle of it. Its spray is constant, but even with its disturbance and the lack of direct sunlight, the lake remains bright and shimmery.

"This is perfect," I say, mesmerized by the scenery. I feel Pan'a'tua observing me.

"You speak American English well, Falu. I need to speak English too?"

I roll my eyes. "If you can stand a teensy-weensy bit of assimilation, sure."

She chuckles. Of course she knows what that word means. She's been fighting assimilation ever since she was born and put on Earth.

After a moment of silent admiration passes, she says, "It is pleasurable to see you, Falu." She leans forward to look at Ben. "It is also a pleasure to see you, Ben Artiste." She touches my jeans. "Also, Falu, you are certainly wearing less garments in these days."

I let out a hearty laugh, and Ben laughs too.

"And using less words!" I counter. "Try saying, 'You sure are keeping it skimpy.'"

She looks severely perplexed. "Keeping it skimpy?"

"Yes, the Americans have learned to economize when it comes to speaking. It's really gnarly."

"Gnarly?"

"See?" I say.

Pan'a'tua laughs.

"It's good to see you as well, Tapeetha," Ben says. He looks at me. "Excuse me while I go join the others."

His smile makes me weak in the knees. I'm so mesmerized by it that I'm unable to verbally respond. Tapeetha watches him go, and when he's no longer in her space, she turns to study my starry-eyed expression.

"These damn Selells," she quips in a dry tone. "They have too much power over us sisters."

I just grin. She's right, but there's nothing we can do except stay away from them, which would only cause more misery.

"I would have come for you if I could," she says out of the blue. There's guilt in her voice.

I link my arm around hers. "I know, Pan'a'tua. It all worked out fine, didn't it?"

"Father said to me Cl'auta made you safe. She is strong, is she not?"

"Very," I whisper.

I listen to the water shifting in the lake. It would be too easy to strip and jump into it. I feel as though there's another world down there. That's how being around Pan'a'tua makes me feel, like an adventurer.

"Leto Danto sees I am here on the Earth," Pan'a'tua whispers, looking far off.

The strained look on her face tells me she's dreading the possibility of coming face to face with her former lover, the Selell bond she slighted for her Wek.

CLARITY

This Finn is definitely serious, and not in the same way as Baron. Since sitting at the table, he's ached to get up and leave. A stream of faces constantly runs through his head, and they're all Selells he could call on to help him. He's making plans to move forward with us, but he's also making his own plans. Since Lario has found a way to use Leto Danto for his cause, killing him is Finn's primary goal. With or without us, he's going on a hunt for him, and he has it all mapped out.

The problem is, I'm so exhausted that I can barely keep from resting my head on Baron's shoulder, which is only a few inches away from me. Fawn, who just joined us, and Zillael are equally tired. Our human side is still made of flesh, and we've been going for two days without sleep.

"I don't know where Exgesis is, but I can get us close to him if Danto is anywhere near him," Baron says bitterly because of the accusatory way Finn just questioned him.

I cannot take it any longer, their bickering or being awake. "Finn," I say his name strongly. "Baron certainly has no association with Lario Exgesis and hasn't in a very long time. If you just ease up on him, he can help, and he can probably get you closer to Leto Danto than I can because the Shams have conjured up all of these barriers that seem to stop me. I don't think they affect Baron the same way they do me, because Lario didn't see this coming. With all of his studying and consulting whomever he consults to learn about us, he probably didn't count on Encaser power transferring to Baron. So if you want to head out of here right this second and track down Leto Danto in hopes that he'll lead you to Lario, then you should be nicer to Baron." I touch Baron on the same shoulder I want to sleep on. "As long as you two are here, on the same team, you're not opponents; you're allies."

The group turns quiet.

Vayle says, "Whoa, Clarity, that was badass. You should go into politics."

"I second that," Zill chimes in.

"Really? Ze Feldis has the power of the Encaser? I thought you had to be Enuian to have that power," Fawn says. She eyes Baron suspiciously. She now knows how I found out about the dreams and flashes she's been having of Lario Exgesis.

"I suspect it happened after planting the leaf in Jari." My words come out slurred. I can no longer keep my head up, so I rest it on Baron's shoulder.

He kisses my forehead. "We'll leave shortly," he says to Finn.

Then Baron stands, and I'm swept up in his arms. He cradles me, and I fall into his chest. I'm too tired to complain that he's overreacting to my exhaustion.

"I'll accompany you both," Artiste says as he stands.

"What about you, Vayle?" Zill grins at him as if she's daring him to tag along.

"What? You think I'm afraid?" he barks.

"No, but I think you'd rather go swimming." She smugly lifts one side of her mouth, challenging him.

That's all I see before Baron whisks me off to

bed. Now my head is spinning for a different reason. His lips are on mine, and our tongues are entangled.

"I'll be back soon," he whispers close to my ear. "Rest, my love."

I whisper, "Okay." I already desperately miss him.

Then he's gone. I turn on my side and let the human part of me sleep.

CHAPTER 8
SEPARATED BONDS
BARON ZE FELDIS

I can still smell Clarity—soft, sensual. I hold onto that memory, needing it to last until we're together again. As I travel alongside Finn Elo, one of my mother's kin, the irony burns inside me. His people were the ones who destroyed our walls, stormed our village, murdered my father, and abducted my mother. They called it "bringing her home, out of the clutches of those filthy Ze Feldises, who didn't deserve to breathe." Yes, the Counsel of Eir had the audacity to speak those words to my face. I killed them all, one by one— twelve of them, my uncles, my mother's brothers.

I'm the last Ze Feldis. My mother's people changed her name back to Elo and forced her to marry some cad from the Askins, and she had six more children. I let them live and die a natural death. I'll admit I share a bloodline with the Elos and Askins, but that's it. It only took me two centuries to ruin them. But as it turns out, Finn Elo loathes me more than I can ever hate him, not because I killed most of our ancestors and the guards of their clan. He doesn't give a damn about the Elos, Askins, or the Ze Feldises. His hate stems from my brief association with Gia, the Siren.

He's leading me, Ben Artiste, and Vayle deep into the earth, using his eyes to make passageways where there are none. I remember setting out to win Gia's heart for no reason other than she gave it to him. He was just another Elo I wanted to destroy. I'm not the same creature I was in those days. Am I remorseful? Yes. Will I ever apologize to Finn Elo for it? No. What's done is done.

"Here," Finn calls.

"Look, I figured someone should say something, and it might as well be me," Vayle says warily. "What the hell are we doing down here? I assure you there's nobody here but us dweebs."

We look around the dark cave that feels more like a tomb. Two lanterns burn on a rickety table made of mildewed wood. Someone had to light that fire and keep it burning, which means we haven't arrived at some insignificant place, nor are we alone. Finn led us here for a purpose; he just hasn't told us what that is yet.

He ignores Vayle's complaint and lets out a loud, earsplitting whistle.

"One thing's for sure," I say, studying the solid granite walls. "We're not going to find Exgesis in a cave."

"Aren't *you* taking us to him?" He's being facetious.

"That's what I thought, but you convinced us to follow *you*," I snap back. He's really trying to push my buttons.

He snarls a little, and that snide tone of his turns into a snider grin. "You're following *me* now, Ze Feldis?"

I tighten my jaw, forcing myself to let it drop. Elo may hate the hell out of me, and rightfully so, but he's a hell of a slayer. If he saw fit to bring us here, then there must be a reason.

I notice Artiste is walking around the perimeter of this tight, airless space, pushing against the rock. He's like a sane man who's been locked in an asylum for a thousand years. He's losing his mind and can only recover it once we get the hell out of here.

All of a sudden, a fifth vampire enters the chamber. His eyes are sunk deep into his face, and his nose is bent off center. His hair is pure black, and his lips are red. I know this guy.

"Chex?" I say.

He's looking right at me, wearing one of those "long time no see" grins. "Ze Feldis?" he grunts in that rough way men like him greet the rare handful of old friends they've managed to keep in their brutal lives. "Where the hell you been?"

"Just give it to us," Finn barks impatiently.

"Around," I answer casually.

Vayle, clearly surprised, asks, "You two know each other?"

Chex unbuttons his long, ankle-length black coat with a smirk that says he's about to make one of his trademark snide remarks. "Not anymore." He chuckles, then adds, "When you've got quid coming out of your ass, it's easy to forget the little guys." His snicker is laced with sarcasm.

I snort, ready with my cynical comeback—our usual ritualistic banter. "I've always had quid coming out of my ass, even when I frequently associated with the likes of you."

"Ha," he barely laughs, then opens his overcoat, revealing his collection of weapons.

I'm not surprised by what he's carrying in the lining. He's loaded with blades of every kind—shurikens, spikes, and more. One by one, he swiftly pulls the weapons from the hidden slits in his coat, laying them across the table.

Elo picks up a dagger, twisting it to inspect the sharpness of the blade. "Mercury?"

"It's what you ordered, isn't it?" Chex replies with a crooked grin.

"Yes, but how did you come by this?" Elo remains equally impressed and shocked by this new and valuable acquisition.

Chex taps on his nose and inhales deeply. "This."

Chex can smell down to the center of the Earth if he so desires. His nose has been his bread and butter for centuries. I've paid him to sniff out a few scoundrels for me.

"Got a newbie, don't you?" He lifts his eyebrows at Vayle, which is his way of pointing at him. "I smell his blood. He's your people too, eh?"

That's news to me and certainly to Elo. It's even enough to distract Artiste from staring at the walls and wishing this leg of our quest will end soon.

"Elo or Askins?" Artiste asks.

"Better." Chex beams at me.

His eyes dance as though he's amused by what he's going to reveal. I've already heard the damn punch line in his head, and it better not be a joke.

"He's a Ze Feldis."

"Damn you, Chex." I lower my arms to my side. That's a bad joke. I'm prepared to drop down, slide out my daggers, and slice off the liar's head. "If you're lying, I'll kill you where you stand."

Chex never backs down from a fight. That's why he's snarling at me, daring me to pull my blades. "I wish I was fibbing because I'd like to know, between you and me, who'd win in a knife fight."

I've already felt his rapid movement. I move too. When we're both still again, the edges of both of my daggers are pushed against his neck, right under his chin, and his blade is threatening to gut my heart out.

"What the hell, Ze Feldis?" Finn calmly says as he runs a finger down the edge of one of the blades, testing its sharpness. "We didn't come here to deal with your family issues and shit." He slices his finger, and blood gushes out of the wound. *Perfect*, he tells himself as he glares at me and Chex, but mostly me.

"You've gotten better with those," Chex says,

wearing a sinister grin. "Drop yours, and I'll drop mine."

A vampire should never trust a vampire like Chex. He has no moral compass. Cash influences him just as much as the thrill of the kill. But we're friends, sort of. Men like him want to be men like me. I'm just as menacing but able to function in normal societies. Chex needs me alive; he needs me as a reminder of what he could aspire to be.

However, I'm a cautious person. I calculate my chances. I can survive the first stab to my heart. By his second thrust, I'll have half of my blade through his neck. Worst-case scenario, we'll severely wound each other.

Vayle hasn't taken his eyes off of us. He's seeing me as the vampire I used to be, not the Selell that Clarity's love has made me. Remembering who I am now, I drop my daggers. Just to taunt me, Chex takes his time lowering his weapon.

"So Baron and I are related?" Vayle asks wearing a big grin.

The longer I look at him, the more I see traits of my father.

"If Chex smells it, then yeah, we are." There's no doubt of that.

Vayle's still grinning from ear to ear. "That's cool." He can't wait to tell Zill about it.

Chex gets a big kick out of our peculiar situation and lets out a loud laugh. "Demand supplied. Happy hunting, Elo, Askins, and two Ze Feldises. I'm getting the hell out of here." He whips around to leave, but Elo takes him by the shoulder.

"How close have you been to them?" he asks Chex.

"Close enough to stay the hell away from them."

"What about the covens they invade? Are they taking them over?"

"No," Chex answers. "These boys, and some girls, have big gonads. Most of them are living right out in plain sight with humans. But if you want to know if their strings are being pulled, from what I gather, I'd say so."

"How many do you think exist?" I ask.

"Seven thousand three hundred twenty. That was my count, three days ago."

"Have you heard of them drinking the souls out of humans?"

Chex frowns hard. "Is that what they're doing? The Sham, Tal, she's good at putting up those smokescreens, and she knows how to hide the humans after a vamp two gets to them. But I've seen a few… and I've seen the vamp after they're done with them—" He stops abruptly.

Though he's not speaking it, I can see it in his thoughts. These humans are Jake and Mary Giles all over again.

"They were doing it more until three days ago," Chex says. "They've backed off."

"That's when Zill killed the two Shams," I conclude.

"That's not your girl, Elo, is it?" Chex says.

"Mine," Vayle proudly answers.

Chex takes a moment to picture that, only he visualizes Glo instead. He sees her in a dark alley, sinewy and tall, having one of the new vampires cornered as she reaches into his chest and snatches out his heart. By the looks of his image of her, Glo's made an impression on him.

"He knows the count of his sheep," Finn says.

Chex grunts thoughtfully. "Exgesis?"

Finn nods. "By any chance, have you seen him around?"

"No. As I said. Shams are hiding him."

"I thought you said Sham," Artiste finally chimes in.

"Tal is the strongest in his stable, but he has others."

"Is there any way you can get to the others?" Finn asks as he lifts an eyebrow at Chex.

"If you make it worth the risk," Chex replies.

"Three hundred fifty thousand per body" is Finn's offer.

"Five," Chex counters.

Finn does that one pronounced nod. As long as I've known him, he's been a man of few words. Lately, though, he's been using them more than usual, and I'm pretty sure a Benel sister has something to do with that. They have a way of getting under our decaying skin, making us want to try this thing called living.

Apparently, it's a done deal, because Chex hurries out, leaving the four of us alone again.

"Did you just barter with him to kill Shams?" Artiste asks, surprised and intrigued.

"The fewer of them around, the easier my job," Finn replies.

"That's your job?" Vayle asks, pointing at the weapons on the table.

Typically, Finn wouldn't bother answering a question like that, but this time he forces himself to say, "Yes."

"Wow," I say, half-amused. "She's really gotten to you, hasn't she?"

Elo smirks. "I still hate your guts."

He's joking, which is a good sign.

"I see I didn't completely break the Elo bank?" I tease, noting how he agreed to five hundred thousand quid without so much as flinching.

"Who said I'm using my own cash, *Baron Elo*?"

He calls me Elo to get under my skin, and I can't deny—it stings a little.

"You should check to see if a Ze Feldis is footing the bill." Finn lets out a cynical laugh.

I feel a surge of anger—he's not joking. He's using *my* cash.

"Well, it isn't this Ze Feldis," Vayle proudly proclaims. "I've never had that kind of money lying around in a bank account or under a mattress. Does that mean I'm rich now?"

I snort, amused. "Yes. I get you all spruced up."

Vayle's eyes widen in surprise. "Really?"

"Yes," I reply seriously, and I mean it.

Artiste steps up to the table, sorting through the weapons. "Enough. Let's get this over with and get out of this tomb." He holds up a pair of matching daggers, testing their balance.

Finn Elo slides his hand under the table, triggering a hidden drawer. It pops open, revealing an assortment of harnesses and straps to hold our weapons.

"There," he grunts.

"Look at this guy." Vayle laughs as though he's pretty impressed by Finn.

I replace the blades on my daggers with ones made of mercury.

"Why mercury and not silver?" I ask Elo.

He shows me why. I see him, Chex, and one of those second-generation vampires in a lab. Chex stabs the guy with all sorts of metals until they find the right one.

I nod appreciatively at Elo. He doesn't growl back, which is another sign of progress.

It's my turn to take the lead. Exgesis's downfall has always been his inability to let go of New York City. If he's hiding, it's in one of its hidden enclaves, with his minions never far from him.

It's nighttime, and a blizzard blasts through the city. Leto Danto roams the streets of Chelsea, moving at a human pace, though his steps are quick and steady. The snowflakes battering his skin don't sting him—he's too angry to feel it. When I delve deeper into his mind, I see what's fueling his rage. He knows Tapeetha has returned to Earth, and he's fighting the magnetic pull to be with her.

I know all too well how powerful that draw can be. I tried to resist it once myself.

Danto reaches a towering residential building, about sixty stories high. He swipes a keycard and strides through the lobby without a glance at the elevators. He opens a door marked "Emergency Do Not Enter" in bold red letters. No alarm sounds as he enters a starkly lit stairwell and hurries down the steps. Reaching the basement level, he touches a sensor on the wall. A door that looks as if it's been painted shut cracks open. Danto pushes it the rest of the way, crosses the cold concrete floor, and stops at the far wall. Without hesitation, he evaporates, vanishing one cell at a time.

I pull Elo into the scene with me, knowing I'll need his sharp eyes to track Danto's movements.

"Elo, come with me," I say, placing my hand on his left shoulder. Now, his consciousness joins me in the basement. Unlike with Clarity, no part of him is visible—just a silent presence.

"Where the hell am I?" Elo mutters.

"Danto's here," I explain. "Look around. Do you see Exgesis?"

A tense silence follows as he scans our surroundings.

"There. I see him," Finn says, his voice steady. "Exgesis."

"Then let's go and get him," I growl, rage building, ready to tear Lario limb from limb.

ELO'S POWER TO TEAR DOWN AND REBUILD IS incredible. He can blow through solid earth that's over a million years old, and pack it right back together, leaving it the way he found it. He's fast too. Mostly we move through the tunnels our kind often uses, taking the upward incline until, to Ben Artiste's relief, we're out of the underground world and soaring toward New York City.

I remember when this island was mostly dirt and trees, when the Haudenosaunee, later called the Iroquois, warred with the Wendat, known as the Huron, over hunting grounds. Then one day, everything changed. I used to be human, but it wasn't until I became this creature that I truly understood how fierce humans are. At their core is a relentless drive to dominate and subordinate, all in the quest for even a morsel of power. I've watched humans live and die striving for superiority, never realizing they'll never possess it. It's not theirs to claim. It's nobody's. Ultimate power doesn't even belong to creatures like me. Believing it can be acquired is pure stupidity.

It doesn't take long to reach Chelsea. We're now standing in front of the same white-stone building I had recently entered using the Encaser power to follow Danto. Seeing it with my own eyes, I can tell it's a newer construct, maybe twenty years old or so.

The city that never sleeps is wide awake, but the shield of blindness I formed around us seems to be holding. We're not blocking the sidewalk, but if humans could see us, they'd certainly notice four vampires standing here. Their eyes occasionally drift in our direction, but their instincts warn them to keep their distance.

"What do you see, Elo?" I ask.

"He's down low, and the Sham, Tal, is with him. Two birds." Finn's priorities differ slightly from mine—he's dead set on ending the Sham, while I'm focused on making sure Exgesis ceases to exist. "Vamp twos are everywhere," he adds.

None of us flinch at that news. There are no cowards here.

"After you, Elo," I say.

"You're still following me, Ze Feldis?" He flashes a sarcastic grin, clearly enjoying this.

"Just go," I snap.

"Brace yourselves," Elo warns. "Things are about to get rocking."

We charge through the lobby and down the stairwell until we reach that open space Danto disappeared from. The floor we're standing on turns to dust. We drop one level, then that floor is pulverized, and we're another level down. This happens seven more times until we're standing in an empty prison cell.

"What the hell is this?" Vayle wonders, checking out our new circumstances.

Barred cubicles run up and down the room. Ben and I are standing in one of them and separated by metal rails, Elo and Vayle are in the cage next to ours.

Before Elo can work his magic on the bars, Artiste uses his force to pull the rails apart, allowing us to step out of the cage and into the aisle. He winks at Elo, who chuckles. The two of them are closer in a way than Elo and I will probably never be.

We have no way of telling who or what has been imprisoned here. If Chex were with us, he could sniff the air and tell us what was once contained here. Elo leads us down the long footpath that splits the rows of cells. We're all cautious and alert. He stops in his tracks when he reaches another red-painted door.

"There's at least twelve vamp twos," he says, focusing hard on what's behind it.

We all look at each other, making sure we're ready for battle. By reading my companions' minds, I know that they are. After Finn is sure of it as well, we hear an earsplitting pop as the door is blasted into metal dust.

Suddenly, we're facing twelve second-generation vampires, and they're charging at us at lightning speed. Vayle's faster. He curls his wrist and unleashes twelve mercury shurikens, catching each of them right in the heart. That shot was more than good; it was poetry. They all fall, convulsing and regurgitating blood. I can smell what they've been drinking: vampires like me. It's sick, and it makes killing them that much more gratifying.

Second-generation vampires are coming out of

the woodwork, but the kid is taking them out. He swings those daggers as fast as lightning. His blades gut their hearts out and slice off their heads, four at a time, six at a time, even ten at a time. We're moving forward right behind him. They don't even know what's hitting them.

Vampires must have endorphins, because mine are pumping. I'm closer to Exgesis. He's only steps away, but he's taunting us. For the first time ever, I'm in his mind. I can feel him, hear him. His ego has grown stronger, and that's his weakness. Instead of ordering Danto to get him the hell out of here, which would force us to chase him down to another location, he chooses to taunt us by showing us what he's stolen from us.

I quickly awaken Clarity and tell her to ask Tapeetha to secure Danto. I know Tapeetha wants to delay their inevitable meeting, but I hope Clarity can convince her to snatch Danto out of here before Exgesis gives him the order to whisk him away. As all hell breaks loose, with Finn pulverizing Selells alongside Vayle, all I can do is wait. Just as Artiste blasts down the door Exgesis is hiding behind, Clarity hits Exgesis's secret weapon, Leto Danto, with severe confusion. Leto looks all over the place as if his eyes are open, but he can't see a thing.

"Danto, now," Exgesis orders.

Danto can't hear him either, and then he begins to dissipate. Exgesis lunges toward him, hoping that wherever he's going, he'll take Exgesis with him, but he falls on his face.

Finally, his day has come.

First draw, first get.

I only have a fraction of a second to act because Ben Artiste's desire to end Exgesis runs deeper than mine. His force has already pinned Exgesis to the wall, but my blades are drawn. We both charge him as the Sham, Tal, is turned into vampire jam by Finn. Then he puts his destructive eyes on my prey.

It's a race, but I'm faster. My blade slices Exgesis's head off clean, sending it flying up. As I watch it rise, he still manages that arrogant sneer. Since I took the head, Finn hits his body and turns it into jelly.

Oh, the exhilaration of knowing that Exgesis is no more. Ding-dong, the devil is dead!

His white, stringy hair is drenched with his rancid blood, and his maniacal eyes are open wide. All four of us watch his head fly for an unusually long time. It's floating, defying gravity. Then the goop dripping from his severed head sullies the ground and starts to bubble. Right before our eyes, his body regenerates. His bloodied head drops onto his newly made shoulders.

Although we're awestruck, we don't wait to repeat ourselves. I slice off his head. Elo turns him into mush, but once again, Humpty Dumpty puts himself back together again. We give it another try, but again Exgesis returns.

"And one more time, boys," he mockingly sings. "We can do this all night, Finn Elo!" Exgesis hisses like the snake he is.

His beady eyes circle our general location, but he still can't see us because of the shields I've erected. What's interesting is that he's only mentioned Finn. He doesn't seem to know the rest of us are here.

Elo looks at me and nods toward the door. He's right; we should go and figure out what the hell Exgesis has done to cheat death. Before we go, Elo and Vayle are struck by the same idea. They turn and unload the rest of their shurikens on him. He may live, but he'll hurt first. And that's how we leave him, writhing in pain.

CHAPTER 9
ALIVE AND LIVE
CLARITY

I had to think fast while Tapeetha deliberated about whether to help us or not. Leto Danto was so close to taking him and Lario out of harm's way. While I was in Leto's mind, reading his thoughts and taking on his emotions—essentially being him—I took away his ability to hear and see. Finally, Tapeetha let her anxiety pass and decided to bring him here.

He has his sight and hearing back. His gaze skips from me to Zill to Glo to Fawn and then rests on Tapeetha, who's put on a sleeveless white dress that's long enough to brush the tops of her feet. The sight of her takes my breath away, so I'm sure it's making him choke. Neither one of them knows what to say to the other.

"Hello, Leto Danto," Fawn says, realizing it's time for someone to say something. "It's good to see you again."

"Fawn?" He sounds surprised to see her. "I thought you were…"

"He thought I was what?" Fawn asks just me. By the look on my face, she knows I've listened to him finish his statement.

"Dead," I tell her.

Fawn frowns hard. It doesn't take a genius to figure out where that lie came from.

"Where am I?" he asks as he observes his new surroundings.

I see that he's naturally intuitive. He recognizes the distinct difference in the weight of the air from where he was and where he is now. He notices the shift in the moon phase and the sounds of summer buzzing all around us. His eyes fall over the fire pit behind him, and then he gazes beyond the balcony and out over the pruned grounds.

He narrows his eyes at Tapeetha. "You brought me here?"

"I did," she barely replies.

"Why?" he says past clenched teeth.

To my surprise, her stony exterior melts. She

wants to flee and find a place to cry in peace. That's how I'd found her only minutes ago, lying in a hammock sniffing back tears and dreading this precise moment. Her throat is tight. She can't answer him, so she looks at me, which is my cue to take the floor.

"I asked her to bring you here," I say. "You were on the verge of using your power to save Lario, and we had to stop you."

"How do you know that?"

I glance over my shoulder and gesture toward a seat. "If you sit and join us, we'll fill you in."

He takes another long look at Tapeetha before obliging me. We all join him at the table and focus our attention on Fawn.

She explains how she and Artiste were separated by Lario and the years she spent believing she loved him. "He made me think that total happiness for him would be being human again. I was..." She shuts her eyes as she relives a former state of her heart. "I was consumed by figuring out a way to make that happen."

She lets out a deep breath. I think she's finally releasing herself from sharing any blame for what she tells him next, about the leaf.

"Ha!" He laughs once, very cynically. "From the Tree of Life? Impossible. That doesn't exist." He sounds very sure of himself.

"You're a vampire. Vampires don't exist either," Fawn counters.

"Ha," Danto laughs again, but this time it's different; he's admiring her clever comeback.

"We first had to find the tree," she continues. "Lario knew another allegorical book existed that told the story of seven seeds that were sprouted from one tree that bore all life. I remember reading the book and thinking, 'This is me, us, my sisters and I.'"

She pauses to reflect. I feel what's affecting her. That was the first time she remembered she had seven sisters and a father, which meant she wasn't alone in the world.

"So," I begin, attempting to take it from there. I think she's too choked up to continue.

She gently squeezes my forearm to let me know she's able to continue. "We figured out that the seven trees in the story were us, my sisters and I."

"There are seven of you?" he asks, studying each of us.

He always knew of Fawn and Navi, and for the first time, I get a visual of her from his memories.

Her skin is bronze, hair golden-brown, and eyes gray; the rest of her is a carbon copy of the rest of us.

"And seven of you too," I say. "Vampires."

He frowns, deeply confused. "So what are you all, Trees of Life?"

"Basically, yes," Fawn replies. "Our blood is linked to the first tree."

I shudder at his thoughts. He's remembering the taste of Tapeetha's blood. He's another Selell who drank the blood of one of my sisters. His memories allow me to taste it on his tongue, mostly lime and mint with a hint of a subtle herbal sweetness. I tune in to Tapeetha, hoping she can give me a sense of how it feels to be drunk, but she's fighting the strong attraction that draws us to our bonds.

Tapeetha's avoiding thinking about Leto Danto or looking in his eyes. Because Danto isn't playing nice. While he's attentively listening to Fawn, he's keeping his eyes glued to Tapeetha's face.

"I was able to call on the Tree, and it actually led me to it." Fawn shakes her head, still amazed that it worked. "Lario already knew that if he ate a leaf, he'd become human again. He said he wanted to spend the rest of his days with me and die like a man should, old and in love."

Danto lets out another cynical laugh. "Exgesis, human? Never."

"Well, now I know that." She rolls her eyes at the obvious.

"How did you become involved with him?" I ask Leto out of extreme curiosity.

"He saved my life. I owe him."

"How?"

"I walked into a blood trap," he says as if we should all know what that is. After scanning our faces, he sees that none of us is familiar with that term. "Shams have a way of turning vampire blood into fire water. If you drink it, it gets rid of the thirst for a long time, but it also kills you slowly. If you'd ever been thirsty, then you'd know how appealing being dead sounds. It's expensive though, and you don't pay for it with cash. You must have something Shams need."

"And Lario saved you from this trap?" I ask. I already sense something fishy about this. Lario wouldn't save a rat from a cage.

"I was numb all over. I couldn't get myself out of there."

I see his memories and take on his experiences. He's being held captive deep in the earth. All around him are rotting vampire body parts, and the stench is enough to knock a person out. He can't move. He can't tap into the power of matter. He's a sitting duck, waiting for his turn to be drained of his blood and left there to decay.

"How did you get out?" I ask.

"Exgesis formed a band of vampires to storm prisons to save those who had been captured so that Shams could make fire water out of them." He takes a deeper look at Tapeetha. "That's what I've been doing since you left me, freeing vampires trapped in those prisons."

"If you think you haphazardly found yourself trapped by Shams, then you are seriously mistaken." I hear myself hiss. I can actually feel the hate stirring inside me. "But no matter, he's dead now."

Danto shoots to his feet. "What!" he roars as if he's ready to move heaven and earth to change that.

Tapeetha stands. "Leto." There's a plea in her whisper.

All the anger and angst that grips him subsides.

"This Exgesis," she continues. "I recognized him tonight when Cl'auta, I mean Clarity, brought me to him. I've seen him before."

"Yes," I chime in, "I would think you have. You fell in love with the Wek after you bonded with

Danto. I don't think you would've ever done that without somehow being compelled to."

Danto falls back into his seat when he hears that. He looks like a human man who just had the air knocked out of him. By the time he hits the chair, all of his allegiance to Lario has vanished. He finally gives Tapeetha a reprieve as he keeps his eyes focused mainly on me and Fawn.

We tell him everything about recovering the script at our grandmother's grave and journeying through Nowhere to get to Jari. It's Glo and Tapeetha's first time hearing about our quest, and both of them are enthralled.

"You mean Jari looked nothing like it does now?" Glo says.

"Thank God," Zill mutters.

"No, before we planted the leaf into that world's Tree of Life, it was as if at one point, the whole place had literally burned to ashes."

"But the trees didn't burn down, did you notice that?" Zill asks. She's remembering every detail about the old Jari. For her, it was not a good experience. "The ashes were at least a foot thick on the ground. That's a lot of fire. Shouldn't those trees have been burned to nothing?"

"You're right!" I darn near shout, struck by illumination.

Her observation deserves attention, but Baron appears with the others, and he's all I can focus on. He's still wearing the icy wind on his skin, and he's my own personal breath of fresh air. In this moment, I see only him. I leap to my feet, but before I can move, he's right beside me, our cheeks pressing against each other. The warmth... I'm so warm.

"He can't die," he whispers.

"Who?" I whisper. I already know the answer, but I hope I'm wrong.

"Exgesis."

I'M NOT SURE HOW THIS MOMENT CAME TO BE. Once Baron confirmed my worst nightmare, all I could see was red. I looked at Fawn to see her reaction to his dreadful news, but she was too caught up in Ben Artiste. Apparently, I wasn't the only one who'd leapt into her lover's arms. Glo did too. Even Zill stood face to face with Vayle; they weren't touching, only grinning at each other.

I decided to storm off to the script, praying it

would show me a way to kill the demon vampire, Lario Exgesis. Every fiber of my being warned me against feeling that hatred, but I wanted him dead. But I didn't make it to the study to consult the script. Baron swept me off my feet and into his arms before I took two steps. We didn't enter the house. He carried me up a stumpy grassy hill and then down to a patch of grass peppered with sweet-scented yellow and white wildflowers.

Now I'm lying on my back, and he's lying beside me with one hand under my skirt. His fingers gently slide up and down my crotch. I can hardly breathe, and the fire that sent me off on a mad dash toward the script has been replaced by the flame of desire. Baron gives me that naughty-boy smirk. I open my mouth to catch a breath and gulp. His finger is already making me climax. He's an effective lover.

"Can I get you naked?" he asks, still wearing that lopsided grin.

"But we have to find a way to kill—" I utter in feeble protest.

"Naked," he says, cutting me off.

I can't fight this desire; it's Goliath, and I'm only an ant. "Go for it," I whisper.

My slinky black wrap dress that kisses the lines

of my figure is off and tossed somewhere to the side of me. His eyes run up and down my body. The low growl trapped in his throat is my favorite sound. With his lips and tongue, he tastes my belly. His fangs throb against my abdomen. Downward he moves, nibbling on the insides of my thighs, teasing me until his tongue makes it to that sweet spot. I clench my teeth and clutch a handful of wildflowers and grass, pulling them out of the ground.

In an instant, his mouth is near my ear. "Let go. Give me all of you, Clarity."

His tongue stimulates me. He wants me to scream, to lose my mind, to grab him and mount him and beg him to make love to me for eternity. I feel it coming on, stronger and stronger. I'm straining to hold in my scream. I know I'm afraid of being heard. He's never afraid of that.

I want to scream like a mad woman, but I'm still clenching my teeth and pulling up grass in an attempt to contain my reaction to what he's doing to me. I'm squirming and fighting the pleasure. Baron doesn't let up, which means I'm forced to give him what he wants. A high-pitched cry echoes in the night. It's so distant from a sound that Clarity Parker would allow herself to make, and it seems to turn him on even more, which I didn't think was possible.

Now I'm not the only naked one. He's inside me, carefully thrusting, making each movement more pleasurable than the last. His warm mouth is on mine. Our tongues dance, yet we're still failing to do what we both want, which is to merge into one. Even that will not be close enough.

"Clarity," he whispers, without breath.

"Baron."

"Will you let me drink you?"

I hesitate. My initial fears of him drinking me to death return, but then I remember Glo and Finn. I think of how satisfied he was that I hadn't given Baron a chance to experience drinking me.

"Okay, yes," I answer. My entire body tenses as I brace for impact.

"This won't hurt," he whispers. He smooths a lock of hair away from my forehead. "I need you to know that."

His eyes assess me, waiting for me to put my trust in him. His eyes are crystal blue. I forget that sometimes. For the most part, we're way beyond seeing little details about each other. Like the way both sides of his mouth turn up into a tiny bow or that slight curve of his nose. All the tiny traits that make him unique.

Finally I'm calm, and Baron's fangs pierce my skin, pressing into my jugular. I can actually feel my blood flowing into him. Clarity Parker, who's always thinking and experiencing life cerebrally, feels as though she's floating toward the moon. He's still shifting his hips, and so am I. I want him to consume all of me. I can think of no better way to die, but his teeth pull out of my neck. He throws his head back to let out a growl that's way more animalistic than usual.

He's not finished. Even while here on Earth, I can hear why, feel why. I can sense Baron.

"I can hear you," he whispers.

"I can hear you too."

"I don't want to stop either, Clarity."

That's exactly what I'm thinking. I don't want him to stop. "So don't." I press my mouth against his. I need to taste him.

ZILLAEL

"Really?" I snap at Vayle. I can hear them, Clarity and Baron. "Do they ever stop screwing each other?"

"I know; it's hot. She's hot," Vayle remarks.

"Sometimes you can be an idiot." I peel my gaze away from him to look at the tops of the tall trees bordering the lawn. I wonder why we have to climb over the fence every time we leave and come back. Why isn't there a real gate?

We're sitting on the rim of the swimming pool, our feet in the water. I must admit, this place is starting to feel like home. Especially at night. There's something about the purple sky above the tops of those tall trees. I never noticed stuff like that before.

"I'm not an idiot," Vayle finally says.

I thought he'd let it drop. I certainly had. What he had said was not idiotic; it was true. If any two people should be having a lot of sex, it's Clarity and Baron. She's always wearing those come-have-sex-with-me-Baron-Ze-Feldis dresses, and he's always in those expensive pants. I don't know, it sounds stupid, but there's something about those dresses and those pants that equals sex.

I face him to say, "I know they're attractive. You're just an idiot for saying it out loud. She's my sister, for goodness sake!"

Vayle laughs and then narrows his eyes at me. "She's hot. He's hot. But to me, you're hotter."

I roll my eyes hard. "Now you're outright lying."

"Not only am I not an idiot, but I'm not a liar. It's going to be tough." He exaggeratedly slumps his shoulders as if he's defeated.

"What's going to be tough?"

"Making you fall in love with me."

I drop my face and giggle. I think I'm blushing, which I don't do often. I'm considering having sex with Vayle. I remember when he first broke into my house and asked to sleep in my bed. As we lay beside each other, he touched me in ways no one else has had the chance to do. I never thought my body could feel things like that.

Once I had been in the restroom at school. Not because I had to go but because I needed a break from the teachers, the kids, and Mrs. Lowenstein. I wonder if she survived the vampire soul-stealing invasion. I bet she did. Who would want to take her soul?

Anyway, while I sat there, using up the full ten

minutes Mr. Whatever-His-Name-Was allowed us to take for a "proper" toilet break, two girls walked in. They were already in the middle of a conversation. One of them had had sex for the first time like an hour earlier, and she wasn't too thrilled about it. She kept saying it was okay, but the other girl ordered a play-by-play of her recent experience.

She said, sounding totally dejected, "Well, it hurt. I just wish... I wish I would've waited to have it with someone else. Because it hurt, you know?"

If she had been talking to me, I would have sympathetically said, "Yeah, I know." But her friend, Miss Lamebrain, could only go on about how "hot" the guy was. Dudley Meyer was his name. I remember thinking that he wasn't even warm, let alone hot! I hate that adjective, "hot." Usually the people who use it all the time are imbeciles. Vayle uses it lot, but always to describe Clarity. Not Fawn or even Glo, who's beyond gorgeous, or Tapeetha.

"You know what I think?" I say.

"I want to hear whatever you're thinking, sexy," he says all sexy-like.

He's lost it.

"I think you have an Oedipal Complex," I say,

happy that my words wash that smug look off his face.

"Why would you think that?" His eyebrows are knitted together, and he sounds serious.

"Look at you, coming all undone. Have you heard that before or something?"

He shrugs as he studies the way his foot causes a minor cyclone in the water.

"It's just that you're so enamored by Clarity, and she's got that mommy attitude," I say. "Like the perfect mom. A real MILF."

Vayle doesn't stop swirling his foot or look up from the pool. I wonder what he thinks about my assessment.

"Do you know who I'm enamored by?" he finally says and then stares right into my eyes.

I'm getting dizzy, but I get dizzier when in, one swift move, I'm on my back and he's on top of me, pushing his package against my pubic bone. All kinds of things run through my mind. Like if it hurts, do I want to experience that pain with someone who can't even acknowledge it? Derek would acknowledge it. He would be gentle, stroke my hair, and tell me everything will be okay. Vayle, however? I'm not sure he'll be that caring.

"By you," he says and slides a hand under my

T-shirt to caress the slope my breast. "I'm trying very hard to keep my vow," he whispers and then exposes my nipple to the moon.

He puts the tip of his tongue on it, then his throbbing teeth, and then his soft, warm lips. I can hardly stand it. I hear myself moaning, but I'm not putting any effort into my reaction. It's just happening naturally. Nothing hurts when he does this.

"You're so beautiful," he whispers. He brings his face up to kiss my mouth. "I'm only enamored by you."

The growling sound that's caught in his throat gets progressively louder, and that bulge between his legs pushes deeper into my crotch. Every part of me throbs for him. The wooziness is turning into vertigo.

"Okay, let's do it. I love you," I whisper. As soon as I say it, I hear a small splash.

I open my eyes. Vayle is gone. I'm alone. But the dizziness hasn't left me. I use all my strength to rise to my feet, but as soon as I'm up, I fall back down. Someone catches me just before I hit the ground, and everything turns black.

CLARITY

"Clarity, it's Zill."

"That's Derek. I have to go," I tell Baron, who's still absorbed in making love to me.

He mutters something—probably the "s" word—and then presses his lips to mine one more time. "I know, I heard him."

To my chagrin and his, he lifts me to my feet. In a flash, he's gone, and then he's back in front of me, dangling my dress on one finger. If only he knew how sexy he looks doing that, but I think he reads it in my mind because he smirks.

"Get your hands up," he orders in a bedroom voice.

I shake my head a little because he's still being naughty, and I lift my arms as if I'm under arrest. He's turned on by that, but instead of pulling me back down to the grass, he slides the slinky dress over me. The fronts of our bodies touch. Our lips touch too, but we both know that we shouldn't kiss. This is an emergency, and we won't be able to pull apart if we do that.

"Clarity…" He clears his throat and straightens his posture. "Are you ready?"

I can't stop grinning as I bob my head like a

giddy schoolgirl. In a few seconds, we're in Zill's room. My smile fades the moment I see her lying on the bed and looking so pale. Vayle is perched on one side of her and Derek is on the other, both hating that the other is present. Zill's eyes are open, although barely, and she's watching me and Baron quite keenly.

"You have flowers in your hair," she mumbles and manages to roll her eyes a little bit. "And your dress..." She points to her chest to show me where I'm having a problem.

I look down. I forgot to button my dress. Not only are my nipples still hard against the fabric, but the fleshy part of my breasts is exposed. Baron can hardly take his eyes off my blunder.

"Down, boy," she mutters.

"Well I see you're doing better," I say sarcastically as I button my dress.

Glo is standing at the foot of the bed, and Finn is close behind her. She has fresh bites on her neck; it's no secret what they were up to.

"It looks like she's recovering from being brought here by Tapeetha's power," Glo says with her eyes trained on Zill. "We have human hearts and brains. Those were the first to regenerate, but the rest of her is taking its time."

I can see Zill's condition in Glo's mind. There's her heart in her chest, her brain in her head, but the rest I don't recognize. I passed advanced anatomy and physiology, and I never forget any subject I've studied. Zill doesn't have human kidneys or even a liver. She's—that is, we're—put together in a peculiar way. Seeing it actually scares me a little, but I work really hard to hide that not only from the faces in the room but from Baron's ability to sense my thoughts and emotions now that he's consumed my blood.

"What about Fawn? Is she okay?" I ask in a panic while looking over my shoulder.

Glo looks in the same direction, but the look in her eyes tells me she can actually see Fawn. "The same thing has happened to her. She's with Ben Artiste, and Tapeetha is with them."

I touch Glo's shoulder. We both feel so miserable, as if by sheer will we can speed up Zill's healing process.

"Goodness, we're not dying?" Zill says and then lifts her eyes higher to focus in on Glo. "Are we?"

Glo presses a hand over her heart as she sympathetically says, "Of course not, Zillael. You'll be fine. I didn't mean to scare you." She sounds so apologetic.

I squeeze Glo's shoulder. "What you've just heard was sarcasm sprinkled with a little sugar."

Zill simpers. Glad I was able to clear that up. In retrospect, Glo gets the humor and snickers.

We decide to leave and let Zill get much needed rest. I raise my eyebrows at the strangest thought she has before falling to sleep. She says to herself that I'm totally mother-like, and Vayle definitely has an Oedipal complex when it comes to me. Baron grunts, also amused by her thought.

She's certainly not very aware when it comes to Vayle. He barely gives me any thought at all. She's the only creature of the opposite sex that he obsesses over. I think he's toying with her emotions, attempting to make her jealous because he's still angry that Derek is a factor. When she's better, I'll put a little bird in her ear. It's always good to give a girl the advantage of knowing the truth.

Finn carries Glo out of Zill's room. Baron is eager to get back to what we were doing earlier, but I'm too distracted. First, by how Vayle and Derek refuse to abandon their seats at Zill's bedside. I thought Derek had relented in his quest to win Zill's heart, but apparently not. He saw something earlier that he's reacting to: Vayle on top of Zill near the edge of that huge swimming pool Vayle loves to dive into. Zill had a look in her eyes of pure surrender, and it was that look that made him realize he doesn't want to see her like that with Vayle, not as long as he exists.

Then there's Tapeetha, whom I can't help but reach out to. She's the only sister I haven't instantly bonded with. Yes, that bothers me, but I'd be negligent if I didn't go to her right now. She's really hurt and confused. She wouldn't let anyone know, but I know.

As Baron and I walk out of the room, he informs me that he has to make some calls anyway. He holds out a hand for me to shake, and I giggle at how sweet and simultaneously silly his gesture is. I shake his hand. Warmth fills me, butterflies flutter in my stomach, and then he's gone.

I'm nervous as I head down the stairway to see Tapeetha. I've never pushed myself on anyone who wanted to be alone, nor have I forced a relationship between another individual and myself. When I think about it, this is the first time I've gone to comfort someone I didn't know so well. I don't know why Tapeetha intimidates me. Maybe because I'm Harvard Business, Park Avenue; she'd probably stab herself in the heart or let an asp bite her in the neck before becoming anything like me.

Realizing I'm merely swimming in a sea of self-loathing, I take a deep breath, hold it, and let it out as I hurry into her space.

She's sitting on the large hammock, staring right at me. "I was wondering when you would come in." She slides off of the sling to stand. "You swim?" she asks as she steps out of her long white dress. She's completely naked, and without waiting to hear my reply, she leaps past the threshold, across the grass, and dives into the lake.

I sigh hard. This was not the plan, but for the second time tonight, I drop my dress. The grass feels supple as it crunches beneath my soles. I've never done anything like this in my life—diving into a swimming pool, the ocean, or the lake. But I'm running so fast that when I jump, I rise so high my legs naturally want to kick up and lead me into the water head first, so I go with the flow.

What does it feel like? Pure exhilaration, maybe better. When I come down, first my hands slice through the liquid, and the rest of me quickly follows. I'm heading toward bright, colorful stones that glow as if somewhere in the depths of the water, they've managed to catch the sun, but there's no threat of me hitting bottom. This lake is deep, hundreds of feet deep.

"Good?" Tapeetha asks me once I swim back to the surface.

"Good." I smile and tread water. I mean it; it's very good. The water is the perfect temperature and refreshing on my skin.

"You care about me?" she comes right out and asks.

She meant worried. I smile because her English is cute. "I am. How did you know?"

"How you look at me. You know what I think."

Again, I smile at her.

"I let Ose go." She sounds as if she's on the verge of crying. Maybe her eyes are watery, or maybe they're naturally that sparkly in the moonlight.

"I know. I'm sorry you had to make that decision. I know it hurts."

"Leto's here…"

"I know," I sympathetically whisper. It's time to get to the bottom of what's really bothering her. "And that means a lot to you. He loves you—still."

"No, no Leto Danto. He hates me."

I shake my head. "No, Tapeetha, he loves you."

"I did love Ose." She looks at me as if she's trying to convince me. She feels as if her love for Leto Danto cheapens what she had with Ose.

I smile warmly. "I know."

"I never should, I mean, I never, I…"

"I know," I whisper. "But remember, your affections for him were more than likely influenced by the magic of some Sham."

"No," she vehemently denies, shaking her head. "Was real, no magic."

I smile at her. This is a sensitive subject for her, so I let it drop. "You love both of them, and that's okay." That's the true source of what's bothering her.

"But…" She stops because what she wants to say hurts.

"But?" I ask.

She needs to confess this in order to move forward. There's a remarkable saying and a valid one too: The truth will set you free.

"I always love Leto more."

The tears that were stuck in her eyes moments ago trickle down her already-damp cheeks. She's staring into my eyes, retelling the history of her heart. She loved Danto more on the day she chose Ose, but she could no longer take the earth and its humans. She cried about that. Ose comforted her. They made love, and the ramifications were immediate. He began gasping for air, and together they made a mad dash to the Enu portal. Over time, her affection for the Wek grew to almost equal the affection she always had for Danto. She grew to love Ose out of loyalty rather than passion.

I gently wipe the tears from her soft cheek with one finger.

She chuckles a little. "You are a good sister, Cl'auta."

"You are too," I say.

Tapeetha laughs, and it's a good, healthy one. "You did not think that when we meet." She scans the natural landscape. "I did not want to come back to the earth, but here I like it."

I'm curious why our father chose this scenery for her. It's so different from the Savannah grass-lands, purple rock mountains, and dense rain forest that her heart conjured in Enu. On my first stay in Enu, my heart's desire gave me a view of my favorite skyscrapers from Manhattan and Cambridge. I stayed in a cottage with carpeted floors, something I wanted in every place I ever lived in, but my father owned those places and designed them to his tastes. Maybe this, the American lowlands, represents Tapeetha's progressed tastes. I mean, could I ever return to the city and be comforted by skyscrapers and the hustle and bustle of strangers? I don't think so.

Since the sun will soon rise beyond the perimeter of our property, we decide to make our way to the Catskills to see Akili. We plan to go deep-water swimming for our first leg of the journey. Baron has been tuned into me ever since we shook hands and parted ways. We hesitantly tell each other, "See you later." I'll admit that all of the time he and I are apart does make the heart grow fonder. I can hardly wait for our next reunion.

So Tapeetha leads the way, and I happily follow.

GLO

"So you're just going to leave?" I hear myself whining like a thirteen year old whose mother is going on a shopping spree at the mall without her.

I feel dirty. I'm completely naked. The love he made to me was the best ever. He told me he missed me while he was away and that he loves me, but now he's leaving? What sense does that make?

"I can't stay here. This is not how I live, Glo. You can come with me," Finn suggests, standing on the threshold of this room, which is a carbon copy of my bedroom in Cleveland.

"You know I can't go."

"I'll be around." His eyes roam around every part of the bedroom that has been designed for me. "But I can't stay here."

"Where in the world are you going?" I'm frustrated to no end.

Finn doesn't say anything. He just stands there, watching me. His mind hasn't changed, that's for sure.

I extend both of my arms toward him. "Just come here, Finn. Please."

In one movement, he's on top of me again and staring into my eyes. His pinched expression tells me he's extremely conflicted.

"Just stay, okay?" I already know I'm asking for more than he can give.

"I can't live like this. Not as long as Exgesis is out there and unable to die. I told you, Glo, I'm a slayer. It's my job to kill him. If I have to do that a million times to make it final, then that's what I'll do."

"We're going to figure out how to do that." Once again, I'm whining.

"You do it your way, and I'll do it my way."

"What if our way is the best way?"

That somehow amuses Finn, and he grins. "It isn't," he says with a sexy snarl.

I lift my eyebrows. "We have more powers than you." I'm joking, of course. Finn's got a bag of tricks that will take us a thousand human lifetimes to accumulate.

He laughs out loud and kisses my mouth, and before I can snap my fingers, he's back on the threshold. "Your sister just asked me if she could use my power."

I frown, wondering who or what could he mean, but then it occurs to me that he's referring to Clarity. She has the ability to be in anyone's head or take someone out of their body and bring them to another place. She explained that it was the power of the Encaser.

I give up. I'm not going to argue with Finn on this issue anymore. He's the sort of vampire who sleeps deep in caves; he blasts through soil that hasn't been turned since the earth was created. I can hear Clarity in my head too, telling me that it's time.

"Well, where are you going now?" I ask him. At least he can tell me that.

He looks up and a little to the right. I follow his

line of sight. He's watching Baron pace with a cell phone pressed to his ear.

"To have words with Ze Feldis."

"About what?"

He winks at me. "Remember, you have your way, I have mine."

I can't help but laugh, especially when I remember how well those two bicker. Truthfully, I think Finn trusts Baron and not just a little. "What's the beef between you two?"

Finn stands there looking at me with that blank stare.

"I think you like him more than he knows, don't you?" Again, he says nothing, and I laugh as I scoot out of the messy bed. "So you're going to Finn Elo me?"

By the time I'm standing, he's right here before me, embracing me. His lips almost touch mine. "I like *you* more than you know."

"Now that's how you change the subject."

We stand together in silence.

"Aren't you going to kiss me?" I finally ask.

He shows me my favorite lopsided smile. "No."

"Why?" The way he's staring into my eyes is literally taking my breath away.

"Because I know I won't stop."

"Oh. Well then, good-bye," I whisper.

"Good-bye." He runs his thumb across my bottom lip with a growl stirring in this throat.

Before I can be a bad girl and go in for the kiss myself, he's gone, and I'm standing here alone. I make myself yawn. I'm not tired, but I do it out of habit. Yawning has always been my way to signify a change: shift over at the diner, time for appointment with Dr. Herman, dinner with Aries, those sorts of changes.

Clarity has instructed me to wrap myself in a towel, bring clothes in my hand, and lay them along the edge of the lake next to her and Tapeetha's clothes. What's crazy is that my entire wardrobe and more is housed here. I would wonder how that came to be if I hadn't experienced what I have thus far. Anything is possible these days.

Already feeling the pressure of being late, I trot to the closet and fish out the warm brown cargo pants I thought I'd left in my apartment in Cleveland. I grab my cream cable-knit deep-cut V-neck sweater and brown tie-up work boots. I slip into a pink fluffy robe, one that I've never owned but I like just the same, and go where Clarity leads me.

CLARITY

"She's on her way," I tell Tapeetha as I look around this underground cave. I'm positive no human being has ever been here.

We got here by spiraling down a vortex no person could ever survive. Once our feet touched the muddy floor of the ocean, I knew we were no longer in our own universe on the earth. I followed Tapeetha as she swam to the surface. When my head emerged from the water, we were here.

The walls are made of coral reef. An ancient but very fresh scent lingers all around us. I imagine this is how places smell where humans haven't been.

"Why is it so light in here?" I ask, searching for any sort of object that could possibly conduct sunlight from the sky that's probably thousands of feet above us. It seems impossible, but this cave is certainly lit by the sun.

"I bring the light from the sun," Tapeetha replies.

"Oh, wow," I marvel, still observing the powder blue coral reef above us and the deep tide pools that bubble all around us.

Glo has just jumped into the lake. I'm a little worried about the vortex she's going to run into, but

I decide to heed Baron's subtle, and sometimes overt, advice to trust my sisters' strength and autonomy. Why shouldn't I? They got along perfectly fine during all the years they lived without me. Plus, I feel Tapeetha's gaze burning a hole in the side of my face.

"You never, um…" She pauses to think of the word she wants to use. "Discover the earth?"

"Not really," I answer with a shrug. "I'm pretty new to all of this. One day I was in advertising, and the next day, I was in Enu…"

"Advertising?" she says, pronouncing the word one syllable at a time. It's a word she's never heard before.

"My job."

"You mean work like humans?"

"Well, I always thought I was human."

"I never thought *I* was human. One day, I take you to the middle of Earth." She smiles at me.

It's hard to think that this is the same woman I saw for the first time on a mountain in Enu. "Sure, I'll take you up on that," I say as Glo's head emerges.

"Okay, that was highly enjoyable!" she bellows from about fifty yards away. She swipes the water out of her eyes and backstrokes over to us, clearly loving the swim.

We don't have any time to flop around in the water although we want to. Tapeetha makes our clothes materialize, and we hop into them. Right away, I connect with Akili so that she can show me where we're going. I call Finn Elo to get us out of here.

To my utter surprise, he and Baron are together, moving outside in the daytime. A bus speeds past them, along with the other vehicles that make up heavy traffic. They're shadowed by buildings on both sides of the street and are catching the eyes of every passerby.

Finn can't wipe that lopsided grin off his mouth. He loves being part of the hustle and bustle of the morning rush. He can't stop reveling in the advantage this gives him over the enemies of his instincts. That's where he gets the knowledge of which vampires to slay and which ones not to slay— from his instincts. Once Finn Elo is aware of my presence, he grabs Baron's shoulders, and they both come to an abrupt stop.

"Where in the world are you two going?" I ask them.

"To track Exgesis and stay with him this time," Finn answers.

Part of me is upset they didn't include us in this plan; the other part of me realizes how effective it is. The power of sight and the power of mind are our best weapons to use against Lario at the moment since the destructive ones can't kill him—yet.

I'm back into myself, and I've brought Finn's consciousness with me. He notices Glo beside me and admires the sight of her. Glo and Tapeetha watch me carefully.

"Finn's here," I inform them.

"Where?" Glo asks.

I touch one side of my head. "Here."

As a joke, she leans over and kisses my cheek. Tapeetha and I chuckle. Finn barely laughs, amused by that.

"Tell Glo to hold it all steady," he tells me.

I relay his message to her. Suddenly, a wide gash is blown through the sedimentary rock and the deep pool of muddy ocean above our heads. I see the gray sky at the end of the opening. I turn to study Glo. Her eyes are shining. What she and Finn just formed together is nothing short of amazing.

I'm the first to lift off and fly through the fissure.

I have a line on Akili, who's waiting for us deep in the woods that frost Slide Mountain. She's outside in the daylight, draped by the green haze that keeps her safe from the heat of the sun.

I surround each of us with shields of invisibility and warmth before we reach the top of the opening. When we're out, we look down to watch as Finn puts it all back together again. Once the show's over, I let go of him.

The early East Coast morning is indeed dank. We're hovering high above the Atlantic Ocean. My long-distance sight isn't up to Glo's standards, but I do see the stretch of snow that covers the Long Island coastline ahead of us. We hurry toward it.

"Doesn't look warm," Glo remarks. She's trying to figure out why in the world she's not freezing.

"I've made it warm for us," I tell her as we pass over Long Island.

I catch a breath as we venture over the explosion of skyscrapers that appear to grow out of Manhattan's soil like ancient trees. Then we're over the symbols of American glory: tidy lawns, bulky houses, swimming pools, long driveways, tree-lined streets, pristine sidewalks, plastic jungle gyms in fenced-in backyards, and wooden dog houses.

We touch down on a lonely trail in the Catskills

that's flanked by spiny trees. All of our senses are on high alert. There's a thick layer of snow with hoof-prints etched into the ice, showing where a creature, maybe a deer, once crossed the path and disappeared into the woods.

"I see her," Glo claims. Then she searches to the north, south, east, and west of our destination. "Everything looks safe."

Tapeetha and I follow her. We're like Ping-Pong balls racing past the posts. The twigs don't crunch under our feet because we aren't touching the ground. I feel faster somehow and in tune with the objects around me. Glo is quick too, but Tapeetha struggles to keep up with us. I slow down so that she can catch up, but she shakes her head.

"No, Cl'auta, you are strong. You go."

"No, we stay together," I insist.

Glo rushes back to join us. "Tapeetha, are you okay?"

Tapeetha touches my neck where Baron sank his teeth into me. "You have Selell power." She touches the two tiny holes in Glo's neck as well. "And you too."

"Then we'll slow down," I conclude.

"Definitely," Glo agrees before Tapeetha can protest.

We finish our trip at our normal pace. When we catch sight of Akili, she's standing on a downed tree that's covered with sticky green moss and snowflakes.

This Selell has a very interesting beauty. Her smooth skin is so dark that she's almost blue, and her facial features are very tiny. Her intricately curly hair is blacker than coal. Her mane is thick and parted in the middle, and her locks fall over her extremely high cheekbones. I saw her when she appeared on our lawn, but I feel as though this is the first time I'm able to fully observe her. She's wearing an ankle-length scarlet skirt and a thick, black, waist-length coat. Unlike us, her shoes are made for keeping a person warm. Akili's a Selell. She's not affected by the elements, so her attire must be an aesthetic choice left over from a previous decade, or maybe century.

She's standing still, patiently waiting. I disengage our shield of invisibility. As we come into view, she rests her eyes on each of us, one by one.

"Hello, Akili," I say cautiously. I don't know why she incites carefulness in me, but she does.

"Follow me." Her tone is naturally brusque. She turns her back on us and walks into the woods at a regular human's pace.

Glo, Tapeetha, and I give each other a look. Glo nods, which is her way of signaling that the coast is clear. After the brief delay, we follow Akili. The snow crunches under my flat, open-toe sandals. The ice gets in between the bottoms of my feet and my shoes, but I can't feel the cold; the heat shield around me melts and dries the ice. It's so bizarre how I notice every insignificant detail. There are squirrels on their hind legs, chewing tiny pinecones and observing us. There are plenty of deer, and they know we're here. They feel safer for it. All of the creatures out here have one or two or all of their senses focused on us.

"The evil is older than any living thing," Akili says with her back to us. "It lives in the air. It does not control wind, sun, seas, or earth. Do you know why?" She stops at the edge of a high ridge made of mud and rock. She turns to face us.

"They seek no power," Tapeetha answers.

"Yes," Akili says, but it sounds more like *jes*. "That is why. That is astute of you." She narrows her eyes thoughtfully at Tapeetha before turning them on me. "Be invisible again."

I do as she tells me. The rock wall we're facing slides open. Beyond it exists a darkness that's blacker than black. She steps into the abyss, and we follow her. Once we're all inside, the wall slides shut.

This coven has a different energy than the Mount Olympus coven, which felt dangerous from the beginning. Even outside in the surrounding forest, there's a sense of tranquility. I know that this peace could stem from it being daytime. The woods are scarier at night, even without vampires. Because it is too dark to see, I add sight to the shields of warmth, invisibility, and numbness, which I formed to keep our scent from driving thirsty vampires mad.

"They are hiding," Akili whispers. "Every second, they hide."

Now that I can see, I observe that we're standing in a tight space, surrounded by two high walls made of jagged rock. The path before us extends way farther than my eyes can see.

"We will go fast," Akili says. She takes Tapeetha's hand. "I will take you." She's already noticed the bite marks on my and Glo's necks.

I can't help but think how very "astute" that is of her.

We race down the path at a speed that's ten times faster than my fastest normal pace. The farther we go, the more life energy I detect, from the smallest creature to the largest. Akili's right; the Selells are dug in deep into the rock. Fear—that's the prevailing emotion.

We travel at least five miles into the mountain, passing entryways to more long, dark hallways. Suddenly we're moving downward. It's a straight drop, and when we get to the bottom, we come to an abrupt stop.

We all twist around, observing how constricted the space is. Akili pushes open a door. We follow her into an empty room with plastered walls. There's an L-shaped wooden desk in one corner with a reading light that's turned on top of it. A simple cot is against the wall, and there's a narrow bookcase next to it. We're facing a dark green velvet curtain. Just as I sense life behind it, a man, an actual human being, steps out from behind it.

At first, he only sees Akili. He asks, "Is it possible that they're here?"

I drop the shield of invisibility. His eyes shift from my face to Glo's to Tapeetha's, observing us as if he's watching a volcano erupt; he looks both terrified and amazed. The man is a peculiar-looking individual. He has to be at least sixty years old. His thin skin is snow white, and he looks to have one foot already in the grave. It's easy to see he hasn't experienced the sun in a very long time, and he doesn't eat much either. He's literally skin and bones.

Akili extends a hand toward the man. "This is Gregory Rudolph. He is a prophet."

I glance at Tapeetha, who rolls her eyes a little.

"This is our help? A human who lives in a cave?" she scoffs. She lacks faith in him. Her feelings come not from dislike but from experience.

"Skepticism, the refuge of the wise," he says, shaking a finger at her.

"Who is he?" I ask Akili. I can't believe how upset I am to see this individual living so far under the earth. I feel his vanity, and it's a trait I have long learned to never trust.

"I've been preparing for this day," he says, a little too overjoyed.

"Gregory is able to see this time before it comes," Akili explains, grinning. "The humans lose their souls, vampires lose their lives, you sisters save all. That simple."

At the moment, I feel as if we're coming up empty. Lario Exgesis is unable to die, the people in Moonridge are practically dead because Selells are traipsing around the world with their souls, and the same Selells are terrorizing vampire covens. I thought Akili would lead us to a team of Shams more powerful than the team Lario's assembled. The witches would consult their crystal balls or mirrors or cast some sort of spell, if that's what Shams do, and stop the magic Lario has been using against us.

"You're dying, Gregory," Glo says to him out of the blue. "Do you know that?"

Instead of answering, he drags himself over to the desk and hits a lever on the wall. A spindle releases a paper map that has a number of thin lines drawn across it in different colors. I'm not familiar with the shape of the land mass behind the lines.

"I understand that's what it looks like to you," he replies. "But you're not here to talk about me. You need help, and I can give that to you if you want it." He's glaring at us. Even in his weakened state, he's pompously waiting for our consent to continue.

Glo sighs hard. "Sure, I'll hear it." She'd rather rush the guy to the nearest hospital for treatment.

I shrug. "If you can help."

Tapeetha remains quiet.

"You and I have something in common," he says and runs a finger across his eyebrows. "We're both intelligently designed." He shakes a finger at us as he tries to organize his thoughts. "See, the evil can only create from what has already been made by the hand of God. From free-willed beings like me, not you…"

"Because we're not free willed," I whisper to myself.

But Gregory hears me and shakes his finger again. "To a certain degree you are. See, you're hardwired to make all the right decisions." He studies Tapeetha as he says, "See, if you make the wrong choices, it will haunt you."

She narrows her eyes at him. Although it doesn't look like it, she's starting to take him seriously.

"So Selells are made by the hand of evil," I say. "We sort of know that already."

"They were conceived by the mind of evil. It drew from a source of this world to create the first of them. The Remuk."

"Remuk, the blood," I say.

Glo frowns, confused. "What does that mean?"

He says, "A tribe that settled in what's now Central Africa. They were fierce, bloodthirsty, and had an insatiable lust for spilling it…" he takes a dramatic pause to really reel us in, "and drinking it.

They were the first vampires. The Remuk. The evil used this." He points at a spot on the map. "The sun."

"So you're saying that if the sun created them, then the sun will destroy them?" I ask.

"Yes!" he exclaims with more energy than I thought he could muster. "But when the blood of life gave the vampire the leaf to eat, the evil gained ultimate power." He drags himself to the bookcase and scans it. "Here." He hands me a book. "Start from the top."

I take it and read. Right away, I notice the book is allegorical and written in a language I have never seen but understand completely. It's a story about a mad man who made a deal with an entity that resembles the devil. As I speed-read, mentally marking the important parts, I notice a shift in the story. It appears to go backward. It says that the entity knew it was weaker than the man and needed the man to make it strong, so it had to make the man believe it was stronger than he was.

"What does it say?" Glo asks. She's growing more impatient by the second.

"It's a story about a man who made a deal with the devil," I summarize and pause to read more. "He steals souls for this evil entity. The souls keep him alive?" A strong force of dread collapses around me and squeezes. "Each time he's killed, he takes a new soul, but the human dies."

Gregory steps back over to the map and presses a finger on the sun again. "The bentu be dun'e is in three days or three suns."

"Day of creation," I repeat what my brain has translated.

"When the full moon and sun meet at sundown." He touches a spot on the map a few inches away from the dot that represents the sun. "You, the Encaser, connect to the sun. Only three of you are here. Where are the rest?"

"There are two more," Akili answers before I can.

He hesitates to consider whether five instead of seven will be enough. "That may work. You'll have to increase the intensity."

"What for?" Tapeetha asks. Her tone is snide; she's still wary of him. "Why the sun and the sisters? To what end?"

Gregory widens his eyes as if he's utterly confused. "I don't know. The daughters of the House of Benel are to draw from the power of the sun to fight against the god of the Remuk."

"And where is this place on that map?" Glo

asks, taking the words right out of my mouth. "It's not marked."

I saw that.

His eyes shift rapidly toward Akili and then back to me. I sense deception because his thoughts and emotions have come to a grinding halt. When I pull from him, I get absolutely nothing, and no one is ever thinking or feeling nothing.

"It's not important," he grunts, still failing to look me in the eye. "The sun shines over the whole earth. On that day, you tap into it to ignite your power when you need it. It will make you strong enough to overcome the opposition. You will win."

"So that's it?" I *am* slightly disappointed. I indeed was hoping for more.

"That is all," he confirms, graciously nodding as he takes sluggish steps toward the green curtain. "Thank you for coming. I've waited a long time for this day."

Glo, Tapeetha, and I stare at the curtain he has disappeared behind. Then it hits me.

"Sentakuloc," I blurt.

"There's no more sentakuloc," Tapeetha says.

"Maybe we use the sun instead of sentakuloc."

Tapeetha grunts thoughtfully. That sounds rational to her. I look at Glo, planning to bring her up to speed on what sentakuloc is, but she's focused on what's going on behind that curtain. I wonder what in the world she's seeing.

ZILL

Simultaneously, my eyes pop open, and I let out a huge breath that feels as if it has been trapped in my chest for decades. I imagine this is how Snow White and Sleeping Beauty felt after their Prince Charmings kissed them awake. I feel as though I could run twenty marathons back to back. I look to the left and then the right of me, and all I can do is wish I were out cold again. I don't want to be caught between Vayle and Derek.

I push myself up to sit against the headboard. "So what have you two been doing this whole time, sitting here exchanging recipes?"

Neither of them responds. In fact, they don't even look at each other.

"So what... You two just sat here all night, not saying anything to each other?"

"No, we spoke," Derek says.

"About what?" I'm so curious about this answer.

"I asked him why you would need a Wek if you had me," Vayle says.

I turn to Derek. "And you said?"

"I'm not only your Wek; I'm his too."

"And Mr. Nice Guy called me a knucklehead," Vayle says as if he's still surprised by that.

"Whoa, that's equivalent to the f-word for you, Derek!" I lift my eyebrows, exaggerating being shocked.

They chuckle. I love these moments when we all get along. I can't ignore how hungry I am. I'm craving a healthy portion of berries, cream, and lots of Goshem tea.

Just when I think about filling my belly, I remember something and leap out of bed. "My sisters! We're supposed to go see the guardian! I mean, the Sham!"

"They're already gone," Vayle says as he and Derek stand.

"Without me?" This news makes my knees buckle a little. I fall down to sit on the foot of the bed.

I sound saddened by that news because I sort of am. I was looking forward to hitting the road with them. I wanted to do my part alongside Clarity, Glo, Falu, and even Tapeetha, who intrigues me to no end. She's definitely from another dimension.

Still dejected, I announce that I'm going to go to get something to eat. Derek and Vayle look at each other as if they're trying to determine the other's next course of action. This is pretty weird coming from Derek. I figured since one roll in the hay with me would kill him, he has decided to back off. But it appears he's back on and making it difficult for Vayle to seduce me.

"Okay," I whisper, standing between them. I'm too hungry to give either of them much thought at the moment. As I step away, both of them follow me. I come to a halt. "Neither one of you eat really, so I can just go to the table, um, alone." I thumb over my shoulder.

They scrutinize each other, each waiting to see who'll be the first to retreat.

"I'll go for a swim," Vayle grunts, and then he's out.

I'm sort of shocked he chose to leave first.

Once Derek is sure that his competition is gone, he leans in close to me. "I'm happy you're well." He kisses my check, and he's gone before my heart can stop dancing.

My head is still spinning as I walk to the

balcony, fully expecting to see a feast of berries, cream, and hot Goshem tea waiting for me. With Derek out of the running, it was easy to fall into Vayle's charms. I'm not one of those girls who's attracted to bad boys over good boys. For me, it's the opposite. Vayle's definitely bad, and yet I'm so very attracted to him.

Derek is definitely good, but something inside me has shifted. I'm no longer as enthralled by his ability to remain calm when all hell is breaking loose, or pleasant even when he's dealing with a severe ass, or being likable and liking every person in the world, even annoying, self-indulgent people like Riley Simms. I can't stop wondering about her. Four years have passed since I saw her last, which means she could've escaped the vampire invasion. I hope she did.

"Zill, you're up!" Fawn sings as I walk onto the patio. She's already indulging in the spread of food on the table.

Everything is always displayed so scrumptiously. The cream is in a beautifully carved crystal bowl, and it's all white and fluffy. The breads and berries are lined up on a gold platter. There are fruity sauces to mix into the cream. My mouth waters just remembering how it all tastes.

"You're still here!" I sing just as enthusiastically. "I'm starving." I flop into a chair and dig in. "Did you pass out like I did?" I'm distracted by the bite marks on Fawn's neck as I take my first bite of the crepe-like bread I've stuffed with berries and cream.

"I was already lying down when I lost consciousness," she replies as she takes a bite of the bread. She narrows her eyes at me. "What are you looking at?"

I press a finger on my neck at the same spot where the tiny bite marks are on her neck. "Did Ben Artiste do that to you?"

"Yes, he did." She smiles at me, very amused by my curiosity.

"Did it hurt?"

She shakes her head. "Nope."

I chew on my bottom lip. I want to really talk to her about something, but I'm afraid of what I'll have to admit.

"You know it's perfectly okay for the Selell to feed from us," she says. "When it happens, we're actually feeding from them too."

"Really?" I gasp, nearly shocked out of my mind. "You drink his blood?"

"No way! We can't drink any blood!"

"Then how do you feed from him?"

"I don't know… I guess it's a sort of a meta-physical process," she says with a nonchalant shrug. "I'm not sure how it works. It just does."

I try to imagine what she's just said, but I can't. A metaphysical process sounds serious. "So," I begin, deciding to just go for it, "that can happen between me and Vayle?"

"If you want it to. Have you two connected?" She asks casually.

I think back to when he pressed up against me in the hallway to the bathroom and when he laid on me near the swimming pool. Both times, I had been willing to give myself to him. I bashfully drop my face. "No."

She reaches across the table to take my hand. "That's okay, Zill. Don't do anything until you're ready."

"I'm ready," I say. I'm certain about that. "But…" I stop, because this is where it gets complicated.

"But?"

"Vayle can be immature. And he's not that… you know…" I'm trying to think of the word, and after a moment, it comes to me. "Nurturing."

"Hmm." She nods.

"What?"

"You two have a lot in common, you know?" She picks up a knife to spread cream on a crepe. "You're both outspoken; you say what you mean."

"You mean we're both impetuous." That's not a good thing.

"No, no way." She takes a thoughtful pause. "Well, yes, but in a good way."

"Well, thanks, Fawn," I say sarcastically.

She shakes her head. "No, no, impetuous people get a bad rap. You're exciting." She balls up her fist and shakes it. "You take life by the balls. One day you think hot, the next day you think cold, which makes you forever willing to move forward and experience everything. You're brave; he's brave. Your heart is always in the right place, and so is his."

She stops, and I think she's finished. So far, she hasn't changed my mind about Vayle. Those are all the things I already know about him.

But then she says, "You know, you're not all lovey-dovey, huggy-kissy on the outside either. On the inside…" She winks at me. "You're all warm and fuzzy there. I bet he is too."

I don't know at what point during Fawn's assessment of Vayle and me that I stretched my lips into this wide smile. I'm happy listening to what my sister thinks about me. Am I really that great? The thing is, I think I believe her!

"Now eat, and give the vampire the benefit of the doubt." Fawn takes another bite of bread, berries, and cream as she lifts her eyebrows.

CLARITY

"Wait," Glo whispers as she pushes the back of her hand against my shoulder. Her eyes are glowing, and she's still focusing on what's behind that curtain.

A loud, agonizing, throat-gurgling yell fills the air. I start to run toward the sound.

"No." She takes my arm to pull me back. "Not yet." She's still staring daggers at whatever she's looking at. "Now," she fervently says once her eyes return to normal.

I remain a step behind her as she pushes past the curtain. On the floor, near the corner of the small room, is a heap of something that looks like charcoal. Gregory is laid out beside it. His arms and legs are spread out, and he's bleeding at the neck.

"Oh my God," I gasp. It's an appalling scene.

"He was attacked." Glo uses Finn's super speed to rush to the corner Gregory's not far from. She squats, scratches at a seam in the tiled floor, and pulls up a slab of concrete. "Selells?"

"Are they still here?" I ask, gripped by panic.

She nods stiffly as she glares past the wall. Her eyes are glowing again. I didn't factor a fight into the equation. Glo is operating as if she's been in the trenches with Finn forever.

"We should hide," Akili cries.

"I'll take us out of here," Tapeetha says. "We might be sick, but we'll be safe."

I lift a hand as a thought comes to me. "No, wait! Glo, show me a Selell who's alive."

She doesn't hesitate. We look at a Selell who's skulking through the cave, searching for first-generation vampire blood. He looks like all of Lario's minions, and he's wearing a pair of expensive jeans and a shirt that cost a pretty penny too. The creature is meticulously groomed, the opposite of what a vampire terrorizer is supposed to look like.

"Show me his heart," I ask Glo, and she does.

I see the leaf inside the creature's heart. I conceive a shield that stretches as far as the borders of the mountain range and into the depths of the earth beneath it. I block hearts that are pierced by the leaf from entering the protection, and there's an acerbic chorus of shrieking and growling. We stand still, listening as the echoes diminish into silence.

Glo searches beyond barriers we're unable to see. "That worked." Her expression is wide; she's amazed by how simple that was.

I'm relieved that it worked. Now I'm certain that not only can Tapeetha move the Catskill Mountains to the west if she chooses, but she can gather up all those vampires with leaf-pierced hearts in one place to meet their demise.

We all stare at Gregory on the ground. I sense his life force. Although it's weak, he's alive, and no part of his soul is missing since Glo killed the Selell who tried to suck it out of him.

"He's almost dead," Glo remarks. "We can't leave him here, can we?"

She looks to me for an answer. I want to say, *No, we can't.*

"This is where he wants to be," Akili answers for me. "This is where he dies. He has waited many years for the daughters of the House of Benel to come. You are here, and now he is a real prophet."

"We're done here," Tapeetha says. She's already looking toward the curtain.

"But what about him?" Glo gestures toward Gregory.

"I will make Gregory comfortable," Akili says.

"What about you?" I ask, thinking of Fawn. She'll want to know that her old guardian is safe.

"I will stay here until you meet the sun." She looks off as if she's seeing into the horizon.

In her thoughts, I see what's left of her chateau —stone, cement, brick, wood, and metal all stacked up on the ground beside a cement foundation. She really doesn't have a home in France anymore. Akili escorts us out.

I lead us to the entrance to the tunnel in Central Park. I figure Tapeetha will appreciate how much traveling through the diamond-walled pathways feels like home. By the look on her face, she does.

IT'S A RELIEF TO BE IN THE WOODS BEYOND THE gates of our estate. I smell the early morning. Tiny birds call to the recently risen sun, and the morning dew is still on the leaves, making them fragrant. It's lovely to be welcomed by such peace. It's a feeling I've grown to anticipate whenever I return home from the world beyond us.

I call to Fawn to let her know we've made it back, and she informs me that she and Zill are eating on the patio and that there's plenty enough for us too. Glo and, surprisingly, Tapeetha race off to join them, but I head to the diamond chamber to consult the script.

In three days, according to Gregory Rudolph, we're supposed to use the sun to fight an enemy and win. This doesn't sit well with me because we have no battle plan. There were a lot of lines intersecting across that map he showed us, and I have a strange feeling they mean something he doesn't want us to know. Simply put, I don't trust him or Akili.

Once I enter the diamond chamber, the essence of Enu surrounds me. I go to the script and read, starting from the point where I last left off. The second-generation Selells steal souls and then what? Surprisingly, it speaks of the light of the seven lost in Rov. She merges with the Mtknv to erase the dark and revive the universes.

Then there's an abrupt shift in the text. It talks about a thief, the mannenkela. He's a master, little *m*. When the possessor dies, the mannenkela steals the life of the man. That explains how Lario can stay alive even after being pulverized into a million pieces. The script mentions the evil again. The

Daughters of Benel destroy its friend, but it transforms all with a lunar eclipse. That makes no sense to me, so I read past it.

Next I see the heart with the fang grouped with the wind. The Tree of Life pulls the two apart and does it violently. Finally I see the outcome I've been longing to see. The fang that pierces the heart that drips with blood is destroyed.

But first we have to separate the wind from the second-generation Selells. I think we need to discover where the separation should take place. Gregory said the location is irrelevant, but I beg to differ. With only three days to figure it out, I'm pretty sure I should return to Gregory's underground cave to reexamine that map.

CHAPTER 10

A DOUBLE CROSS
AND A FAREWELL

CLARITY

T he best way to get inside the cave and stay undetected is to stay right here in the diamond chamber. I connect with the coven deep in the core of Slide Mountain and end up in the same room where we met Gregory. I keep a shield of blindness over me and block Akili from sensing me in any way, shape, or form.

Everything is just as it was when we left. The desk is here and the cot and the bookshelf, but the map is missing. I picture the map and allow myself to travel to wherever it is, which sends me hurtling through darkness. I reach a dimly lit atrium where I'm surrounded by booths like the ones in the Mount Olympus coven. Not all of the booths appear to be bar dives though. A number of them aren't open to the atrium. They're walled up with signs that have nothing but peculiar emblems on them. The three I can read right away are Medes Craft, Akshur Voice, and Belta Donis.

My quest for the map leads me behind the wall of Akshur Voice. A freestanding bonfire burns in the middle of the room, and Akili stands over it, waving her hands through the tops of the blue and green flames. She's chanting in French.

She says, "Look at the Remuk, see their creation, no curse, no damnation, with eyes to see the making." She repeats that over and over.

I gasp when I see Gregory here with her. He doesn't look as wan as he did earlier. As a matter of fact, he doesn't look as human either! He's a Selell. The scent of his blood defies all I know about vampires. He's first generation *and* second generation.

He bites into his wrist until it bleeds, holds his arm over the blaze, and lets the liquid drip into the fire. He jumps back to avoid the explosion of flames that turn from blue and green to blood red. To my utter and complete shock, Lario Exgesis steps out of the fire.

He's such a grandiose individual. His back is straight and chin lifted, truly reveling in being the kind of creature that appears out of fire. He feels godlike. He was a cavalier individual when I first met him, but now he's so superior that even in the state I'm in, his energy puts a sour taste in my mouth.

"It actually worked," he spits.

Akili snorts. "Of course it did." She's offended he could think otherwise.

I can't help but shake my head at her. If I had a destructive power like Glo or Zill, I'd be tempted to strike her dead where she stands. To be so deceptive… she would have fooled us if I hadn't trusted my instincts.

"Where's the map?" Lario asks.

Akili flicks her arm, and the map appears in her hand. "Here."

Lario snatches it as if it's the last morsel of food left on the planet and he hasn't eaten in years. "She looked at it?"

"Of course she did," she hisses as she takes the map from him and unrolls it. "Her eyes are here."

She dips the map into the flames, which are green and blue again. The paper doesn't burn. She pulls it from the fire and nudges a spot on the map where there's a shadowlike image of two eyes. On close examination, I see that they're definitely shaped like my eyes.

"I used the power of Benel to see the bentu be dun'e, as you asked," Akili adds. Lario reaches out to snatch the map away from her again, but Akili draws it back. "I am not done, Exgesis. But when I am finished, you promised." She eyes him, reading his intentions.

He just sneers at her.

I cannot let Lario get his hoofs on that map. Thinking fast, I engage in some old-fashioned encasing. I take over Akili. I'm inside her hollow, decrepit body and bring blindness and confusion with me.

Finn and Baron show up. Lario still hasn't figured out that Baron can make shields, so they continue to go undetected. However, I'm in full control of Akili, and I use her eyes to stare at Baron, hoping he'll recognize me. He's always able to see me in whatever form I take.

"I guess you'll have to trust me, won't you?" Lario says, but Akili can't hear him.

"Clarity?" Baron asks in a deeply curious tone.

Lario is unaware that extra people are in the room, but I can tell by how he's frowning that he detects the change in Akili's behavior. Acting fast, I rush her over to hand the map to Baron.

"Take it and get back to the study," I say in a hurry.

All Lario sees is Akili holding out the map, and then it disappears into thin air.

The last thing I hear is Lario whining, "What the hell just happened?"

I'm in the diamond chamber, waiting for Baron and Finn. I was prepared to leave Akili blind and confused, but lucky for her, I was born a sympathetic creature. In less than a minute, the cousins come rushing into the study. I hurry out of the diamond chamber.

Baron is perplexed by the map. "What is this?"

I take a second to drink him in. I'll always love the smell of the wind on his skin and clothes whenever he returns from traveling vampire style. Only when he looks at me do I notice I'm holding my breath. The effects of him sharing my blood have worn off. I can't hear or feel his thoughts behind that smirk of his. Come to think of it, I like it better this way.

I walk over to him, and his nearness makes my insides tickle a little. He's so close, so warm. It's hard to believe that he's in love with me and vice versa.

"Here," I say as I point at the image of the eyes. "When Glo, Tapeetha, and I went to the coven, this man who calls himself a prophet showed this to me. Did you see him? He was in the room with Lario and Akili."

"I did," Baron says.

"He's a mixture of a first-generation and second-generation Selell, but when we first met him, his aura was human. And he was really human, because Glo saw his organs and was concerned he would die at any moment."

I glance at Finn, who's looking off toward the patio. It's no mystery who he's watching. He still considers his love for Glo a weakness that he can't shake.

"He could've been changed in the very short period of time between then and now, but I doubt it," I say.

"No," Finn says. "His name isn't Gregory Rudolph. It's Jill Falslow, and he's a fifteen-hundred-year-old vampire."

"What's his story?" Baron asks as he forces himself to look away from my face.

"He's a future spinner, and he's not in the business of being wrong."

"Then his predictions are accurate?" I ask.

"As accurate as he makes them. He's a hack, a dangerous one. He's on the list. He's lived long enough," Finn says with narrowed eyes.

I get a feeling that's a list no one wants to end up on. It dawns on me that Finn is accusing Gregory Rudolph of rigging the future.

"You know what's funny?" I say. "He said we're going to win whatever battle we're to fight in three days. Why would he make that happen if he's working with Lario?"

Baron, Finn, and I look at each other, searching for an answer none of us appear to have.

"Well, look here." I point at the trace-out of my eyes on the thick paper. "Apparently, this was captured after I looked at this map. My theory is that the power of the mind can uncover what this all means." I take a hard look at the intersecting lines, etched in red, green, blue, or regular pencil. So far, I have no idea what any of it means. "But I would have to sit down and toil over it for a while." I sigh, exhausted by just the thought of it.

"You never have to toil alone, Clarity," Baron says, wearing that naughty smirk.

I lift a finger in warning. "We have to work, not…" I lift my eyebrows to suggest what I mean.

"Tell me when you find something," Finn says

before he darts out of the room. He was not at all happy about our flirting.

Now it's just Baron, me, and the map. We waste no time getting down to business. First, we try to figure out the shape of the land mass on the page. Neither of us can place it by sight, but great minds surely think alike. He and I look at Lario's extensive library at the same time, the one my father had confiscated.

"You take the right, I'll take the left, and we'll meet in the middle," he proposes.

His face is so close to mine. It would be natural to kiss him for no reason other than he's only inches away from me. I swallow the lump in my throat, wondering if I'll ever stop having these physical and emotional reactions to Baron Ze Feldis.

"Okay," I croak.

He simpers at me again. "Okay."

We stare into each other's eyes. I'm torn about what to do next. My eyes won't let me look away from him, and my feet won't allow me to spin around and face the bookcase.

I feel my lips pull up into a crooked smile. "You should go ahead and move to the left."

He chuckles a little. Yes, I still love the sound of that.

"I was thinking," he says, "we'll be better at this if we, you know..." He taps two fingers against my neck.

I smirk. "So all you want me for now is my blood?"

He doesn't stop touching me. One of his hands smooths the side of my neck while he draws me into him with the other. I'm dizzy and floating on air. For the moment, I've forgotten what we're supposed to be doing.

Baron is ready for me, and I'm ready for him.

Nevertheless, he kisses my forehead, and we both chuckle. Because there's a sense of hilarity in this moment. We've just stolen from three vampires a map that has an image of my eyes on it. One of the vampires is a witch, one's a con man, and one's a self-fulfilling prophet. All three of them are allied against us. This is a heavy moment indeed, and yet we want to make love. Zill is right; we do have to learn to cool it.

"So I go right. You go left." I sigh.

Baron does that sensuous sniff and darts over to search the stacks. I go to the opposite side and start my own search.

TAPEETHA

They only have the ci'ke, ton'rek, and the ci'cha fruit to eat here. There are many more fruits to eat at my home. This is not enough. I want my home. At this table, I see Gu'he, Falu, and Zillael. They don't know how it is to be here like I'm here. The inside me hurts. I need to cry all the time.

"Are you going to eat?" Falu asks me. She is concerned all the time.

I see the ci'ke, ton'rek, and ci'cha, and I am ill. "No. I need rest." When I take to my feet, so does Falu.

"Do you want company?" she says to me.

"No." I want to be by myself.

Gu'he and Zillael watch me too. They are like humans in how they think. I know what I must do to make them feel better.

I smile and say, "I need rest. I will be okay." I say it as I mean it. It is true. I will soon not be sad anymore, but for now, I am.

Falu sits down. I'm happy to see this. She can be —persistent. I can go on my way now.

This house is big. There are things inside it that I never saw before. There is the long pole with a light on top of it. There are lights above, inside the ceiling. We do not need these in Enu.

I see the steps that dip down to where I stay, and it is there I see Leto. He waits for me. I cannot understand it. I close my eyes. When I open them, he has not moved.

"Tapeetha," he whispers.

We do not speak at all since he arrived. He sees me. I see him. But we say nothing. We do not get close. We used to touch a lot. I pat his hair. He pats my hair.

Gon tek, I used to say to him a long time ago. *Love you.*

"Come," I say to him. As I walk past him, the inside me tickles.

He follows me. I hear his steps go *plunk, plunk, plunk* when his feet touch the floor. We move slow. I and Leto never move slow.

The long poles with light are not here. The fire burns in the pit. The daylight comes inside from outside. Leto is beside me, and I still feel the tickle, like the slow wind tickles the blades of grass.

"How do we do this?" Leto asks me.

"I am…" I can't think of the word. Is it *I am sorry? My apologies?* Is there a word in English for what is inside me? "Se'nuko, ze'nerum'a." It is the same as sorry and apologies but means more than those words can ever be.

He does not answer. He does not look at me. He watches the lake, the grass, and the sky. Does he hear my heart like before?

"You hate me?" I ask him, because he is still silent.

"No. Gon tek." It is good when he looks at me. "Always gon tek." He stops, and then he speaks. "I was angry at you for a long time, Tapeetha. But I know it wasn't me you didn't love. It was the earth. I just thought you could love me more than you hate it."

How do I say this in the right way? I close my eyes to think, to make my English better. "I stayed with you here, with humans, as long as I could. You could have come with me. I wish you love me more than you love the earth."

"I guess Ose took care of that for me." His tongue is sharp. He says he doesn't hate me, but I hear he does.

I hear the wind humming. It is light and a little warm. I want to run with it. I want to be free of this hurt in my heart. I want to go back to when I left Leto. I would say, *Leto, please come with me. I cannot breathe without you, but I cannot breathe here.*

"You are made from the dust of this earth, Leto. You cannot know why I made my choice," is all I can say.

He looks at me. He puts one hand on my yellow hair. He touches my face. He is warm. I breathe, and I burn, and I smell him. I close my eyes. This is too strong. It must stop.

It does stop.

I open my eyes.

He is turned away from me. "No matter. We can't change the past, but since I love you, I want to help you and your sisters."

"That is good."

We are quiet.

"We can't go back to the way we were," he says.

My heart hurts when I hear that. I want to cry again, but I don't. "Okay." It almost sounds like a cry.

Leto's eyes see me one more time. They are blue but not like the sky because he is a Selell. His skin is white but not like the sand. He is like the snow. His mouth is red, his lips tender because he is not thirsty.

"Okay?" he says.

I don't think he's happy about my answer. I sigh

and look at my feet. "I don't want to hurt anymore."

He touches me again but more this time. We are close. My breasts are against his chest. *Does he feel my heartbeat now?*

"If you let me go this easy, then you *will* hurt me. Is it always this easy for you, Pan'a'tua?"

I shake my head because I have no words. I don't stop shaking my head because he does not understand me. He will never understand me.

His arms hold me tighter. His lips are on my cheek… my mouth… our tongues are tied in knots.

"Pan'a'tua," he does another whisper.

My eyes open. I see that he is not here. Now I know why. It is Cl'auta calling.

CLARITY

THIRTY MINUTES AGO...

After taking more than an hour to get through half of the books on the top shelf, I decide Finn and Glo's ability to see through inanimate objects with precision may help speed up the process. Unfortunately, I interrupted a passionate moment between them. Although neither was thrilled about it, they joined us straightaway.

When I show Glo the map, the first thing she asks is how we got it.

"I thought we left it with that Gregory guy?" she says.

"We did." I explain the rest of it.

"Fawn's old guardian tried to double-cross us?" she asks, surprised.

"It appears so," I mutter. I have my own thoughts on the matter.

I know for a fact Freda would *never* betray me in such a way. There has to be more to Akili's actions than what we saw. One day, we'll probably learn what that is, but for now, we have to believe she's a double-crosser.

Glo and Finn search the stacks. They're fast and precise. Baron and I stand out of their way as Finn takes the books on the high shelves and Glo takes the lower ones. They don't even touch the books. After staring at the spine of one for a few moments, they move on to the next.

When Glo narrows her eyes at Finn and he grins back at her, their searching turns into a competition. I don't pick sides, but I have to stop myself from cheering when Glo slides a book off the shelf first.

"Maybe this?" Glo says as she hands it to me with a wink at Finn, who continues to grin at her.

I take it. "*In the Days of Drought.*"

"The map's on the last page," she says.

The book is thin, and the pages are made of papyrus. A mixture of words and symbols are burned onto the material, just like the script I recovered from my grandmother's grave. I flip through the pages. I'm still amazed by my ability to understand foreign languages.

As far as I can tell, the book is written like a textbook; the content is technical. It details how to harvest certain fruits and vegetables during seasons of low rain. The writing goes into detail about a process I interpret as *moving sun*. It's basically using sunlight as water in the way that it provides oxygen to stimulate growth. It's a quite interesting technique, but to make it work requires exact positioning and an object made of gold to conduct the sunrays.

When I flip to the map, it's clear the two land masses are not similar. However, I notice that they have something in common. The image in the back of the book has two lines that run over the land mass, crisscrossing in the middle.

"From what I read, these lines are sun guides," I say, tracing the lines.

Baron is reading over my shoulder. "Yes, I see that."

I flinch, taken aback. "You can understand this?"

"I'm pretty sure that I can do whatever you're able to do."

I take a moment to ponder that. I've always been alone in possessing my frightening abilities. I almost feel as if I've cursed him; I certainly don't wish this on him. One thing hasn't changed: Deep down inside, I still want to be normal.

If I take the time to consider it, regular humans have the optimal status. They're only as ignorant as they allow themselves to be, and in many cases, ignorance *is* bliss. They can just say no to every element of evil, and it can't touch them. They can live. Then they die, and they're done. Not to say that they're free of burdens, but boy, if they make the right choices, they can live a lovely worry-free life. I've come across those people, the happy ones. I've always wanted to be one of the happy humans.

"Clarity?" Baron asks to reclaim my attention.

"Yes?" I quickly put my focus back on the moment.

"Do you think the lines on the map are these sorts of sun guides?" he asks.

"I do. And I don't think these are *my* eyes, because I don't have the power to see."

Baron and I turn toward Glo at the same time.

"Study this closely," Baron says to her as he hands her the map.

She nods before looking at the page. As soon as she begins to read, I feel her dizziness. Finn catches her as her legs turn weak, and she drops toward the floor.

I felt that, and so did Baron. The good thing is she's already recovering. Strong magic is prohibiting her from reading the map. I turn to gaze at the diamond chamber. So far, it's been our most effective weapon against Sham magic.

So I point at it. "Let's go in there."

BARON AND FINN STAND OUTSIDE THE CHAMBER, their eyes trained on Glo. In the confines of this chamber, her thoughts, emotions, and everything she senses are free from Baron. But not from me. She and I are going on this journey together.

She takes a steadying breath, hoping to God the dizziness stays away. I felt it the first time and understand why she's hesitant. First her breathing turned shallow, then everything around her spun. As soon as she closed her eyes, it all went away. That experience is singed in her brain. But it doesn't stop her from moving forward. Glo lifts her eyebrows at Finn. I think that's a smile—not a smirk or a cynical grin, but a warm, encouraging smile— he just showed her.

She lowers her face to study the map. She sees the lines and braces herself for the adverse reaction. Nothing happens. She continues to study the lines carefully.

Then something miraculous happens. There's life on this page. I see the lines as beams of light that hover over changing landscapes, including gravelly semi-arid desert regions holding fanned-out trees. What gives me a clue of the general region I'm seeing are the grasslands where herds of giraffes graze on high trees, zebras chew the dry grass, and shanties constructed of sheets of rusted metal or plywood are erected throughout the terrain.

I go there as the Encaser, taking in the lukewarm, late-afternoon air. I can draw in the energy of whatever my eyes see, but I can only see so far. So I bring Glo here with me.

She gasps. "Whoa."

"Sorry," I say. "I should've warned you first. I used to be more mindful about that, but since I've been using my abilities so much, I'm always on automatic pilot."

"No, it's okay," she says to assure me that it's no big deal. She means it.

"Okay, I need you to search out as far and wide as you can, more eastward than westward," I tell her.

Suddenly, I can see past the crispy dry desert with its thirsty trees. The Mediterranean Ocean is to the north, and the Red Sea stretches down the eastern coast. They're the first large bodies of water that I can identify, but the lines that crisscross and intersect in the atmosphere are way west.

"The lines are off by a number of miles to the north," Glo observes.

What she's able to do with the power of sight is impressive. I see that in her head, she's comparing the map, the book, and the actual lines in the atmosphere.

"I see what you see," I whisper.

"But they're moving; can you see *that*?"

I shake my head. "I can't. Are they moving south or north?"

"South."

It clicks. Two of these same lines were crossing paths in a book that was basically about farming. Water brings sustainability to the body, and the sun brings nutrients.

Life…

Sustainability…

The bentu be dun'e.

The day of creation.

The sun and moon together.

Excited, I clamp a hand around Glo's arm. "I think I've got it!"

We're both fully back inside the chamber. Baron and Finn are still watching us with their eyebrows crinkled. They look as if the entire time we were literally out of the country, they didn't move an inch.

I give Baron two thumbs up and the biggest smile ever. I'm *that* confident we're on our way to figuring out how all of this can help us destroy Lario's second-generation Selells in a single swipe.

IN THE PRESENT...

I call for the rest of my sisters to join us in the study. They show up and bring their bonds with them. As I gaze around the room, I'm amazed at how far I've come.

For me, this all began one morning when a frightening fog rolled into Manhattan. I hardly noticed how chilly it was as I walked to the office because my world had just been turned upside down. Baron Ford, who I now know is Baron Ze Feldis, was back in my universe, and he had requested that I handle his account.

Several weird occurrences unfolded after that. The talking butterfly, who I now know as Lorenzo, was my Wek. A stranger in an alley tried to slice my neck open, which I now suspect was perpetrated by Sham magic. My neighbors became catatonic, and I learned Freda wasn't my mother, which I must admit was quite a relief. Then I was whisked away to Enu while being chased down by the evil.

One by one, the sisters came into my life. First Adore, then Fawn, then Zill, then Tapeetha, and finally Glo. I wonder, did the Shams know about this day even back then? I'm certain that what I'm about to reveal will be a game-changer.

I hold up the map for all to see.

"How did you get that?" Tapeetha takes her time constructing the question.

I tell everyone what I've already told Glo about how I returned to the coven and saw Akili engaged in a ritual involving Lario Exgesis. Fawn looks at me without blinking. I take on her emotions. She's tense. Her head feels as if it's floating as she tries to fully absorb the possibility that what she's just heard is completely true.

But she doesn't ask me anything. She swallows the lump in her throat and forces herself to give the matter no further thought. Thank goodness Ben Artiste is sitting beside her. He pulls her closer to comfort her. It works. She feels much more secure, and I take that as my cue to get on with it.

"This is equivalent to the equatorial line," I say as I run a finger across the one straight line on the map. "Here, the number of daytime and nighttime hours are equal. This is the balance of energy that was needed to create the first Selells from the Remuk. I think—no, I know—that the evil isn't finished creating. When these two perpendicular lines line up the right way, the second-generation Selells will be transformed into something else.

What that is, I don't know. But whatever they become won't be good for us."

"Glo filled us in on what happened during your first visit to the coven," Fawn says. "We're supposed to connect with the sun somehow. How does what you just told us relate to that?"

"That's a good question, Falu," Lorenzo says.

I turn to the right.

He's standing there, as beautiful as ever. "One you know the answer to Cl'auta."

"Right," I barely say, studying him. A lot of questions run through my mind at once. I want to know where in the world he's been all this time and how he's holding up in the wake of Ben Artiste's return.

However, his eyes are on me. Like the dutiful schoolmarm he is, he waits for me to answer Fawn's question.

"Well…" I stop to ponder the details.

If I use reason, I have no answer. But there's a life force within me that isn't separate from who I am, and it unequivocally knows the answer. It's the Enuian me, or it could be the divine me. For years, the human part of me has been dominant, but now that isn't the case, and it hasn't been for a long time.

I answer him with confidence. "I presume that

the sun was used to transform the Remuk into bloodthirsty creatures, but so was the moon. The time of creation took place at a time of day when both planets faced each other."

Information is coming at me so fast that I can barely keep up. I massage my temples in an effort to slow it down.

"But something didn't go according to plan," I continue. "Because Selells can't live in the sun, but they can walk under the light of the moon and live. The sun must've cursed them. The Remuk wants to try its hand at creation again now that there are Selells who are linked to the leaf from the Tree of Life. The evil wants the outcome it first intended. I think that if we were to tap into the sun from the wrong position on Earth, then our power will just fuel the evil's power. That's why Gregory, or Jill, didn't give us an exact location."

"So the evil intends for the Remuk to prey upon humans and have the ability to walk in the daytime," Glo concludes.

"Yes, that's what I think."

Lorenzo beams at me, clearly satisfied by my conclusion. "Everything you just said is correct"—he points at me—"because you've finally accepted who you are. You're using the full power of mind. It hears the truth when lies are spoken, and if you let it, it can know the intentions of the evil. That's why it wanted to kill you. It will always want to kill you. You have to fight it, or it *will* kill you. Remember that."

The way he's looking at me makes me feel as if I'm a graduate student who just passed my oral exams after years of studying to be an Encaser. But it's more than that. Is he saying good-bye? I don't want to accept that, but I'm sure he is. I look at Baron. He sees the anguish in my eyes, and now he's up and holding me from behind.

"Cl'auta," Lorenzo continues, "you know it's time for me to say good-bye." He looks at Fawn, above my head at Baron, then over at Vayle and Zillael, who are standing beside each other behind the sofa and quite close. He came to know us well on our venture through Nowhere to Jari.

I can't move, but I want to hug him good-bye. I don't want to let him go. I thought things would end differently for Lorenzo. He was obviously attracted to Fawn and vice versa. I wanted her to find love, the deep love I have with Baron. She did find it, but it wasn't with Lorenzo; it was with Ben Artiste, the Selell fate bonded her to. I guess there's never truly a reality outside of the will of fate.

"What now? Where are you going?" Fawn asks to my surprise.

I know the answer to her question, and she does too. He's going to do what Ose and her own Wek did: become nothing. He hasn't a soul that will live on or a spirit that continues to be the life that is Lorenzo the Wek. I wonder what part of him is able to love, feel, and desire. Suddenly, it hits me.

"You choose to disappear, don't you?" I ask only him.

He looks at me. He has no thoughts, no words. Lorenzo won't give me an answer, but I know the truth. He chooses this for himself because he cannot continue to live if Fawn loves Ben Artiste. He knows that I know, and he's satisfied with that.

We're all watching him when it happens. There's no fanfare. He doesn't glow like an ornament on top of a Christmas tree. No voice from heaven calls out for him. Felix Benel doesn't appear to bid him farewell.

Lorenzo just disappears. He ceases to exist.

Forever.

CHAPTER II

RENDEZVOUS IN TWO SUNS

CLARITY

T he finality of Lorenzo's departure lingers in the air, which makes this all the more real. I can't believe that after all I've experienced, I still require proof of this life at certain times. A large part of me still believes I'll see Lorenzo again one day, because the fact that he's gone forever is something I cannot believe.

However, what's crystal clear is what our next course of action should be: destroy the second-generation Selells.

"If what you're saying is correct, then second-gen vamps have to be at this site to be transformed into more powerful vampires," Finn says, looking at me for corroboration.

"I believe so, yes."

"You believe so…?"

"No, I know so."

He lifts one side of his mouth into a lopsided grin. "Good. Because like the Wek said, you know everything. Not Ze Feldis."

I snort, but Baron doesn't find Finn's humor amusing. I think it's because he doesn't like Finn smiling at me that way. Finn knows it, which is why he did it. These two will probably never get along.

"Let me see the map." Baron holds out his hand. I give it to him, and he examines it. "See this?" Baron walks over to the onyx coffee table and spreads the map out on top of it. "These are the same lines that are in the book, *The Days of Drought*. I think we need to be where those two sets meet— the ones in the book and those on the map."

"Sounds like a plan. I'll be there watching," Finn announces to Glo's surprise.

We all hear her let out a loud gasp as she straightens her back.

"So what are you going to do, just stand in the jungle and *watch*?" she snaps at him.

"No," Finn replies. "We are."

"Ha!" she scoffs. "I'm not living in the jungle."

"Whoa," Vayle sings out of the blue.

Zill chastises him for this outburst by punching

him in the shoulder, although she can't stop grinning either.

"You're a vampire slayer, Glo. This is what we do," Finn says, ignoring Zill and Vayle.

He's rendered Glo speechless. She's thinking about what he just said. She's asking herself, *Am I a vampire slayer?* I wish I had an answer for her, but I don't. Regardless, she's decided to join him, only because she knows he's leaving and she'd rather not be without him again.

"Then go to the intersection and keep an eye out," Baron says.

Finn snarls at him. "Thanks," he says facetiously. He doesn't like being ordered around by Baron, and he clearly took that as a directive.

"You're welcome." Baron's tone is just as sharp.

I thought after spending so much time together keeping an eye on Lario, they would have ironed out the kinks in their relationship. *Apparently not.*

"What about the rest of us?" Ben Artiste asks.

"We wait," Baron answers, but he's staring at me in a strange manner. Something's turning in his head, and I have no idea what.

"You mean we get a break?" Vayle sounds excited.

"At the second sunrise from today, we'll meet in Libreville, Gabon," Baron announces.

"They're five hours ahead of Eastern Standard Time," Fawn says.

"Is that what those clocks are for?" Glo stares at the floor beneath the bookshelf.

"What clocks?" Fawn asks.

"The ones lined up in the hall beneath this room."

Fawn and I look at each other.

"If there's a room down there, then how do we get in there?" I ask.

Before Glo can answer, the ground gives way. I drop into a dimly lit room that's designed like a museum gallery. Among other peculiar artifacts, all the clocks that were once in Lario's possession are lined up against the wall. But there are more of them, at least a hundred more.

When I'd asked Lorenzo where they were, he told me that Felix had secured them. I wonder why he didn't tell me they were here! I wonder if, back then, I would have the impulse to study every object in this space like I do now.

"Thanks, Finn," I say as I take in all of it, even the objects I don't recognize.

"All the times are different," Glo says.

Fawn walks over to the only one that has a pendulum made of sapphire, and she taps the glass. "This is the one that tells East Coast time. I remember that."

"Ten thirty in the morning," I say.

Baron looks at the time on his very expensive watch. "That's what I have."

"Me too," Leto Danto adds, studying his wristwatch.

"Then it's settled," Finn says while staring at Glo. "We'll meet where the two lines intersect at sunrise."

We all consent with nods and burps of "Okay."

ZILL AND VAYLE HAVE DECIDED TO JOIN TAPEETHA and Leto for a swim in the lake in Tapeetha's backyard. Interestingly enough, Fawn and Ben head out to the Mojave Desert. Before leaving, she asks me to put shields of invisibility around them. It's risky leaving the estate after stealing the map from Lario. I'm sure he's figured out that it didn't just disappear into thin air by now. To put me at ease, Fawn promises to keep me dialed into her and to be very careful.

Me, on the other hand… My skin is grimy and needs to be washed. After I announce this to Baron, he sweeps me up into his arms.

"You smell like a bed of roses," he says, inhaling me deeply at my neck.

I shove him back with one hand. I must strip off all of my clothes, crawl into bed, and sleep for most of the nearly forty-eight hours we have before we confront the evil, which is planning to supersize the second-generation vampires. "Baron, I really need to clean up. Sorry." I step away from him.

But he holds me from behind. "Your wish is my command," he whispers seductively.

I chuckle because he's being frisky at the worse time. "Doesn't sound like it to me."

"Come with me, and you can take a shower there."

I sigh. "You know it's not safe to leave here. Not while Lario is probably on the warpath. He can't find us here."

Baron kisses the side of my neck. I feel his sharp fangs against my skin.

"He's already handled."

"What do you mean?" I ask.

"Elo has what we call a sniffer on him."

I'm too tired to ask what that is. For the first

time since the bond between Baron and me was ignited, I want something more than I want him. That's a shower, plus rest, and I want to do both right here at the House of Benel.

"Baron, please," I feebly plead.

"Trust me. I want to be alone with you and share something with you. Something that's important to me."

I want to sigh, but it comes out as a yawn instead. All of a sudden, my feet are off the ground.

Baron is cradling me. "Sleep, love, and I'll have a bath drawn for you upon arrival."

"Arrival where?" I'm starting to slur.

"To my home. My real home."

Now I'm alert. I used to long to see where Baron lived. I always thought he resided in Manhattan, since his company Red Yard was, or is, there. Funny, I haven't heard him mention Red Yard in a long time. However, my curiosity causes careful Clarity to throw caution to the wind. I would *love* to sleep between sheets that have a faint scent of Baron Ze Feldis.

"Okay," I whisper with as much enthusiasm as I can muster.

He smiles and kisses my forehead. The touch of his lips makes me catch a breath. Hearing my unrepressed response turns him on, and he kisses my lips, deeper and deeper, until we're hot and heavy.

I notice that I'm literally speeding through the air even though Baron hasn't pulled his mouth from mine. I'm probably as light as a feather in his arms because as he's holding me with one hand, the other hand is in my dress, in my bra, massaging one of my breasts. He gently stimulates my nipple. I want to scream with pleasure. I bet Baron wants me to cry out as well, but I don't. However, he's made me want more than a shower or a bath, maybe both, and some sleep. I want to make love to him too, and do it forever.

We're moving at warp speed. At first, we were high in the sky. Then we moved downward, entered some sort of portal, and now it's safe to assume we've journeyed way farther than the eastern coast-line. Time is ticking away one minute at a time. I wonder where in the world he's taking me.

"We're here," he finally says.

Once again, there's a stark change in air quality. By the smell of it, I conclude that it's icy cold. I can't feel it though, because any contact with Baron keeps me nice and toasty. The light of the cloudy day flows over my face. Our hot and heavy kissing and petting stops. We're standing in a snow-covered clearing, and tall evergreens horseshoe around us. Baron is still carrying me, and together we're facing a massive white metal dome.

"Where in the world are we?" I wonder.

"At the tip of Kiruna," he says, still staring at me with fire burning in his eyes.

"Sweden?" I'm shocked. "How in the world did we get to Sweden this fast?"

"I commissioned a tunnel. Makes it easier to cross the ocean."

"Wow." I'm still marveling. "How were they able to build that?"

"Creatures who are already dead can do work that kills the living."

I laugh because as morose as it sounds, it's true. I take a harder look at the massive dome. "Looks like an observatory. You live here?"

"Not as much as I used to. I've been spending a lot of time in this peculiar place in Vermont lately." He grins at me.

I kiss him because that was a sweet thing to say. Before I pull back to smile at him, we're inside the great dome. I curve my neck to look at the ground; Baron's feet are on grass. The same evergreens are scattered around a flat, square-shaped complex of boxlike structures. The walls are old and dusty and made of clay.

"Is this where you were born?" I ask as I pat his shoulder, my way of asking him to put me down.

He does. The grass is wild but soft, like a fluffy pillow under my feet.

"Yes, this is it."

"You preserved it for all of these years? This place has to be at least four hundred years old."

He wears a severe expression as he looks over the relic of his past. "Nine hundred. The Ze Feldises were Vikings. That's how we acquired our riches." He smirks at me. "And women."

I smile.

"Are you ready to go inside?" he asks, looking into my eyes.

I do want to see what a household that bred the likes of Baron Ze Feldis looks like, but I need a moment first. This place is nothing less than Baron's broken heart on display. To comfort him, I gently massage the nape of his neck, but he seizes my hand and kisses my knuckles.

"It's not like that anymore," he assures me. He feels the sympathy emanating from me. "I wanted to bring you here because I only loved three people before I met you—my father, my mother, and myself. I wanted to bring you here because it's time for me to know if—" He abruptly stops, and he appears to be more conflicted than ever.

"What?" I ask. My heart thrashes. The suspense is killing me.

But he doesn't answer. He scoops me back up into his arms, and in a flash, we're inside.

The change of scenery distracts me. In unequal parts, it's both antiquated and modern. For instance, there's an electronic fireplace and wrought-iron floor lamps twisted into archaic patterns. The silk benches and armchairs have definitely been reupholstered in recent times; the material is too untarnished. An old chair that resembles a throne made of high-glossed wood and outlined with woven gold commands one end of the room.

"Your father was a king?" I ask.

He lifts his mouth in my favorite gesture. "King of his lair at least."

"I don't understand."

"He was a man of means who built himself a village behind strong walls. He made the laws and enforced them. But there were hundreds of men just like him in this country. The ambitious ones waged wars against men like my father and stole everything they had."

"But that's not what happened to your father."

"No," he says, surprisingly without any bitter-ness. "Wait here. I'll be back shortly."

He's gone before I say okay. I love learning about Baron and the life he lived before he should've been dead and buried.

I'm distracted by sand-colored burlap curtains that cover a vast opening. The two sides don't quite join, so there's an opening between them. If I squint really hard, I can see a courtyard past the gap. There's a stone structure in the middle of it. As I take the first step toward it, Baron appears before me, and I'm in his arms.

"The bath is being drawn," he says, following my line of sight.

"Is that a statue?" I ask.

"What's left of it," he answers.

I want to walk past the curtain actually to look at it. It's evident by the one broad shoulder still intact that it's a replica of a man. I assume he's the same person the throne belonged to. It would be nice to see any part of the person who helped create Baron. However, Baron doesn't budge, even after sensing where my curiosity is directed. He's gazing into my eyes, and I don't have to be able to read his mind to know that he doesn't want to talk about that at the moment. I won't push him.

I crack a tiny smile and ask, "Okay, so who's drawing the bath? Do you have the same sort of ghosts that we have at the estate?"

He lets his head fall back as he graces me with his delightful laugh.

I stare at him with googly eyes because he's so gorgeous with his neck-length wavy hair. Even when he laughs, his eyes remain intense, and I feel alive in his mind because of the way he's looking at me.

He's still grinning at me. "No, I have servants here, but they stay out of the way, like your ghosts."

"Well, then," I whisper and kiss the tip of his nose. "Take me to the water."

With that, he sweeps me off of my feet.

GLO

"Ha!" I let out a loud sarcastic laugh because Finn just asked me if I was pouting. I take a deep breath to calm myself a little... well, a lot.

Zill and Tapeetha have gone swimming, Fawn is

trekking through the desert, Clarity is getting some much-needed sleep, and *me*? I'm in the jungle where it's smoldering hot and mushy and wet. We're just standing here. No, really, it's just the trees, the gorillas, hippos waddling in the deep lakes that cut through the grasslands, a whole lot of green-and-orange parrots that have gathered in the trees around us, and Finn and me. The parrots' squawking is so loud that all I want to do is run away.

"Yes, Finn, I'm pouting," I growl while slapping a mosquito on my cheek. I end up giving myself a good whack on the face.

Finn Snickers, I guess I find my misery entertaining. He takes one of my hands and points at the sky with his other hand. "Look."

I force myself to forget my despair and look past the leaves and birds. The lines are indeed moving toward the equator, but they're farther away from the center point of the two intersecting lines that we're focusing on. I can see the intersection moving toward a tiny island with Spanish charm and lots of palm trees.

"That's São Tomé," Finn says, grinning at me.

"That's where we need to be?" I feel as if I'm discovering that the mirage of a fresh lake is actually real after trudging through the barren desert for days, thirsty, starving, and knocking on death's door.

"Done pouting?" he asks, smirking at me.

He's so smoking hot, especially now that he's shown me that volunteering to half of the advance party may be worth it.

"Let's just get there first," I say, joking with him.

"But"—he puts his lips close to mine—"I like the idea of doing you right here in the mud *first*. What about you?"

He's standing too close, hindering my ability to give his question any serious deliberation. Sex around baboon feces and beetles isn't ideal. But when his lips touch mine and I feel his fangs and other parts of him throbbing, I forget about those details.

"Damn, I love you," he whispers as we make our way down onto the soggy earth. He stops to look into my eyes while his hand is in my pants, his fingers under my panties and inside me.

"What?" I say, confused by that look on his face. His expression isn't his typical puzzlement or one formed by bridled passion.

"Nothing," he says. His tasty lips are on mine again, and his fingers bring me pleasure.

"Wait." I tuck my chin to stop myself from

kissing him. "I think I love you more than you can ever love me."

"You can't," he counters.

"I can, and I do."

He sneers at me while his fingers touch me down there. He's so damn good at that. His kisses are just as exploratory and stimulating. Finn remains a careful and indulgent lover. He lets my every expression be his guide to pleasuring me.

I'm breathing deep and fast. My eyes are closed, but I can't see his beautiful face from behind my lids, so I open them. He's studying me with his mouth agape. I can't ask him what he's thinking even though I want to. A high-pitched moan gets away from me, but I don't take my eyes off of him. He growls at the same time I cry out. My heart and thighs are pulsating, especially down there.

When the sensation subsides, he withdraws his fingers and buttons up my pants. "Let's get the hell out of here," he whispers with his mouth close to mine.

I'm as limp as a ragdoll, but I can shift my head enough to nod. That's when he leads us away.

ZILL

After a bit of encouragement from Tapeetha, I stripped and jumped into the lake outside of her cave. Now I'm underwater, laughing so hard my cheeks ache. I'm still shocked that I can breathe under here. My backside is pressed against Vayle's belly. He has me by the waist, and we're torpedoing through the lake, spiraling, free-falling, stopping before we hit bottom, and then blasting through the white ringlet clusters that grow on the floor of the lake.

This started out as a race from one side of the lake to the other, but he beat me so badly that he decided to offer "the broken-down Porsche a tow." I dared him to carry me one hundred laps around the lake in less than a minute, but he said that was too easy, and we cut the time down to fifteen seconds. He finished in ten. Then we challenged Tapeetha and Danto, who'd been streaking up and down the pond but not together. Those two acted as if they just happened to be in the same lake. However, they did accept our challenge.

First we won, then they won, then we decided to go three out of five. We won! Then in a surprising move, Danto carried Tapeetha off somewhere, and we haven't seen them since.

Vayle and I are heading toward the surface at a record speed. When I no longer feel water against my face but the fresh, crisp air of the night, Vayle lets go of me. I regain control of my body and flutter like a leaf that's falling to the ground. This is an experiment. I want to see if I can control my body like this, and I can!

Our backs hit the grass at the same time. I'm all wet, and I stare at the sky. There are loads of stars —all of them twinkling brightly. This night looks as if it was snatched out of one of those bedtime story books that used to be in my kindergarten classroom. Deanna never bought those books for me. She said I was too advanced for them.

I used to dream of one day seeing some of that stuff in real life. I liked *A Cricket Ate the Acorn* a lot. It was about a cricket who carried an acorn. It was too heavy for him, of course, but he traveled all around the world asking all these different creatures if they could break the shell so he could eat the seed. No one would do it, and after the black widow spider chased him, threatening to eat him, he decided to roll the acorn off a high bluff.

The bluff stretched over a stony desert. The sky

above was solid blue, and all I wanted was to be there with the cricket, looking out over the cliff with him. I wanted to crack the acorn for him. I mean, the gecko, the colony of worker ants, the squirrel who tried to steal it from him, and the blue jay who would've eaten him but was already full, all of them said no because crickets don't eat acorns. But back then, all I wanted to do was to see that bluff and crack that acorn.

Those books were fun. As I lay looking at this scene, I feel as though the biggest dream I ever had has been answered. I no longer live in the ordinary world.

"Why are you smiling like that?" Vayle asks me.

Gosh, I'm grinning. I've been doing a lot of that since Vayle returned from Jari. I believed he would choose to be human again and return to his family. But he didn't. He chose me, and that keeps me feeling all giddy. I love all of this. I love being able to breathe underwater and walk on air. I love that I can lie here on this spongy grass, totally naked, and not care. A lot about me has changed, and it's all worth smiling about.

"Because I like this—all of it," I answer.

"Me too." He studies the parts of my body that entice him the most.

I playfully punch him in the shoulder. "Stop. Don't ruin this for me."

He props himself up to lie on his side, and he runs a finger up and down my abdomen. I skip a breath upon his first touch.

"I wonder where your sister and Leto went," he says with his eyes pinned on my breasts.

They are something to look at. I didn't realize that until I saw Tapeetha's. Our racks are identical.

"They're probably off doing you-know-what."

Vayle laughs loudly. "You're a prude, Zill."

"No, I'm not," I whine. Now that I think about it, I'm probably the only sister who isn't getting it on with her bond. "I mean, why do they all have to have so much sex anyway?"

"I don't know. You want to try it and see?" Vayle jokingly asks.

"Right, like I want my first time to be with you," I say with a laugh.

Vayle withdraws his hand and lies on his back. I think I hurt his feelings, and boy, I feel bad about that. As I study his profile, I can really see his faint resemblance to Baron and the other vampires.

"I'm sorry," I say. "I didn't mean that. It was a joke."

"You meant it."

Now it's me who runs a finger up and down him. I touch the point of his nose. I never described a guy as handsome before, but Vayle is simply handsome. His eyes were really dark when we first met, but now they're pale gray. He has messy dark hair, and although he's dead, he isn't pale like a corpse, like the other vampires. His skin is a little olive toned.

"It's just that you're not…" I don't finish what I was saying because I'm no longer sure of it.

"I'm not your Wek," he says for me.

"No, Derek has nothing to do with the way I feel about you."

"How do you feel about me?" He looks at me again, but this time, he stares into my eyes, not at my nipples or crotch or hips or butt.

I swallow the lump in my throat. The question isn't how I feel about him. "The question is how do *you* feel about me?"

He grunts. "You already know."

"No. I know you want to have sex with me, and we have fun together. I know you're attracted to me, and you love the thrill of chasing me. I've heard guys are into that, the thrill of the chase."

"I don't want to chase you. I want to have you,

but you're making it so damn hard." He puts his hand on my belly.

With that one touch, warmth fills me again.

"My parents are divorced," he continues. "I've never been bitter about that, though. When they were together, my mother never smiled, and my father was never home. But then they got a divorce, and it all got better. But I know that if we were married, you would always smile, and I'd always want to come home to you. I'll never get tired of seeing you."

I study Vayle's face for signs that he's screwing with my head. I'm waiting for him to crack a smile or laugh off everything he just said, but he does neither. His sincerity allows me to confess, "I'm afraid you won't be gentle with me. I heard it hurts."

Vayle remains silent. His hand slides up past my breasts to cup my cheek. The look in his eyes takes my breath away.

He carefully mounts me. "I'm going to make love to you. Are you okay with that?"

There's a full moon out tonight, and its rays illuminate his face. I feel as though we're in a fairy tale, and Prince Charming is asking to put himself inside me. Who could say no to Prince Charming?

"Yes," I whisper.

"Okay?" He sounds shocked.

"Okay."

He shifts, and I brace myself. I feel him slowly slide inside me. He pauses, reading my reaction. I remember the girls in the restroom saying the first time hurts a lot, but this doesn't. I've never felt anything like *this* before. I mean, I felt it when Vayle did the thing with his tongue down there, but this is different. The sensation is threatening to be only the beginning of the pleasure that's stirring deep inside me.

"Are you okay?" he asks breathlessly.

I'm glad he asked. I smile. "Oh my God, yes." I sort of moan because as soon as I smiled, he shifted his hips back and forth. I'm being seized by pure pleasure.

I'm not alone either. Vayle is growling and moaning too. His eyes are wide as if this sex we're having has taken him by surprise too.

When my first orgasm grips me, I cry out at the top of my lungs in order to bear it. I grab Vayle's shoulders, digging my fingernails into his skin. He pulls me close. He's growling over and over.

"Shit," he whispers. He shifts deeper inside me, moving faster.

The more he does it, the more I can hardly stand how magnificent this feels. No wonder Clarity and Baron are always doing it. I'm already addicted. And Vayle... He... Well, he must have a soul because mine is entangled with his. He hasn't stopped staring into my eyes.

Then he closes his eyes and his lips find mine. We're kissing, and I want him to swallow me whole. Both of us are grunting greedily. Why has it taken us so long to get to this point?

He lets out another series of growls, and I feel him release his warmth inside me. At first I feel a strong tickling sensation, like I'm free falling down a rollercoaster, but it doesn't stop. It continues as if it's never ending. We can't stop.

I roll him over, and I'm on top of him. Then he rolls me over so he's on top of me. We're all over the grass, moving from one spot to another. My nipple's in his mouth. His is in mine. He lets out a wild howl when I do that. He likes it. Then his teeth are in my neck, and he's drinking my blood.

I didn't think this could get any better.

I scream when the next sensation takes over me.

I'm screaming at the top of my lungs. If I even have *lungs*.

. . .

MANY HOURS LATER…

I LIFT MY HEAD OFF OF VAYLE'S CHEST. "YOU HEAR that?"

"Crickets?"

"They're far away, but it's like they're close."

"I hear them all the time."

Not only can I hear every tiny sound—like the wind shifting around us, my own heartbeat, the water rippling in the soft wind, and the grass crunching beneath us—but my reflexes are sharp. I feel as though if I leap, I could probably reach a hundred or more feet high.

"So, Zill…" Vayle's voice pulls me back into the moment.

"Yeah?" I sound spastic because I feel like my mouth can talk faster.

"Are we together, one hundred percent, bonded like Clarity and Baron?" There's uncertainty in his tone.

"I think it was inevitable. Don't you?"

He shrugs beneath me, and in a flash, we switch positions. Now he's on top, and I'm on the bottom.

"Not really," he says. "You were really into Derek."

Guilt pricks at me as I think about Derek. I'm caught in a mess of emotions—part of me feeling guilt-ridden, while the other part is unapologetically in love with Vayle, the vampire.

"I still care about Derek," I admit. "He's a good guy."

"And I'm not?"

I roll my eyes. "Come on. Don't ruin this."

He softens, his gaze steady. "I still love you, even if you love him."

"Goodness, I love you, so stop being jealous. Some things aren't cut and dry," I say, exasperated. "He liked me even when I didn't like myself. As I said, he's a good guy. I don't want you throwing what we have in his face. Okay?"

He raises an eyebrow. "What we have? So, it's set in stone."

I resist the urge to kiss his mouth when I reply, "In stone, we're set."

He narrows his eyes, teasing. "Is that a promise?"

I groan, half-weary. "Come on, Vayle."

He grins, enjoying himself while I frown. He never makes things easy, always keeping me on edge. I never know what he's going to do from one moment to the next, and while it frustrates me, I'll admit it's also exciting.

"Just messing with you. I love that look on your face—it makes me want to..." His lustful gaze burns into me, but then he suddenly perks up. "By the way, where the hell are your sister and my cousin?" he asks, his eyes scanning the horizon over the lake.

TAPEETHA

Leto and me have not spoken. We are dekun'ra, that is make sex, and we do this over and over. He drinks me. He kisses me. But we have no words. We are in the cave that Clarity and Glo and I came to earlier. We brought the light with us so I could see him, and he could see me. He laid me on the reef and did everything to me, like the olden days.

"Promise you won't leave me again," he whispers.

I shake my head. "I cannot stay here." I hate to say it.

"You're saying no?" He is, um, surprised.

"I say… I mean, I'm saying I cannot stay. Do *you* have to stay? You will come with me this time?"

He stares at my eyes and moves inside me. He kisses my lips then drinks my lifeblood. I weep because he makes me feel good. He does what is needed, but still, we do not speak. It's love we make. Dekun'ra. We make love, and that is for the better.

GLO

TWELVE AND A HALF HOURS AGO...

Finn never ceases to amaze me. We're underground. This place is like a cave with a deep, clear natural spring, but what makes me sniff cynically is the king-sized bed—with a satiny golden duvet and fluffy pillows—against the wall about twenty feet from the pool. I'm standing on a wooden floor. In the jagged rock ceiling are ducts that usher in light and air.

"What's this, the vampire slayer's love nest?" I lift my top lip sarcastically.

He sniffs. "No, this is a rich vampire's love nest."

Now my interest is piqued. "Really? Who?"

He lifts one side of his mouth and winks. "It's

for me to know and you to find out, but we're crashing because he's an ass."

"You mean this place belongs to Baron Ze Feld-is!" I exclaim, thoroughly amused.

"What gave it away, the ass part?"

I say, "He's not an ass, but you think he is; *that's* what gave it away."

As I give the luxury suite another once-over, Finn appears in front of me. All I can see is him.

With one side of his mouth lifted, he says, "I'm going to strip you out of your clothes; you should get ready for that."

"Go for it," I say. I'm already naked.

He carries my clothes away. I take another look around. Baron lives like this. Finn lives like a rat in the sewer, a scavenger in life, and I'm in love with him. It's nonsensical. I can't deal with him as if he's a passing fascination of mine.

Finn is here to stay, which leaves me wondering whether dark, muddy tunnels, hovels with one bed and no sunlight, and deals in places that look like abandoned parking lots with scary vampires like Chex will be my future too. All of a sudden, dread grips me. The answer to that is a resounding, "Hell no!"

Obviously I have to work harder to make Finn

see things my way. This luxury cave that belongs to my sister's lover is a start. If I weren't with Finn, he would've never come here. Feeling more confident about our future, I leap into the water. It's soft and warm. I close my eyes, spread my arms, and fall back into it. I go under, letting the mineral water cover me. When I re-emerge, Finn is holding up a pair of black skinny jeans and a red, sheer button-front blouse in one hand.

"You wear this kind of thing, right?" he asks.

"Where did you get those from?" I ask, highly curious.

"Ze Feldis has wardrobes for Clarity on all of his properties. He thinks of everything. You know, having the power of mind and all…" He dangles a pair of lacy hot-pink panties in his other hand. That's when I laugh, especially when he asks, "Really, is this your sister's taste? Nice."

He streaks away and comes back nude. He faces me in the water. It's time to finish what we started in the jungle.

TWELVE HOURS LATER…

We've been here for a while. We've been out of the pool and on the bed, and now we're back in the water. My back is against the smooth rock wall, legs floating around Finn's waist. His fangs are inside my neck, and he's gently consuming me in more ways than two.

Suddenly he stops everything, the kissing, drinking, thrusting, and deep breathing. "Did you feel that?"

"What?" I'm confused.

I'm feeling a lot right now, but he's looking up and over the top of my head, which is a clue he's not referring to whatever's going on between us. Then I glance downward because the water around us shifts left and then right.

"Was that an earthquake?" Now I'm alarmed.

"No. That was a mass rising." The look on my face urges him to explain, so he does. "It's nighttime, and a lot of vampires have broken through the soil to rise."

We both stand and rotate as we scan out into the distance. There are so many of them. They're young and mostly male. They skulk in the night across the wild grass that's rich and green in the daytime. Finn and I, and the volcanic mountains that rise and fall around them, are their only spectators. Bats and birds that follow the moon scatter out of their path, escaping the creatures in droves.

"Where in the world are they going?" I whisper past my tightened throat.

We observe them as they make their way to the southern coast. These guys wear serious expressions, and their steps are deliberate; they'll stomp down anyone or anything that gets in their path. If a branch from a floppy tropical tree slaps them in the face, they rip the tree out of the ground, breaking roots and all, and toss it hundreds of yards away. They're destructive, having no concern for preserving the beauty that's millions of years older than they are or ever will be.

"You should get Clarity," Finn says as we watch them skulk toward the white sand shores, into the ocean, and disappear underwater.

"No need to," I mutter. "She's already calling *me*." I'm still mesmerized by the ghastly spectacle.

CHAPTER 12

LEFT IN THE DARK

CLARITY

THIRTEEN HOURS AGO...

Baron gently rakes a hand through my tresses. "Your hair is already drying."

I sit between his legs in the bathtub. I'm safe against his powerful chest, between the strong arms he just used to pour a vase of warm water over my hair. He gently lathered it, massaged my scalp, and rinsed the suds with a handheld waterspout.

"I know," I say. "It used to scare me. It doesn't anymore."

"I remember scaring you when I first saw you at Lario's seminar."

I bury one side of my face in the crook of his

neck. He smells fantastic. "Gosh, that seems like ages ago. I remember you wanted to kill me. Why was that?"

"I don't know," he whispers. "Something took over me. I wanted you so badly. More than anything, I wanted to drink you dry, but..." He takes a long thoughtful pause. "I didn't want to kill you because I knew I couldn't live without you. But you were a stranger, and that puzzled me. I could smell that you weren't human. At first, I thought you were a siren because you were so beautiful. But I didn't smell that on you either. When I did identify what you were, I couldn't believe it."

I kiss his jaw. "What a terrible conundrum. But why couldn't you believe it?"

"I knew about Fawn. I always thought she was one of a kind and that's why Exgesis kept her hidden away. Then I realized how much you looked like her, with the obvious difference in coloring." He lifts my arm and slides his hands up and down my skin.

"Did you ever think we would be here together like this?" I ask after he kisses my elbow.

He's rising beneath me. "I'd be lying if I said that I didn't. I knew."

As I giggle, he lifts me by the waist and turns me

around to face him. I gasp as he slides into me. My nerves, or whatever I'm made of that makes me respond to him, are already reacting.

"It's like we're married, Clarity. You know that, right?"

We stare into each other's eyes. His mouth is close to mine.

"That's one word I've always been afraid of," I manage to whisper.

He moves my hips with his hands. The feeling is too unbelievable to be mere sex.

"You're mine forever," he says. "I want you to know that if you choose Enu instead of Earth, I'll go with you. If you choose hell instead of heaven, I'll go there with you too."

I close my eyes, wrap my arms around his neck, and hold on tightly. This feels too good, but I'm able to confess, "I feel the same way about you."

The kissing, the lovemaking is hot and heavy now. He's drinking me, and I'm soaring.

TEN HOURS AGO...

I'm lying bare between, I don't know, million-thread-count sheets! These linens must have been carefully hand crafted. After three hours of making love, Baron excused himself. He said he had a surprise for me, but he's been away for a good while. My eyes have grown heavy.

Am I still awake? A force is carrying me through a mist of bright light. The rays are not so blinding, but I can't see beyond them either. But the confusion has passed. I know what's happening to me. The Enuian and divine parts of me are being summoned. I don't know where I'm being led, though. This isn't Enu, because upon entering that universe, one is instantly hugged by the warmth, peace, and goodness that emanates there. I must still be in Earth's realm, but I've entered a domain that has been tempered with the power of Enu.

The extreme light disintegrates. I'm standing inside the diamond chamber, facing my father, Felix. I remember that I have no clothes on, but when I fling my arms to cover myself, I touch a blousy white linen dress. I sigh with relief. How humiliating would that've been, being naked in front of my father?

"Cl'auta, you have to do something," he says, getting right to it.

"What's that?" I say spastically, trying to control how fast my mouth moves.

He slides a finger down the script. "Start here."

I squint at the etchings. The writing is a mixture of symbols and words. My mind has become more lucid since Baron drank my blood.

"The seeds of seven steal the sun to stay." I decipher the entire paragraph in my head. It says something about the sun being transformative, protecting the daughter of light and releasing the hidden souls. She is a captive, it says, which I believe as far as time, it's chronologically out of sequence. The paragraph ends with, "The seeds of the seven bring the sun to the night before the creation, there is none."

I look at Felix. "We have to stop the sun guides from aligning?"

"Read more," Felix calmly urges me.

I hesitate at the thought of there being more than what the script has just revealed. If we let those lines shift into place, who knows what the second-generation Selells will turn into. It will be daytime, so obviously the sun won't kill them. Will they become what the Remuk intended them to be?

I'm filled with anxiety. I'm ready to rush out of here, return fully to myself, and alert my sisters that it's time. But then I read something even more challenging.

"We have to bring back the noon sun from the previous day because it has the power of sentaku-loc, but the moon is the gateway to redemption? I don't understand," I say to him.

As I turn to get an answer from my father, my eyes pop open. I'm in Baron's bed, naked between the messy sheets, and he's lying beside me, facing me.

I sit up and look around the room. Everything looks the same. "How long have I been out?"

"Almost ten hours."

TEN MINUTES AGO...

"So what did your father reveal this time?" Baron asks.

We stand at the foot of the bed, facing each other. My heart is still pounding. Every second that we stand here doing nothing, we're losing valuable time.

"We must destroy every single one of Lario's minions *before* the lines are in place," I say, and further explain that we have to somehow bring back the sun as it was yesterday at noon to stop the bentu be dun'e, but we have to do it while the moon is still in the sky. If the moon isn't present, then there's nothing we can do to stop the evil.

"I gather the power of the sun can help with that," Baron says.

"Zill and Vayle should be able to get it done."

"We should go," he says, feeling the same sense of urgency.

I call them: Glo, Fawn, Zill, and Tapeetha.

IN THE PRESENT...

Glo and Finn guided us here to the island of São Tomé. Under different circumstances, this would be a gorgeous place. It's a tropical island rich with rolling green fields, volcanic mountains, forests of floppy tropical trees, and clear-water beaches. We're all standing in a grassy field at the base of a fifty-foot hill. A skeletal moon is still in the western sky, and the third sunrise is imminent.

I look around at my sisters and notice that we're all wearing the same marks on our necks. I'm surprised to see them on Zill and even Tapeetha. My eyes flick back to Zill. She's standing closer to Vayle than she normally would, and the way his arm is around her lower back and his hand rests on her hip displays possession.

When Derek appears out of thin air beside her, her shoulders curve away from him because she's struck by guilt. Vayle stares at the Wek. I can see his thoughts and feel his memories. Zill and Vayle have consummated their bond. I stifle my exclamatory reaction to this new revelation. *Wow!* Where have I been? I didn't see that coming!

"See you've made yourself comfortable here..." Baron snarls at Finn.

Apparently, Glo is wearing *my* clothes. I've never seen any of them.

Just to rub it in, Finn thinks, *"And those pink panties are really sexy. Glo's wearing the hell out of them."*

But Baron's comment is the extent of his reaction to the whole ordeal. I kind of think that deep down inside, he's okay with Finn trespassing on his properties. It keeps them connected in a familial way.

Everyone knows what we have to do; I've already filled them in.

Glo gazes out toward the ocean to our left. "They're still out there, under the water and waiting." A chill runs down her spine.

We're all tense, but nothing's changed. We still have no time to waste.

"I'm starting," I announce. "Tapeetha, Danto, do you see this?" I feed them the image of the heart pierced by the leaf. The organ is yellow, jaundiced, but the leaf is healthy, green. It appears to be the only thing alive in their bodies.

"Got it," Leto Danto reports for the both of them.

We all link hands to unite our powers. This gives us an influx of extra strength.

"Move the sun," I instruct Zill and Vayle.

They look toward the horizon. Something within them connects to the tiny rays of light that threaten to rise in the east. With great force, they shove the sun toward the west.

Derek looks to the east to observe the movement. "It's working."

It's a relief to hear that.

"Tapeetha, Danto," I say, continuing to orchestrate our assault, "when the sun is directly overhead, bring them out of the water."

"We will do it," Tapeetha says while Danto nods at me.

The sky is dark again. It starts slowly, but the ground trembles under our feet. We all lift off of it to keep steady.

A flank of Selells shoot out of the sea and fly toward us. I almost expect to see Viesel Egos and his sword, but he doesn't appear. Instead, Glo sets them on fire. Those who were lucky enough to meet her power retreat back into the water. Those who met Finn's power exploded into fragments.

A second flank of about two hundred more Selells escapes the sea, but before Glo and Finn can take care of them, the sun rolls back to early evening. It's just enough light to burn them where they stand, which isn't too far from us. They all dart back into the ocean as smoke pours off of their skin like a chimney.

"It's heavy," Zill complains as she strains. Her neck is tight, and a vein in her forehead is protruding.

Derek rushes over and puts an arm around her waist. Vayle pulls her closer to him. They almost look as if they're playing tug-of-war with her.

A familiar wind smacks right into us. The pressure of it sends us all scattering like loose leaves in a tornado. I'm pinned to the side of a hill. The air rushes up my nose, hindering my breathing. It's the force of the evil, and it's actively trying to smother me.

The sky shows as if it's late evening, but it's stopped there. It's not progressing backward toward noon. Zill is nowhere in sight. The strength of the wind has increased, and I have a hard time trying to find my footing. Baron, who's standing over me and strong on his feet, lifts me off the ground and holds me against him.

"The light!" he shouts against the deafening roar of the wind.

"Right!" At first, I cannot lift my arms. They feel as if they'll tear away if I shift them outside of the crook of Baron's strong shoulders. But I dig deep to tap into the power of the Selell that was transferred to me when he consumed my blood. My arms go up high, unmoved by the evil's destructive power.

Baron takes my hand. We raise our arms high and stare down a deep red hole in the sky—the eye of the evil. I use all of my strength to face off against the same force that bends the blades of grass at their roots and snatches the elephant ear trees out of the earth. My extremely long hair finds its power too and moves toward my face. The light that made its first appearance when Baron and I made love in Miami sets me aglow like it did back then. He's glowing too.

"Ready!" he shouts.

"Ready!"

We unleash the light. A strong beam shoots out of our eyes and stabs the red hole. The wind subsides, and the sun once again moves toward noon. Fawn and Ben Artiste are helping Zill and Vayle shove it backward by using their own power of force.

"It's almost time," I announce in everyone's head.

"What the hell!" Ben Artiste yells.

Hundreds of wild pigs charge toward us, snorting, grunting, and foaming at the mouth.

"I don't want to kill a bunch of pigs!" Zill shouts. She's seriously torn and still fighting to keep the sun moving into place.

"I'll handle it! Just keep pushing!" I spread a shield of calm over the ravaging beasts.

As their hooves slow, the strong wind lifts them off the ground, and they go flying toward the rain forest. It's evil to kill what one can no longer use, and that's exactly what the evil has in mind for the pigs. I add buoyancy to the shield of calm that covers them. Whatever they end up hitting, the impact will not injure them.

"It's noon!" Glo shouts as she works to maintain position against the force.

There's a thunderous boom. That's the evil's roar. It's rebelling against the progress we've made despite its efforts to stop us. The field is now populated with Selells, thousands upon thousands of them. My God, they're all too young to meet the kind of demise we have planned for them. They should have their whole lives ahead of them, full of friends and family and leaving their mark on the world—the life of a human being.

Fawn and Ben engage their power of force to keep them rounded up and away from us.

"It works!" Tapeetha shouts.

I've never seen her this jubilant. She feels nothing like the way Fawn and I do. There's sadness in Glo's eyes too as she watches what's happening before us.

The Selells' rotting flesh is smoking like wet meat on the barbecue pit.

I recall the young girl I once saved from Lario. She'd come to him to receive a favor from Sham magic. After nearly molesting her, Lario handed her over to one of his human goons so he could to have his way with her. But Lario fully intended to turn her into a Selell afterward. She would be here on this field if I hadn't saved her that night. I look out over all of the stunned faces that are realizing they're close to going up in flames. *What if all of them need to be saved from Lario, from the evil?*

The moon, a voice says in my head.

It sounds like me, my instincts. I look up. The moon is still there and tilted east. Instinctively, I know what to do. If there is a hell or a lake of fire, then that's what's spread out before us. We have judged and condemned these vampires. I'm certain that if we just destroy them, then we're falling short of our goal. We are not judges; we are empathetic beings.

The power of sentakuloc has set them on fire. Their clothing burns off of them, and their hair is on fire, but it's taking a while to char their skin.

I turn toward Baron and shout, "This is not right!"

He frowns at me. I have no time to explain.

"Trust me," I say to him. *"Link hands,"* I yell as loud as I can in everyone else's head.

The evil's effort to stop us has picked up again,

but my sisters and I are operating at an optimal level, as evidenced by the way our hair shoots toward our faces. I move toward Zill and Vayle since they're bearing the brunt of this operation. I take her hand, and Baron takes Vayle's. The others connect with us.

Every single cell in my body is energized. As my sisters fight to keep things as they are, I shield the Selells on the field to guard them from the sun. Glo and Finn see it, but Baron senses it.

"What are you doing, Clarity?" Glo shouts.

"Make it cold. Cool them," I tell her.

She hesitates.

"You have to trust me!"

With that, Glo gives the vampires relief from the heat. It's all happening so fast, but I feel Tapeetha's alarm. She's about to act first and ask questions later. Before she can move the Selells out of the safety I've created for them, I connect with all of the keys to Jari—at least those that are present.

I appear at the main gate to Jari, and I'm not alone. All five keys are on my heart. I breathe in deeply and release it, blowing on the box that serves as the lock. The gate glows as it opens.

"Where did they go?" Zill shouts as the wind stops wreaking havoc on São Tomé.

I return to myself, and so do Glo and Finn. I took them with me because of the power of their eyes. Glo watches me with widened eyes.

"They're in Jari," I say. I ask Glo, "What happened to them?"

She hesitates, still rattled by my decision. "They were swallowed up by the ground." The sight of it lingers in her head.

I catch a look between Finn, Baron, and Vayle. Although Baron tries to hide what he remembers of being underground in Jari from me, Vayle and Finn can't. I see it all. The souls. The blackness.

"You let them *leave*!" Tapeetha shouts at me.

"We couldn't kill them. That's not what we're supposed to do. We're supposed to help them." I sound as if I'm defending myself.

"This was not the plan, that's all," Zill complains. "I mean, that nearly knocked me out."

"But it *was* the plan. We needed the sun right where it was to get that done."

"But where did the sun go?" Glo asks, staring at the sky.

That's when I notice that it's darker now than it was before. The sun is gone!

"Maybe it's nighttime now," I offer as an explanation.

"No, it's not," Finn replies. "The earth's sun is under Jari."

We all take a moment to absorb what Finn just revealed. That cannot be possible. But the longer we gaze at the sky, the more convinced we are of that reality. I think I just swallowed my throat. I'm so afraid of what we've done that I reach out for Baron. He draws me into him.

"How could this happen?" I'm barely able to say.

We all look at each other, confused and wondering what in the world we should do next. I'm blaming myself for this, and Baron knows it. By the look on Tapeetha's face, she blames me too. I bury my face in Baron's shoulder.

He takes my chin and lifts it. "Clarity, you did nothing wrong. Let's just go figure this out, okay, love?"

I nod stiffly. It's nice to be called "love" when the moment requires it.

www.ingramcontent.com/pod-product-compliance
Lightning Source LLC
Chambersburg PA
CBHW072114250626
47159CB00007B/2444